COLDERO RIDGE COWBOY

Amber Leigh Williams

HARLEQUIN®
ROMANTIC SUSPENSE™

Recycling programs
for this product may
not exist in your area.

ISBN-13: 978-1-335-73841-7

Coldero Ridge Cowboy

Copyright © 2023 by Amber Leigh Williams

For questions and comments about the quality of this book, please contact us at CustomerService@Harlequin.com.

Harlequin Enterprises ULC
22 Adelaide St. West, 41st Floor
Toronto, Ontario M5H 4E3, Canada
www.Harlequin.com

Printed in U.S.A.

Amber Leigh Williams is an author, wife, mother of two and dog mom. She has been writing sexy small-town romance with memorable characters since 2006. Her Harlequin romance miniseries is set in her charming hometown of Fairhope, Alabama. She lives on the Alabama Gulf Coast, where she loves being outdoors with her family and a good book. Visit her on the web at www.amberleighwilliams.com!

Books by Amber Leigh Williams

Harlequin Romantic Suspense

Hunted on the Bay

Fuego, New Mexico

Coldero Ridge Cowboy

Harlequin Superromance

Navy SEAL's Match
Navy SEAL Promise
Wooing the Wedding Planner
His Rebel Heart
Married One Night
A Place with Briar

Visit the Author Profile page at
Harlequin.com for more titles.

To my grandmothers, both of whom smiled when I said I wanted to be a writer...even after they read the first draft. Thank you for your encouragement, your example and your grace.

I love you!

Chapter 1

She drove so fast, the hounds of hell might've been chasing her.

It had been so long since Eden Meadows—or Eveline Eaton, as she was known in her hometown of Fuego, New Mexico—had driven down this long stretch of country road. The high desert stretched far into the black of night. It was a new moon tonight. The only things lighting up the shrubby plain were her headlights.

She pushed the rental car to the point of redlining. There were no taillights in front of her, no headlights in her rearview. Streetlights? Forget about it. She was alone with her grief and a sudden thirst for recklessness.

Her heart pounded at her ears. Panic nipped at her heels. If she let it, it would take over.

She choked it back, breathing in and out in a steady wash. She was calm. She was collected. She was in control.

At least that's what she told herself as she stopped

watching the speedometer and kept her eyes over the steering wheel. The dash marks next to the center line streamed together in a yellow blur.

She hadn't driven in years, not since she'd left home to live in the Big Apple. Definitely not since the accident that had left her scarred and in therapy for almost a year.

Signs flicked past like flies on either side of the road. The turn for Fuego was near.

The Eaton family cattle ranch, Eaton Edge, was in the middle of nowhere. For once in her life, she preferred it that way.

I am in control.

Forget the grief. Forget the fear. She tightened her grasp on the wheel and lowered her chin, listening to the engine whine. She pushed the rental to its max.

Knowing she had a good five hundred feet before she needed to break for the turnoff, she pushed the car that last little bit. Just to prove—to herself, to whoever and whatever was looking down at her—that she could.

She didn't have to live with fear anymore.

Eveline didn't see the shape until it was in front of her headlights.

She slammed on the brakes automatically. What looked like an animal stalking across the road on all fours suddenly stood up on thin legs—all too thin—and turned to look at her. The beam of the headlights reflected off its eyes, piercing her straight through.

The face was an animal's. But the stance…

She screamed, tires skidding on old pavement. She yanked the wheel, trying to avoid whatever it was—

She heard a *thwunk* against her rear quarter panel a split second before the car flew off the road.

She screamed again as it bounced hard into and out of the ditch. She was flung back against the headrest, then forward. Her seat belt locked, saving her from face-planting into the wheel.

She didn't have time to scream at the fence post looming toward her. Lifting her hands to shield her face, she felt every muscle in her body brace for impact. The car seemed to drop out from under her. It yanked to a stop, as if someone had tied a lasso around it and dropped it back like a roped steer.

Eveline sat frozen in the driver's seat with her hair in her face. Then a long, shaky breath escaped her. A sob chased it, followed by others. She wanted to lower her head to the steering wheel and shake.

However, that face…those eyes… They made her head swivel back to the road.

What had it been? Why hadn't it run?

Why had it felt like it was staring into her soul?

Eveline shuddered once, then again—so hard her bones rattled. She gripped the wheel until her knuckles felt like they were going to pop out of her skin.

She was afraid to move.

The memories that plagued her dreams reeled like a bad movie in her head.

The smell of asphalt, brake dust… The sound of metal dragging across pavement incessantly until the car finally stopped skidding across the eight-lane highway…and came to rest in oncoming traffic…

The panic she'd been trying to outrun sank its teeth into her. She curled in on herself, wrapping her arms over her chest. She swore she felt the scars on her shoulder and neck burning, like they, too, remembered everything.

Everything—with far too much clarity.

"You're okay," she breathed. She tasted tears and covered her face. "You're okay…" She didn't believe it, but she said it.

She'd frickin' say it until she believed it.

Isn't that what she'd done for the better part of twelve months?

Nothing was broken this time. She was just in shock.

"Talk yourself down," she coached. "Think your way through…"

Her thoughts were a jumble of instability. She couldn't wade through them if she tried.

She clawed at the door of the car to get out, then stopped, jumping when the shadows outside the car seemed to move in a furtive rush.

Her teeth chattered. The creature was imprinted on the backs of her eyes. She couldn't get out. There was no way she was getting out. Not when that thing might still be out there…

She ran her hands roughly through her hair. Already she could feel the headache coming on—from strain—from being jerked around like a rag doll in the driver's seat. The spot where her shoulder met her collarbone felt bruised. There'd be an abrasion there from the seat belt, just like last time…

"Not like last time," she chanted with a hard shake of her head. "It's not like last time." She looked around. The road was just as before. No headlights. No taillights or streetlights as far as the eye could see.

No terrifying creature.

She fumbled for the ignition switch, missing several times. She finally found it and tried cranking the car. The engine gurgled once, then stopped turning over at all.

There would be no driving the rest of the way. Fuego couldn't be that far. She'd seen the sign. She could walk it…

A yipping noise made her jump out of her skin. It echoed off everything and nothing.

Coyotes.

They weren't out to get her, she told herself. But she hated the sound of their yipping. It'd kept her awake as a child with visions of mountain lions and skin-walkers.

Her big brothers' idea of bedtime stories hadn't exactly made for restful nights.

What she'd seen in the road was the stuff of her nightmares as a child. For a moment, she felt like a child, tempted to curl up in the fetal position and whimper.

She fumbled through her purse on the passenger seat, telling herself to get a grip. She couldn't hide in the car all night, though it would take a miracle to get a cell signal this far out. She had installed an app at the recommendation of the person at the rental car company that might help. Time to put it to the test.

Her hands were still shaking. It took longer than it should have to dial her passcode, then find the app. She scanned her options and saw *tow truck* on the list.

Old Hyde Meechum's face popped into her mind. He'd bailed her eldest brother, Everett, out of many scrapes over the course of his ill-fated drag racing career. He was likely only a mile or so away. If his response time was anything like it used to be…

She toggled the tow truck request. Her heart pounded as she waited for it to go through. Glancing over the dash, she looked into the black. She really didn't want to walk. Not only was nighttime out here in no-man's-land not her favorite thing, the town was just that—a town. It was three hundred and fifty strong, at best.

Small towns like to hit the beddy-bye switch early. Every business along Fuego's main drag would've closed hours ago.

Her phone beeped. She saw the message: Tow truck en route.

An unsteady sigh left her. She centered herself in the driver's seat and did her best to settle down to wait.

Eveline was so busy looking ahead to Fuego for headlights, she cried out in shock when she saw them filling the mirror above the dash. She sat up and watched them grow…then slow.

When the vehicle pulled onto the side of the road behind her rental, she groaned. "Please don't be a lunatic," she pleaded. She tried pressing the button to crack the driver's window. When it didn't budge, she cursed and tried again. Same result.

Trying not to think of the creature in the road, she unlocked the door and pushed it open. Her legs wobbled at the knees as she got out, but she managed to keep them steady. Her purse was in her hand. She reached inside until she felt the Taser near the bottom.

She licked her lips. They still felt dry as she waited for the large figure that got down from the truck's cab to come into the light. "Thank you so much," she began to say, then stopped.

He was a cowboy; that was clear. Tall. Wide at the shoulder. His jeans were dark-tinted. His shirt was plaid, just like all the other cowpokes she remembered. His Stetson was black and pulled low over his brow.

All very typical. But that walk…

Her lips trembled. "Wolfe?"

He stopped, somewhere between her and the back of her car. Even with the light behind him, she knew.

She gathered a careful breath. "Wolfe Coldero." It wasn't a question anymore. She knew it was him—as much as she knew that her reintroduction to Fuego was going to be more awkward than she'd thought.

He came forward until the light hit what little of his face the hat didn't shade. He stared. Damn if the man didn't have the loudest stare in the universe. When he was younger, real young, his skin had stretched taut across the broad bones of his face, giving him a haunted look to go with the history he kept hidden.

He'd grown into them, limbs and facial features. His jaw flared out from the point of his lengthy chin. The ridges of his cheekbones were still prominent, but muscle had grown over the rest, giving his face definition.

She took a step back. She was caught—between the past when she'd known him and the present and the tumultuous mess that had happened between.

When he started walking toward her again, she tripped over her feet to get back. "I…" She shook her head when he stopped coming. "I…had a bit of an accident," she said.

He glanced over the wreckage. His narrowed eyes swung back to her.

She huffed a breath, lifting her hands. "I was being stupid, okay? I was driving too fast. A-a-a…*thing*… I'm not sure what it was. But it walked right out in the middle of the road and stopped. At first I thought it was a coyote… But then it almost like…stood up? No, it *definitely* stood up. On two legs. And it looked at me and…"

She trailed off because Wolfe was looking at her like she was growing antlers out of her head. She huffed. "I know what I saw. Or…at least I think I do. Only… it had to have been bigger than a coyote. It was more the size of a mountain lion. Or… I don't know. I just know it looked at me and I swerved. I might have hit it. Actually, I'm pretty sure I did clip it. *Wait…*"

She walked around the back of the car to the rear quarter panel. "Look, right there! I hit it there!"

There was a sizable dent in the panel. She covered her mouth when she saw a smear there, too. "Oh, God. It's blood. I *did* hit it. I…"

Wolfe was beside her. He raised the flashlight in his hand. The beam passed over the smear and the dent and…

Eveline felt her gorge rise. "That's fur, isn't it?"

He held up a hand. He lowered his brow and gave her a look that told her to wait. Her knees locked up and she could do nothing but watch as he walked off in the direction her car had come.

She wrapped her arms around herself, wishing she had a sweater. It was cool in high desert country at night and she was chilled for other reasons. She wished he'd come back so she wasn't alone. And yet, she didn't want him to. Everything was so damn twisted and complicated. She didn't know what to think or what to feel.

After several minutes, she heard the sound of bootfalls on the road and saw the swing of the flashlight beam. She shivered, not wanting to know but unable to stop herself from asking him as he returned. "Did you find it?"

He shook his head. Then stopped, shining his light on something in the brush.

She'd thought it was a boulder. But then she saw the tread of a tire.

He walked around the other side of the car. She followed and saw the empty rear well. "I…"

Wolfe eyed her from underneath the hat brim.

She found herself fumbling for an excuse. "I swerved off the road. That frickin' crater there must've ripped it off." She jerked her hand in the direction of a nearby pothole.

He continued to scan her. She took another automatic step back when she saw he was perusing the scars on her neck under the flashlight beam. Of course, she looked a good deal different from the last time they had crossed paths...

That would've been her mother's funeral. And her stepsister's funeral. They'd been buried on the same day, a result of the same tragedy—a result that had split Fuego in two. It had culminated with her father's decline in health and prison time for the man in front of her.

How long has he been out? she wondered. And since when was he the town tow truck driver? She swallowed hard at the lump in her throat. "What happened to Old Man Meechum?"

Wolfe didn't answer. He looked at her a second longer, then turned on his heel and walked back to his truck.

She closed her eyes. She didn't know why she'd expected an answer.

It'd been so long since she'd interacted with him she'd forgotten he was mute.

She'd tried not to think about him at all. She hadn't wanted to contemplate the crazy circumstances around her mother, Josephine's, and her half sister, Angel's, deaths. She hadn't wanted to think about the fire that had killed them or the man that had set it: Jace Decker, or "Whip" as he'd been known.

Before Wolfe killed him out of vengeance.

Old Western justice, the judge had called it at the sentencing.

Wolfe had never said a word to anyone since he'd been found roaming the outskirts of Fuego at ten years old. Eveline remembered it well. She remembered *him*. Who he'd been. How he'd looked——like a wounded animal coming out of the woods under the supporting arm of her father's then foreman, Santiago Coldero, the man who had taken Wolfe in and who had made a home for him at Coldero Ridge on the other side of Fuego.

The talk around town had been incessant. Where had the boy come from? What had been done to him? The bruises had faded from Wolfe's face over time. He had stopped limping. And he hadn't stayed starved-looking for long once Santiago's sister, Paloma, started feeding him. But people never stopped asking questions.

Accident? Runaway? Some said he'd come off the rez, run all the way from the Apache Nation…

No one ever uncovered the truth. Wolfe never said a word about his past. He'd never said a word about anything to anyone. Not his real name. Who his folks were. He'd held his silence well into adulthood. Long after he'd become a part of Fuego, the mystery around him had lingered.

The only person Eveline had seen him bond with other than Santiago was her brother, Ellis. It must have been their quiet natures. They'd even formed their own brand of communication through gestures and whistling.

When she'd come of age and was gearing up to leave New Mexico for her dreams in New York, Wolfe and Ellis had already gone to work for her father, Hammond, at Eaton Edge. She remembered clear as day watching Wolfe herd cattle with both of her brothers.

That was before he'd started hanging out around the rodeo…mostly to avoid Everett, she was sure. Their feud had been as long running as the mystery surrounding Wolfe's origins.

She tried not to think about that now. Or the fact that around the same time Wolfe had gone to work for her father, Eveline's mother had run off with Santiago to Coldero Ridge, sparking a scandal that had made her all too happy to pack her bags and leave days after graduation.

Maybe if Josephine had stayed at Eaton Edge with her, her brothers and her father none of the rest of it would have happened. Whip Decker would've stayed away from her and Angel. She might not have died. There never would've been a trial…

Her brothers might still be speaking like they used to…

Her father's heart would've never been shattered. He, too, might still be alive…

Eveline saw Wolfe come around the front of the truck. She straightened.

He bent over the loose tire. She galvanized herself to speak again, leaving the questions out this time. "I'm sorry it's so late."

He carried the tire to the truck. She could hear the coyotes yipping again, this time at a farther distance. She'd rather hear her own voice than theirs. "You were sleeping when I sent the ping, I'm sure."

She heard the clatter of the tire hitting the truck bed. When he started back to her, she saw the fanning motion of his hand. *Get back.*

She obeyed, putting distance between herself and the car.

It took a while for him to maneuver the truck around so the vehicles were back-to-back, lights flashing, siren beeping. The hydraulics hissed as he lowered the bed, then got out to attach the back of her car with chains. The truck whirred as it tugged her car onto the platform. It went by inches. Wolfe lowered the platform back to the truck bed, then inspected it to make sure everything was secure.

She clutched her elbows. She was going to have to get in the truck with him. Fuego might be a hop, skip and a jump away, but Eaton Edge and its fourteen hundred acres of cattle lands was on the far side.

For a second, she contemplated walking it again.

Wolfe's arms strained under the sleeves of his shirt. His back was wider than she recalled. He'd been tall long before either Everett or Ellis had been. Another thorn in Everett's side, Eveline was sure.

Wolfe had gotten bigger in prison. She licked her lips, feeling very, very nervous.

Ellis's voice popped into her head from years ago. *He's done nothing wrong. He did what any of the rest of us would have done, had we been there.*

She wasn't sure, even after all these years. Western justice seemed like something from another time, especially after living in the modern world of New York for so long. Shooting someone point-blank. Watching him die...

It had seemed almost as savage as the crime Whip Decker himself had committed.

She wasn't sure what to feel, even after all this time. For her mother. For the circumstances surrounding her death. For Wolfe.

He finished loading and turned to face her.

Once again, she eyed the distance between her and Fuego. She wished she was braver. She wished she wasn't wearing heels. She wished she hadn't seen that thing in the road before she swerved.

Out of options, she moved toward Wolfe instead. He must've sensed her indecision because only then did he start around the side of the truck—the passenger side. He beat her to the door and opened it.

She paused, gauging the distance between the ground and the cab. She'd need a boost. She frowned at him. "I forgot my suitcase. It's in the trunk."

He gave a nod, passing between her and the truck. His scent washed over her. It struck her off guard. It was the same. He'd eaten at her father's table. They'd ridden the same ground throughout the years. They'd shared stable duties and time with Ellis. Of course she remembered his scent.

What she didn't expect was the wave of emotion that came with it...or the memories. Memories of racing across the Edge, both of them bent low over the pommel of their respective mounts, heads tipped down to keep their hats from flying off...

He smelled like freedom, of all things. Freedom, exhilaration...wilderness.

Those were the things that had slipped her mind, along with all the other positive things she'd stopped associating with her New Mexican upbringing.

Before she could change her mind, she slipped out of her heels and clutched them in one hand. She grabbed the edge of the seat and boosted herself up. When he came around her side again, she was in the seat, reaching for the seat belt. She lifted her feet so he could slide the suitcase across the floorboard.

"Thanks," she said simply, trying to smile. Failing miserably.

He shut the passenger door and she closed her eyes. It was going to be a long ride home.

Chapter 2

She was back.

Eveline Eaton—or Eden Meadows as she'd taken to calling herself in the big city—was back in New Mexico, big as life with her green eyes and her model-esque legs reaching into forever. If Wolfe had been prone to small talk, or talk of any kind, he'd have found it impossible on the drive into Fuego.

Clearly, she didn't have much to say to him, either. She kept her eyes on the road, not sparing a glance at him or the shops along Main Street.

Not that much had changed in Fuego since she'd left. Same couple still owned the bakery on the right. Same bastard still owned the bar on the far corner. The bank was still managed by Turk Monday, even if he was training a replacement ahead of his retirement.

The laundromat still sucked down one too many quarters. The pool house still reeked of cigarettes and cheap beer, even though both had been banned there for years.

Still, nothing was the same. Nobody was more aware of that than Wolfe.

He ached for what it used to be—to both of them. He should've gotten out, perhaps, when she did—left for bigger if not better things, too. He wondered, not for the first time, if he should've come back after he got out. A good many people had questioned his coming back to Fuego after prison.

Wouldn't it be easier if you went someplace else? they'd asked.

It was hard to leave the only thing you'd ever known— the only place he'd ever associated with *home*—even if half the people in that place thought he'd done wrong, thought he should've stayed behind bars or disappeared altogether.

It would've been easier—going somewhere, anywhere else.

He'd never done things the easy way. He'd fought against the tide his entire life.

He turned the wheel to point his headlights out of town. The truck's big engine revved into gear and he stomped on the gas. Eaton Edge was a good ten miles past the last house in Fuego—past the rodeo arena and its small set of stands.

He knew why she was back. A day late for the funeral, but she was no doubt here to pay her respects to her old man. Heart attack. Hammond's third, apparently. He hadn't been healthy, Wolfe knew, not in years. He cursed himself for not checking in like he should've before the end.

He'd wanted to stop in and visit Ellis, to make sure he and the girls were all right after the funeral. It'd felt better, safer, maybe, to let the grief sink in somewhat before he turned up.

He had grief of his own. Santiago might've given him a home, but it was Hammond Eaton who'd given him a place—a job. Who'd taught him to ride a horse, for God's sake. Brand calves. Wolfe hadn't known a thing that went on on a cattle ranch. Hammond had ignored that, passing up better, more experienced hands by hiring Wolfe.

There'd been talk of making him foreman, before everything went to hell and Whip Decker lost what was left of his goddamn mind and Wolfe had to listen to Jo and her and Santiago's little girl die.

Before he'd lost his own mind and his job and the reputation he'd built with it from nothing.

Wolfe wondered if Eveline knew Hammond had been the first to contact him when he'd come back to Fuego—had even offered Wolfe his old job back.

He wondered if she knew Hammond had gotten him the best damn lawyer there'd been to find to keep him out of jail. Or that Hammond had paid for Santiago's treatment and aide while Wolfe was away.

Wolfe owed Hammond Eaton a lot. It was a shame he was gone. Everett Eaton had some big frickin' boots to fill.

"Do you see Ellis anymore?" Eveline asked suddenly.

The question caught Wolfe off guard. He gripped the wheel and nodded at the expectant turn of her head.

"Good," she said. "He needs someone to talk to. Even…"

Even if it's you. He nodded, in agreement and because he didn't blame her for implying as much.

"He doesn't tell me much," she added. "About Liberty."

He raised a brow at the stripes on the road.

"You didn't like her much, did you?"

He didn't have to answer. It was a good thing, too. He didn't have much good to say about Ellis's recent ex-wife.

"Me either," she revealed.

If he didn't know any better, he heard some satisfaction in her voice. Had Eveline had time to know Liberty? Her visits from New York had been sparse. Wolfe knew because her arrival always caused a stir among the locals.

Ellis and Liberty had only been married long enough to hit the seven-year itch—not that things hadn't been on the outs before that, from what Wolfe knew.

The lights caught the sign for Eaton Edge with the logo Jo had drawn up when she'd married Hammond and they'd bought the fourteen-hundred acres for their future business in cattle. He slowed for the turn.

"They paved it," she said with some surprise.

He didn't have to worry about the tow getting bogged down in the ruts of the old dirt road. They'd been deep enough to hide in at one point.

"That'll be Everett's work," she muttered. She shook her head. "Maybe he does know what he's doing. He used to drag race down this stretch. Do you remember?"

He remembered the entertainment of seeing Everett dragged home by the sheriff one afternoon, busted, bleeding and drunk off his ass after totaling his Corvette. Hammond had nearly had a coronary.

As Wolfe pulled the tow truck into the driveway for the ranch house, he heard Eveline inhale sharply. He caught her sitting up straighter out of the corner of his eye. He passed the cottonwood tree with its wooden swing big enough for four. Motion lights picked up the truck's movement and flickered on.

There were several dusty trucks in the driveway, all of them with the intertwined *E*'s for Eaton Edge.

Even as he pulled the truck to a stop, she didn't move toward the passenger door. He watched her pull a little silver disc out of her bag. She flicked it open, revealing a mirror.

He switched on the cab light.

"Thanks," she said. She ran her fingertips over her mouth, then her cheek. They trailed over her jaw, down her neck to the wavery lines of scars that trickled beneath the neck of her T-shirt.

The compact shut quickly and she tossed it back in her bag. She clutched the purse in both hands and looked for a long time at the sleeping house.

"Did you go to my daddy's funeral?" she asked him.

He blew a breath out through his nose and put the truck in Park with jerky motions. She didn't turn her head so he didn't bother answering. She already knew.

She rubbed her lips together. "I wish he'd gotten over my mother. Maybe…" She sighed. "I don't know. Maybe things could've been different if he'd just moved on. If he'd let himself be happy. He stopped loving it after she left. The Edge. Life. He stopped…living."

He was a good man. If Wolfe could have said anything, it would've been that. He missed Hammond. He missed Santiago. He missed everything about what used to be.

"Do you think he thought I left him, too?" she wondered out loud.

He frowned at her. Guilt was easy for the living when the dead went. He hadn't thought he'd ever see regret from Eveline Eaton, though. She'd left this world behind, hadn't she? She'd fulfilled ideas for a future many in Fuego had thought impossible. *Pipe dreams*, they'd called them.

She'd done everything she'd set out to do. She'd modeled—in New York. In Paris, from what he understood. She'd been splashed all over magazines at the convenience store in town.

Would she be having these regrets if she hadn't been in that car crash a year ago?

He'd seen the scars. Or some of them. Her body wasn't exactly the same, no. But neither was it ruined. She still looked good.

Damn good, if she asked him.

That isn't what she asked, he reminded himself, and shifted uncomfortably.

She sniffed. "Sorry." She unbuckled her seat belt. She took a few moments to put on the fancy shoes she'd been cradling in her lap. "Where're you dropping the car off?"

He grabbed the business card from a stack on the console between them and passed it to her. It had *Rowdy's Auto Repair* printed across the front.

Her fingers lifted, long and slender. She took it between her first and middle fingers and tilted it toward the dash light. It made a golden halo on the crown of her honey-blond head. "'Rowdy,'" she read. "Rowdy Conway?" At his nod, she made a noise. "Last I heard, he was a rodeo clown."

Rowdy was still a rodeo clown. And the local bar's biggest customer. He talked more smack and stirred more pots than any other male in Fuego.

"Thank you again," she said, looking at him at last. She was dry-eyed and devastating.

When she was younger, he'd thought she was too

tall and skinny, her features too striking for a little girl. Then she'd grown and he'd eaten that assumption. She was perfect. Did she know she was still perfect?

"Guess I better go face the music," she mused. She paused before getting out. "Um, could you not mention what I said about what I saw? The creature in the road. I'm not sure I was thinking straight at that moment. In fact, I know I wasn't thinking straight. Would you mind keeping it quiet, or..." She trailed off and rolled her eyes. "Wow. That was stupid. I'm sorry."

He shook his head slightly. *Not stupid*, he wanted to say. *You're not stupid*. He wanted to reach out and take her hand because he could see it tremble slightly, the way it had when he'd found her on the side of the road. She'd been as jumpy as prey.

Would she grimace if he touched her?

He didn't think he'd be able to stand that.

Eveline cleared her throat. "See you later, Coldero."

He lifted his fingers off the wheel in return. She took the suitcase and jumped down from the cab, shutting the door behind her. He watched her walk to the house and up the steps to the door.

When he caught himself watching the movement of her hips, he put the truck in Reverse and got the hell out of there.

"That Coldero?"

Eveline jumped a mile high. She lowered her fist from the door of the hacienda-style house she'd been about to knock on and frowned at the shadows of the porch. "Everett."

Boot heels clunked across the boards of the porch as her eldest brother came into the light, a trio of loyal hounds close at his heels. He was slender in his dirty

Wranglers still. His eyes, however, had lost their smile under the brim of his hat. "You're late," he said in his baritone.

She set the suitcase down as the dogs surrounded her, sniffing her ankles. Their tails wagged in a show of friendliness. She couldn't count on as much from Everett. He wasn't going to let her in until he'd had his say. "Yes. I'm late."

"Care to explain that?" he drawled.

"There were…complications," she said. "My flight was delayed. Then cancelled. I got another flight. It was going to San Francisco but got rerouted—"

"Excuses," he cut in. "You were always good at those. Dad ate 'em up any way you served them, too."

She closed her eyes. "Let's not do this now, Everett, okay? We're both hurting."

"You weren't here," he stated. "Ellis and me, we buried him ourselves. Just like we took care of him ourselves, all these years."

"You're angry," she granted. "I get that. Hell, I can even understand it. But it's late and I haven't seen a decent bed in what feels like a week. We can have a nice go at this when we're both fresh in the morning."

"Paloma wouldn't have it," he noted.

"Paloma still works here?" she asked.

"Who else is going to nag the hell out of me?" he wondered out loud as he moved to the door. He pulled out his keys. "You?"

He hadn't been home yet, she realized. Probably out in the hills or the barn, catching up on work. She saw the lines around the corners of his eyes. "You've always loved her," she murmured.

He made a noncommittal noise and swung the door open. "After you, Manhattan."

She sighed and picked up her suitcase. "Thanks a lot." As she entered, so did the dogs. Their nails ticked against the hardwood floors.

"Sorry there's no red carpet," he added as he followed her into the long front hallway with its row of benches on both sides and hooks and boot cubbies. "We save that for the important folks."

"You haven't stopped being an ass," she observed as he switched on the lights and she had a look around. The living room was still sparse on furnishings. Her father hadn't been the decorating kind. Everything was wood except for the stone fireplace and the cushions on the couch and chair. The ceilings were low and strong beamed. No television. An old-fashioned radio sat on a secretary in the corner. The scents were all the same—leather, old oak, a hint of horsehair... "At least you're consistent."

He gestured to the stairs. "Your room's still up there to the right. He saved it for you."

Her gaze seized on his face. The bitterness. The grief. His collided with her own.

"Always thought you'd be coming back," he said, devastating her further. "He said you'd get tired of it, eventually—the city. The publicity. The high life."

She blinked at tears. "I can't do this. Not now. I told you…"

"And of all people you had bring you home—Coldero."

His voice took a dark dive. She frowned. "He was the only one I could call. There's no cell service out here."

"You'll need a radio," Everett said, "if you plan to be here more than the cursory few days."

"I do," she admitted.

"How long?" he wondered. "How long before you

go screaming back to the city? I'm no fool, Eveline. It's what you do."

"Everett," she said carefully. "I can't go back."

He stilled. For the first time, she saw him study the scars on her neck. "They don't want you back?"

She fought a wince and managed it just fine. Still, the reverberations pinged off every surface inside her. "Not exactly."

"The hell with them, then," he spat. His features vibrated with fury. "To hell with all of 'em."

She would've smiled if she hadn't been so tired. "Well, that's something."

His shoulders leveled off and the tension seemed to leave him. Suddenly, he looked as tired as she felt. He looked as if he had aged a good deal since the last time she'd seen him at her bedside in the hospital in New York.

"Go on," he said, nodding up the stairs. "Fighting's no fun if you're liable to keel over."

"Are you expecting Ellis tomorrow?" she asked.

"I expect so," he said. He reached up to scratch the center of his forehead. "Bozeman will be here around ten thirty. For the reading of the will."

Her hand fumbled over the railing. "The will."

"Yeah." He pursed his lips. "I guess, in a way, you got here right when you needed to, didn't you?"

She frowned as she turned away from him completely. "Good night," she said, resigned, and took the stairs two at a time.

Chapter 3

The dream didn't wake her. She slept like a corpse and woke, mildly surprised, at the sun. It fell heavy against her bleary eyes. Exhaustion had claimed her. It'd claimed her so hard her subconscious had forgotten to send her screaming out of nightmares midway through the repose.

At the last second, however, something else chased her from the heavy blanket of sleep.

Something that crawled on all fours then stood up, eyes shining. Head like a wolf, dripping fangs…body like an emaciated man's. Its teeth bared and it leaped at her.

She woke up, a cry locked in her throat.

With her heart banging to get out of her chest, she realized she was in her room—her childhood room. She'd forgotten to close the blackout curtains on the east-facing windows before she'd crashed face-first onto her lavender bedspread.

She pressed the backs of her hands to her eyes and shook her head, taking herself through the ragged pants that washed through her like waves. She looked around and tried to gather calm from her surroundings.

She didn't get calm. She got heartbreak.

Everett was right. Her father hadn't changed a thing. The same lace-trimmed skirt on the bed and the matching cut of the curtains. Several porcelain dolls sat wide-eyed and shoulder to shoulder on the built-in window seat. Her barrel racing trophies gleamed like new atop her dresser. The furniture was white. The chest of drawers came up to her breastbone. Everything had received a good dusting.

It was a girl's room, through and through—down, or up to, the glow-in-the-dark stars strewn across the ceiling.

This wasn't Eden Meadows's room, not by a long shot. It was Eveline Eaton's—the girl she'd left behind… or hoped to, all those years ago.

Eveline sat up slowly. She'd slept on her face. Her neck was stiff as hell. She turned her head, hissing as muscles seized. Everything was sore. She reached up to the point where her shoulder joined her collarbone. Her fingertips slid over scar tissue and she pulled it back with a wince.

Last night's accident came back to her. That would explain the aches and pains. She dropped her feet to the floor and rose cautiously to standing.

Nothing broken, she remembered. Just a bruised shoulder and a messed-up ego. And visions that were the opposite of sugar plums.

Neither she nor Wolfe had thought to call the police. Or, if he'd thought about it, he hadn't let on. She'd been so anxious to get away from the scene, out of the night, she'd been only too happy to leave it without reporting anything to the local authorities.

Telling herself not to think about what she'd seen or experienced last night on the road to Fuego, she took her time in the connected bathroom. She hadn't taken her makeup off the night before so she washed her face thoroughly and brushed her teeth. She dug into her toiletry bag for the vitamin E cream she'd used habitually since the accident a year ago, smearing it heavily on the roadmap of broken skin along the left side of her neck, down her shoulder and across her collarbone.

She freshened up as best as she could and raided her suitcase for a pair of jeans. It would be hot. It was always hot at the Edge in summer daylight. She chose a black T-shirt, then threw open the double doors to her closet and hunted her battered white Stetson.

A run into town would be unavoidable. She needed new boots. T-shirts wouldn't do with all this high desert sunlight. She'd need something lightweight with more coverage, more jeans, a new hat... She had to keep the scars shaded. God knows what damage the New Mexican sun would do to them...

She left the room and moved to the stairs. As she crept down, she could hear Everett's acerbic voice coming from the direction of their father's office. She avoided that part of the house entirely and sought the kitchen instead.

There was whiskey ready on the sideboard, as always. She grabbed a snifter from the shelf and reached for one of the bottles with amber liquid inside.

"Ahem."

Eveline jumped, guilty. "Jesus!" she exclaimed, turning wildly in the direction of the stove.

"Whiskey for breakfast." Paloma raised a penciled

brow. "You need Jesus—much as your big brother does, apparently."

"I…" She blew out a breath, laughing off the knee-jerk urge to make excuses. "Paloma. You scared me."

Paloma raised a pot holder. "You're the one sneaking 'round the place, *niña*." She tossed the pot holder on the counter and pulled a mug down from the cupboard. Picking up the coffee pot, she poured it black and offered it that way. "Let's try this again. *Buenos dias*, Miss Evie."

Paloma was the one and only person allowed to call her Evie. Eveline crossed to her, raising both hands to take the mug. She met the woman's dark eyes. Paloma was a diminutive four-nine to Eveline's five-eleven, but that had never gotten in the way of her status around here. "*Buenos dias*, Paloma," she greeted warmly.

"Hmm," Paloma grunted. She smiled. She'd always worn heavy makeup, enough for a television news anchor. Her dark hair was pulled severely back from a wide brow complete with a widow's peak in a low, heavy bun. It was shot through with silver, but still immaculately kept.

She looked…the same, Eveline thought with surprise. Paloma had to at least be in her sixties. How did she look the same as she had when Eveline was fifteen?

"I'm shocked you could sleep through your brother's racket," Paloma said with a shake of her head as she went back to the stove. "He's been hollering into that phone since daybreak."

Eveline clutched the mug. She was relieved. Paloma's gaze hadn't lingered on her neck. Choked up, it took Eveline a moment to find a seat at the table in front of the bay windows. She'd always been able to count on Paloma. They all had, even when they least expected it.

The woman was practically a mother to her. She'd been a permanent fixture at the Edge—ever since Eveline's mother had walked out.

Eveline sipped the coffee. She closed her eyes. "Everett doesn't deserve you," she muttered.

"You let God be the judge of that," Paloma said, bringing a plate and a small basket to the table.

Eveline suppressed a grin. Paloma had been trying to get them all to church for decades. Rarely had she managed to rope all three of them into a pew. Eveline rustled through the gingham cloth in the basket until she uncovered the magic tucked underneath. "Your sopaipillas," she sighed. She breathed in the aroma. A million different memories bubbled up. Heaven could wait. "It's been forever and a day since I've had one of these babies."

"You need it," Paloma commented. She pinched the skin of Eveline's arm. "They're still not feeding anybody up north, I see."

"Not like this," Eveline granted, pinching off a corner of the dough pillow. "Mmm." There was no need for butter, honey or jam. It was that good.

The indulgence quickly became a feast as omelets with chorizo and mushrooms joined the table and bacon and fresh fruit and… "Kill me now," Eveline invited. "It's never going to get better."

Paloma harrumphed as she took the next seat. "You've been all over the world and you expect me to believe this is the best there is?" She shook her head as she raised her mug to her mouth, elbow perched on the table's edge. "*No me parece.* Familiar's what it is. There's comfort in the familiar. Comfort's what we all need right now."

Eveline thought for a split second Paloma would admonish her, too, for missing the funeral. The lecture never came. She felt ashamed. Paloma had admonished her plenty over the years but never in her low moments. She'd always known when to lay the disappointment on thick and when to let it lie.

Grief and gratitude comingled and brought on a rash of new aches—these deeper than the physical ones. They stole Eveline's breath. "How are you?" she wanted to know.

Paloma set the mug down gently. "Everett's got everything handled. Or so he says. He didn't let me lift a finger to help with the arrangements. He's shut us both out, me and Ellis. It's his way of grieving, I suppose. Ellis is holding up but you see it in his eyes. He's taking it hard. His eyes never lie."

"No, they don't," Eveline said. "How are you taking all this, though? You loved him, too."

Paloma took a long draft of air through her nostrils. She picked up the string of her tea bag and dipped it in and out of the mug. "Hammond's lucky he didn't go sooner. I did all I could to take care of him through the years but…a person can only do so much. A soul's got to take care of himself up to a point. He lived for everyone else. Never for himself…"

For a moment, Eveline thought Paloma was going to tear up, too. She looked away quickly. She'd never seen the woman shed a tear. It'd destroy her to see it. "You still haven't answered my question. How are you?"

"Oh, Evie, *niña*, how are any of us, really?" Paloma asked. She reached out and cupped the point of Eveline's chin. "I'm not going anywhere, okay?"

"I wasn't asking—"

Paloma cut her off with a tsk. "I know where I'm needed. Everett may be a pain in everybody's rear, but he and your daddy had one thing in common—neither one knows how to take care of himself."

"Are you still doing his laundry?" Eveline asked.

Paloma chuckled deep, dropping her hand so she could help herself to an omelet. "The man wouldn't know a bottle of detergent from a bottle of bleach. And neither would the other one."

"Oh, my God," Eveline said, finding she, too, could laugh. "Not Ellis, too? He was married!"

"Ever since the divorce, he's been bringing his laundry back and the girls', too."

"And you indulge him," Eveline murmured with a shake of her head.

"It's those puppy dog eyes," Paloma said with a shake her head. "Even I can't resist them. You look rested."

"I am," Eveline said with some surprise.

"Sleep doesn't come easy to you anymore," Paloma guessed, correctly as always.

"No," Eveline admitted. She could admit that. Here. "Last night was the best night of sleep I've had in months." She neglected to mention the terrifying creature that had stalked her out of her dreams.

She fought a shiver. Her eyes fell on the cheery rays of sun across the porch. She could hear the birds. "I always forget."

"What's that?"

"How beautiful the Edge is," Eveline said as she looked for the horizon line. The Edge seemed to go on and on without ceasing. Growing up, she'd thought it went to the ends of the earth—that her daddy's cattle wandered along the equator and lowed across other country's savannahs.

The truth was that the Edge went as far as the distant mesa, which formed a natural barrier to the west.

To the east, there were two large buttes. In the center ran a river in all seasons, which made cattle ranching in the desert possible. There was a mountain to the north, also a natural barrier, and the southern quarter was split between gentle hills, tiny canyons and the desert plain. Fencing wasn't needed all the way around the Edge, thanks to the many landforms on the outskirts.

"It's healing weather."

Eveline hummed in answer, her chin sliding into the palm of her hand. "That's timely."

They heard the backdoor open and close.

Paloma made a noise. "That'll be Ellis. He's here for the reading."

"Oh," Eveline said. "The will."

They didn't have time to discuss it. Ellis veered off the hall into the kitchen. His eyes found her and he came to a stop. "Christ on a cracker. You're here."

"Mm," Paloma muttered, satisfied. "That's three for church."

"Ellis." Eveline had to swallow her emotions.

Ellis was broad—not as tall as Everett, but he'd stood toe-to-toe with their father. He held his hat in his hands, respectful where their big brother never had been. She saw his hands tighten on the brim. "I missed you yesterday. We all missed you."

"I missed you, too," Eveline replied. She rose as he came forward. "Oh, Ellis." She didn't so much hug him as attack him, throwing her arms around his shoulders. "I'm so sorry."

He took the brunt and held his own. "It's all right."

Ellis had always taken it upon himself to be the family counselor. He'd consoled her more times than she could count. He'd been their father's trusted ear and

he'd weathered more tirades from Everett than any of
the rest of them.

He'd weathered them so the rest of them wouldn't
have to.

Eveline pressed her face into the soft plaid of Ellis's
shoulder. "I wanted to be here."

"I know you did," he murmured.

"Everett said—"

"Don't pay any attention to what Everett says. Not
right now. He's doing his best, okay?"

She squeezed her eyes closed, fighting for composure. "Damn it. I didn't want to cry today." She pulled
back and snatched the hankie he had ready. "Why're
you so perfect?"

"I'm not." His dark eyes were so sad but he smiled
the crooked smile that was his own. "Nobody's angry
with you. Not me. Not Everett. No one. Okay, kid?"

"Sit," Paloma said as Eveline continued drying her
face. "Conversations like this always go down better
with—"

"Whiskey?" Everett said as he trudged into the room,
the dogs with him as always. "Damn right."

"Everett Templeton Eaton, don't you touch that poi-
son before you've had your breakfast!" Paloma threatened.

His hand fell away from the sideboard and he
growled his displeasure. "You didn't tell me the gang's
somehow managed to assemble itself, in spite of everything."

Ellis took the chair next to Eveline. "Let's eat before
Bozeman gets here."

Everett dropped to a chair, too, without his whiskey.
The dogs settled on the floor, eyeing the tabletop hope-
fully with lolling tongues. Everett reached for an om-

elet and earned a swat on the hand from Paloma. "Hat off," she said smartly.

He scowled at her but pulled the hat off anyway, hooking it over his knee. "May I?" he asked with false grace.

"Lose the sneer," Paloma said. "It'll make you old before your time."

Everett grumbled and cut himself a large egg from the hot plate. "We're Eatons. It's our lot to age quick and die young." He shoveled a huge forkful into his mouth.

"Dare I ask who you've been jawing at all morning?" Paloma asked.

"Mechanic," Everett said around a mouthful. "Tractor's on the fritz."

Eveline's eyes narrowed. "Rowdy Conway?"

He eyed her over the length of the table. "How the hell do you know that?"

"Wolfe gave me his card last night," she said.

"Coldero," Everett muttered darkly.

Ellis raised both brows. "You've seen Wolfe?"

"He got me out of a tight spot last night," she explained, sidestepping any mention of the wreck…or what had caused it. "I needed a tow."

Ellis looked the other way at his brother. "No wonder you're in such a fine mood."

"Don't get him started," Paloma said as she dropped to her seat with her hands raised. "When's the lawyer supposed to be here?"

"Ten thirty," Ellis and Everett said as one.

"And who's he called for the reading?" Paloma asked. "Will I need to make lunch?"

"No," Everett answered brusquely. "He said to expect family only. That's Ellis, you, me and Manhattan over there."

"I don't see why it's necessary for me to be in the room during the reading," Paloma stated.

"You'll be there," Everett told her.

"We want you to be there," Ellis said, more gently.

Eveline nodded her agreement and Paloma raised her hands again. "I'll make lunch anyway. You'll need to eat. The lawyer can stay, too, if he likes."

"Don't go all out," Ellis advised. "We don't need much."

She got up from the table and escaped to the pantry, already talking about the menu. Eveline leaned toward her brothers, hushed. "She's taken care of us for twenty years."

"Us?" Everett said pointedly.

She ignored him. "Dad must have left her something. Didn't he?"

"How should I know?" Everett asked as he piled another omelet on his plate.

Ellis frowned at him. "I can't make myself think Dad would want it any other way," he said in an undertone. "We'll see, won't we?"

Why was Eveline dreading this, more than she'd dreaded coming face-to-face with Everett or anyone else from town?

Lionel Bozeman had been her father's lawyer for as long as Eveline could remember. Their partnership dated back to before Eaton Edge was a working ranch. Even Everett trusted him—and since Everett trusted maybe three people in the entire world, that was saying something.

Everett made it clear that Lionel was to sit in the brawny armchair on the far side of the desk. Two cowhide chairs served as guest seating. Eveline let Everett and Ellis take those, knowing they would feature most heavily in their father's wishes.

And there was nothing wrong with that. They hadn't only been here for Hammond on a daily basis. They'd worked at the Edge since they were boys. They knew the business. They knew the land, the hands, the animals and all the little details in between.

She and Paloma took the more discreet reading chairs in the corners of the room. They were deep-cushioned leather and squeaked when either of them budged, just as Eveline remembered. She'd spent several weekend mornings watching her father work from the one closest to the window. She'd liked watching the light shift from high and harsh to slanted and lazy. She'd liked watching the clouds and the hues change.

She'd liked hearing Hammond's voice. He'd never raised it. Not to anyone. Not even Everett. His voice had sounded like old suede and cigar smoke. There was nothing that said home like her father's voice.

As she listened to Lionel discuss the formalities, she missed Hammond more than ever.

She'd never hear that voice coming from the other side of that desk again. She reached out with her foot to the dog lying supine on the rug nearby and rubbed its belly. The gesture was meant to soothe her as much as the canine.

"…to Paloma Coldero…"

Eveline saw Paloma startle. She wanted to reach for her, but she was too far away. Ellis turned and winked at her to set her at ease.

Lionel continued, glasses perched low on his nose as he read from the documents on the desk. "Hammond has left a sum of fifty thousand American dollars…"

Paloma made a choked noise. "Fifty thousand?"

"...as well as instructions for her yearly salary if she chooses to stay on at Eaton Edge as housekeeper..."

"She'd better," Everett opined.

"Let him read," Eveline told him.

Everett sent her a long frown.

Lionel added, "...as well as the added option of the mother-in-law suite above the stable. If she does choose to take the suite, it is to be renovated in accordance with her needs and tastes."

Paloma's mouth had dropped open. "Oh, Hammond," she muttered.

"Yes," Lionel said with a smile for her. "He was determined that you should be well cared for, even after your retirement. The mother-in-law suite is to be your residence even after you retire, if you so wish. On a related note, Hammond has asked that an amount be set aside—whatever's needed—for the treatment and care of your older brother Santiago Coldero."

"Do what?" Everett said.

"Don't say a word," Ellis advised.

Everett narrowed his eyes on him. "You knew about this?"

"He said, and I quote," Lionel said carefully, "'No expense spared.'"

There was a stunned silence. Then Paloma made a sound that could no longer be mistaken for a broken sob. Before any of them could get up to comfort her, she pushed to her feet and rushed from the room.

Eveline would have gone after her if she wasn't in such a state of shock. "He left arrangements for Santiago to be cared for?"

"It's a generous arrangement," Lionel confirmed. "Hammond was firm about this, however."

"I'll be damned," Ellis said.

"He wanted the man his wife left him for to be taken care of," Everett said slowly.

"Don't start, Everett," Ellis commented.

"It's insane," Everett stated. "He couldn't have been in his right mind—"

Lionel cleared his throat loudly. "I assure you, Everett, that your father was in a clear and present state of mind when he made these wishes clear to me. You will let me continue?"

Everett's jaw clenched. He blew out a breath, then waved his hand.

"Very good," Lionel said, dropping his incisive gaze back to the documents. "Next is the rights and shares of the family business, Eaton Edge."

Eveline could feel the tension in the room. She couldn't think why. Everett would get the bulk of the shares. He would also receive the big job behind the desk as chief of operations. And there was nothing Ellis would do to counter. Ellis had never been interested in the top job. He was happy working behind the scenes.

"...to each of his children—Everett, Ellis and Eveline—Hammond wrote, 'I leave a twenty percent share of the ranch.' Another ten percent should be left to each of his existing grandchildren, the girls—Isla and Ingrid when they come of age..."

Lionel paused and Everett stared down the end of his nose at him. "I can do the math, Lionel. There's another twenty percent floating around out there."

"Yes," Lionel said. He cleared his throat again and kept his eyes averted.

A sense of foreboding crept over Eveline. She hugged her arms, bracing herself.

"...the final twenty percent is to be left to Wolfe Coldero—"

Everett jumped to his feet. "The hell it is!"

The dogs jumped up as well. The one at Eveline's feet barked a long, howling bark, startled out of its slumber.

Lionel raised a hand. "He knew you would be displeased, Everett—"

"What was he thinking?" Everett said, passing a hand through his hair. "Coldero? He left an equal share of the Edge to—the son of a bitch!"

Ellis stood to face his brother. "Take it easy."

Everett rounded on him. "You knew about this, too. Didn't you?"

"No," Ellis said. "But you heard Lionel. Dad was in a clear and present state of mind when he put all this together. There's not much you or anyone else can do to fight it."

"You can have my shares," Eveline said, coming to stand as well. "You can split them evenly between you. That would give each of you thirty percent of the Edge."

"What the hell would that do?" Everett snapped. He waved his arms. "How the hell is that supposed to fix the fact that Coldero is now a shareholder of our birthright!"

"It's not like he's going to walk up on the ranch and take possession!" Ellis argued. "I'm sure he doesn't want any part of this."

"I'm going to have to buy Wolfe Coldero out of twenty percent of shares!" Everett said, pacing now.

"Stop saying his name like that!" Eveline cried, earning a curious look from Ellis.

Everett was beyond hearing. "Twenty percent!"

"Management of the property and holdings," Lionel interjected, "is, of course, in the hands of you, Everett. It states that very plainly. Hammond was confident in your capabilities to maintain the land, cattle and business. Ellis is to have a comanagement position to make sure you don't take on too much. He didn't want you working yourself to death."

"Like he did?" Everett snarled. "He could work himself to death, but I'm not allowed to?"

"Precisely," Lionel said as he rose to his feet and began stacking papers together. "Your father was a very generous man. A compassionate one. I suggest you all honor that and, further, abide by his wishes."

"We'll see about that," Everett said, all huff and fury as he turned on his heel and clomped out of the room, the dogs trotting to catch up.

Bozeman stacked papers, shaking his head. "Ellis, you're going to have to talk him down. It will be difficult for him to fight this. Very difficult. He'll be tying Wolfe and himself up in court for years."

"I understand," Ellis assured him. He placed his hat on his head. "And I'll speak with him."

"Are you in agreement with your father's wishes?" Bozeman asked, eyeing him carefully.

Ellis nodded thoughtfully. "I have no doubt Dad knew what he was doing. Though I'm not sure why he's done it this way…"

Bozeman looked to Eveline for the first time. "How about you, Ms. Eveline? Are you in agreement?"

She exchanged a look with Ellis. There was apprehension in his eyes, but his jaw was square, the picture of assurance. "I am." Though she couldn't help but think that her father had had a sense of humor and he'd picked a strange time to show it.

Chapter 4

"Twenty frickin' percent!"

Eveline blew out an exasperated breath, hard enough to lift the hair off her cheek. "This is going to kill you, isn't it?"

"If it's not fixed," Everett muttered as he hunched over the steering wheel, staring daggers at the road in front of them. "Dig me a grave next to Dad's and let me pass on peaceably before I see that son of a bitch take over."

She shook her head. "*Why?* Why have you always had it out for him?"

"You're kidding, right?" he asked out the side of his mouth. He stomped on the gas as he hit the straightaway between the Edge and Fuego.

Eveline gripped the handle of the door and closed her eyes. Her anxiety about cars wasn't limited to her own driving. It was worse, in fact, when others drove—which made living in the city where the bulk of transportation was in the hands of cab and Uber drivers a living hell.

She hadn't been the driver the night she was in the car crash in the city. She'd been helpless to stop any of it.

Everett was known to have a heavy foot. He was notorious for driving with his ego. Eveline tried several breathing exercises as he continued to rant.

"The asshole shows up at the Edge and suddenly becomes everyone's charity case. Santiago made him his own. Paloma fawned over him. Jesus, Mom left so she could be his mother instead of ours."

"That's not true," Eveline argued. Trees blew by on either side of the road. They were a blur, just like the signs last night.

In through the mouth. Out through the nose.

"Dad puts him on a horse and gives him a job. The guy couldn't use a radio!"

An idea struck Eveline. She'd heard talk of it the last time she was in Fuego…for her mother's burial. "Is it true Dad wanted to make him foreman before the fire at Coldero Ridge?"

Everett steamed in answer.

Eveline's lips parted. How would that possibly have worked—with Everett in a management position and his so-called archnemesis foreman? Why would Hammond have even considered it knowing the chaos that would ensue?

Why had he done *this*? Even Bozeman had said it. Hammond had known how Everett would feel about shares going to Wolfe. And he'd done it anyway.

"It's some kind of test," Everett muttered. He mimicked the long drawl of Hammond's old suede voice. "'Here, boy. Here's what I promised you. But only if you pass your own personal version of the Kobayashi Maru.'"

"The what?"

Everett hesitated. "It's from *Star Trek*. A training exercise with a no-win scenario so no one would ever pass."

"What's the point of that exactly?" she asked.

"I don't know," he snapped. "To test a cadet's character or some crap."

"Huh," she said. She bit the inside of her lip when he slammed on the brakes for the stop sign ahead. Turning her face to the window, she willed herself not to say anything…like "Please don't kill us both."

"Are you upset about the twenty percent he left to me?" she asked out loud.

"You're his daughter," Everett said. "*That* I can get behind. It's your birthright, same as me."

She breathed a quiet sigh of relief. She didn't want Everett bitter at her. She'd never wanted that.

"Whether or not I think you deserve it," he added.

She nodded. She should've seen the sour sidenote coming. "And you're okay with me staying for a few weeks? Just to get my bearings."

"Even if I didn't, Ellis and Paloma would form a league against me. Between the two of them, I wouldn't have much say in the matter."

"That tells me nothing," she said. "Do you want me there or not, Everett?"

"*Dad* would've wanted you there," he rumbled. "I can honor that, all right?"

It was as close to uncovering Everett's actual feelings on the matter as she was going to get. "Thank you."

"I expect you to work," he stated. "There's plenty to

be done. What with the last few weeks, we're behind in every department."

"I can work," she agreed.

"Won't be no catwalk or day on the beach like you're used to."

"I said I can handle it."

He made a noncommittal sound. "You still ride?"

He went off the road a little and hit a pothole, jarring the teeth she'd had clenched together since they left the Edge. She was going to lose her mind before they closed the distance to Rowdy's Auto Repair. "Of course, I still ride."

"When was the last time you were in the saddle?" he asked, always skeptical.

"I, ah…" She cleared her throat when her voice wavered. She couldn't tell if Everett's driving was better or worse with her eyes closed. "I have a palomino mare, Sienna Shade, stabled in Upstate New York. I ride her as much as possible."

"In the last year?"

"Especially in the last year," she admitted. She propped her elbow on the sill, cupping the messed up side of her neck. "Pretty sure that's all that's kept me sane over the last twelve months."

He said nothing to that. The silence in the cab was easier this time.

They were all different—Everett, Ellis and Eveline. While Ellis liked to take the peaceful way out of most of the time, Eveline and Everett had always butted heads. They hadn't had much in common—not with her aspirations so far outside of Fuego and his fixed firmly at the Edge. There was also a good eight years between them. However, the one thing they had both always loved was riding. Horses. Being in the saddle.

He understood horses had held her together. He understood why. He spent every day astride his red mare, Crazy Alice.

Over the last year, she'd thought seriously of pulling up roots in the city and disappearing into the countryside with Sienna Shade—buying a barn with enough land for the mare to run and enough space for Eveline to forget everything.

Now she was back in New Mexico. She felt nerves crawling around in the pit of her stomach as Everett pulled onto Main Street—back in Fuego, the last place she'd ever thought she'd contemplate living again.

"If you're going to stay awhile," Everett began carefully, "you might as well send for her."

"What?" she asked, trying not to make eye contact with anyone on the sidewalk.

"The mare," he answered.

"Sienna?" she breathed. "You'd... There's room for her?"

"You're part owner now," he reminded her. "If I've got to get used to it, then you might as well. We'll make room. Hell, we'll build another stable if we have to."

"Everett," she said, treading lightly, "I can help. With expenses. I have money."

"I know about your money," he grunted. "I don't need it."

"If the estate ever did—"

"We'll talk," he said shortly. "But not before then."

She nodded. "Having Sienna here... That would be amazing."

He said nothing more before pulling into the parking lot for Rowdy's garage.

Here we go, she thought. Maybe it was her brother's driving, but she felt nauseous. It took her a moment to find her footing on the pavement outside the vehicle. She leaned against the passenger door until she felt steady.

"Comin'?" Everett asked as he headed for the open garage door.

She followed him, keeping the brim of her hat low. Nobody had to see her until she stopped looking green.

It didn't take Rowdy long to call her out. He had a gut now. His coveralls hadn't been fastened at one shoulder. There were rags hanging out of his pockets, all of them smudged. The sun had turned the upside of his cheeks burnt rose. "I'll be damned. If it ain't Eden Meadows in my own garage."

"We're here about her car," Everett told him.

Rowdy wasn't to be deterred. His dark eyes took a dive where they shouldn't over Eveline's torso. "Do you go by Eden now, exclusively?"

"No," she answered. "I'm still Eveline in places."

He gave a nasty little chortle. "Where might those places be?" he asked, suggestively.

Everett snorted. "You've got balls."

"Hold on a minute," Rowdy said. "I've got something for you."

"It better be the effing bill," Everett said, starting a slow pace that would work its way up to a fine stew if Rowdy didn't stop leering and step into gear.

Rowdy came back, magazine in hand. He'd found a pen, too. "You mind signing?"

"What?" Everett snapped.

"It's the swimsuit edition from last year," Rowdy said with a wide smile. "Your finest, in my opinion." He thrust the magazine at her.

She saw that it was crinkled, as if it had been handled quite a bit since its place on the newsstand.

"You looked real good in that yellow one. With the cutouts," Rowdy said, his eyes alight as they found the vee between her legs. "Your legs go on for days."

"Do you not see me?" Everett asked. "I'm standing right here!"

"Not right now," she told Rowdy. "But we would like the bill, please."

Rowdy's grin died. "Huh." He balled up the magazine and stuffed it in the pocket of his coveralls. "Just as well. It wouldn't be worth as much now, would it? Not with your looks all messed up after—"

"*The car*, Conway!" Everett shouted. "I'm liable to strangle you and I don't feel like dealing with a lawsuit today!"

Rowdy eyed both them wearily before he ambled back to his computer station.

She turned away, breathing carefully.

"Don't let Rowdy get to you," Everett told her in a tone that brooked no argument. "He's an everlasting douche-bagger."

"I'm fine," she replied. "It's not my first time dealing with this sort of thing."

Rowdy came back, no faster than before. He hitched his back belt and handed Everett the bill. Eveline took it for herself and surveyed the fine print. "What's wrong with it exactly?"

"It's fubared," Rowdy said.

She narrowed her eyes. "Is that your professional opinion?"

"It ain't drivable," he said. "And won't be, ever again. When you mess up a car, you really mess up a car, sweet pot."

"Don't call me that," she warned.

"Don't call her that," Everett snapped, simultaneously.

"You hit something, didn't you?" Rowdy asked.

"What?" Eveline asked. Her jaw dropped and her lips trembled. "W-Why would you say that?"

"That big dent in the back quarter panel," he said, lowering his brow. "Looked like blood on it."

Everett glanced at her. "*Did* you hit something?"

Eveline swallowed. "I…don't really remember. It happened so fast…"

Everett must've seen her nerves underneath. He cursed. "Let's get out of here."

"What about the bill for the tow company?" Eveline asked. "Do I settle that through you or…"

Rowdy chortled, going up to his toes. "Tow company. That's a good one."

"Conway and Coldero aren't affiliated," Everett informed her. "That's one thing I don't blame him for." He watched Rowdy scratch at the front of his pants. "The *only* thing."

She waved the bill. "I better call the rental company and see how to take care of this."

Everett snatched it. "Go wait in the truck."

"You are not paying for this mess," Eveline said.

"As you're not getting the car back and it looks like he did little more than take a look at it before deciding it was totaled, I'm going to rag on the man until he agrees he jacked the price up knowing it was you who's bankrolling this."

"Then you'll let me foot the bill?" she asked. Before he could walk away, she grabbed his arm to stop him. "Everett, we're not riding back together."

"Why the hell not?"

"Because you drive like you're on the lam," she informed him.

His chin jutted forward. "My vehicle isn't the one that's been totaled."

"Nonetheless…"

"If you're not riding with me, how're you getting back to the Edge?"

She lifted her shoulder. "I've got the radio you loaned me. I'll call Ellis. I need to go by and see the girls."

"Liberty's got the girls. She's moved them to Taos."

Eveline's lips parted. "She…took them all the way to Taos?"

"Ellis sees them every other weekend," Everett explained. He nodded when she shook her head. "It's messed up. Worse that Ellis won't fight much of what she demands."

"He loves them so much," Eveline said. "How could she keep them from him? He doesn't deserve it."

"Try telling Liberty," Everett said before he walked off to deal with Rowdy.

Eveline told herself her current impulse was because she had a bill to settle. And she wanted to get off Main Street. She was already drawing stares and whispers from the locals. When she ran into Javier Rivera, a longtime hand at Eaton Edge, she took it for luck. After chatting with him for several minutes in the parking lot of Ol' Pat's Pool Hall, she eyed his company truck. "Are you going to be here a while?"

"Oh, yeah," he said and shrugged. "Me and the guys—we like to let loose after work. You know how it is. We'll probably hit up the taproom across the street, too."

She put her hands in her back pockets. "I need to

run a quick errand and I was wondering if I could use your truck. It should only take twenty minutes or so."

"Yeah, sure, Ms. Eveline," he said, readily digging his keys out of his jeans pocket. "You take it out for as long you need. You know where to find me."

"Thank you, Javy," she said with a smile. She considered him. His eyes still sparkled, big and brown. He'd been eighteen when she turned teenager. Back then, he'd been eye candy like no other.

Hell, who was she kidding? You never forgot your first crush—even if his hairline had since receded. "It's good to see you."

"You, too. Hey, you staying a while at the Edge? The rest of the boys would love to come by and say hi."

"I'd like that," she said. "And yes. I'll be staying— for a while at least."

"Good to hear."

"One more thing," she said before he could join the other hands in the pool hall. Following impulse, she asked, "Could you tell me where I can find Wolfe Coldero?"

As it turned out, Wolfe now lived outside Fuego limits. She drove past the point where she'd wrecked the car the night before. She knew it was the spot because of the tire marks on the pavement. She looked around, keeping her hands firmly at ten and two on the wheel. She peered into the brush on the roadside, shivering when she thought of what she'd seen before she ran off the road.

Or what she'd *thought* she'd seen. In the daylight, it seemed absolutely ridiculous.

She was so distracted, she nearly missed the turnoff Javier had told her to watch out for.

She followed the dirt road, which was smooth and grated, and the treads of tire tracks through a small stand of ponderosas. Off the highway about half a mile, she pulled into a clearing.

A clearing that reached hither and beyond. As she stopped and put the truck in Park, she blinked for several moments at the vista. The property was adorned with a small barn, a paddock and an RV with the tow truck pulled up next to it. In the distance, some two hundred feet or so, she saw a concrete slab—the footprint of a future house.

But that view. It was a stunner. She got out of the truck slowly and walked toward what would be a spectacular sunset in a few hours' time. She could see mountains, buttes and mesas that would soon be painted desert red.

She licked her lips when she realized her pulse had gathered tempo. Again the word *freedom* popped into her head—second time in less than twenty-four hours. And both times she'd been within earshot of Wolfe Coldero.

She heard barking from the direction of the RV. The screen door swung open and a sheepdog let itself out, leaping over the metal steps and racing in her direction. With its ears pinned back, it barked a montage of "Stranger Danger" before putting its nose to the ground.

She stopped when it didn't come straight to her. It milled around before weaving back in her direction, sniffing incessantly. Finally, its nose found the toe of her sneaker. When its head lifted, she saw its eyes.

They were milky white.

"Oh," she said, stunned. She reached out and touched its snout. "You poor thing."

Its tail thumped on the ground several times and she

smiled. It might be blind, but it certainly wasn't deaf. She crouched to its level so she could rub the long fur along its front. It didn't have a collar but it was clean and well-fed. "Hello. I'm Eveline. What's your name?"

A whistle answered. The dog turned and trotted toward the stable as Wolfe came around the building. His eyes fell on her in the shadow of his ten-gallon hat. His steps hitched and he came to a stop.

Eveline pressed her hand to her stomach. He wasn't wearing a shirt—just jeans and boots—and she nearly lost her breath.

Screw it. She did lose her breath. For the love of God, the man looked good—so good it took her a moment to gain her feet again. He was lean in the center and wide at the shoulder. Muscle rippled everywhere, like lazy ocean waves. Everywhere.

She looked studiously at his boots. She was staring. She hated when people stared at her. She could imagine how he felt when people stared at him. "We were just saying hello."

Wolfe reached down in an automatic gesture and touched the dog's head.

Of course, she thought, her smile coming back. The man who didn't speak and the dog who couldn't see. They made a picture. "He's friendly," she said. "What's his name?" Then she cursed herself and shook her head. "Sorry. I'm out of step again."

Wolfe held up a hand. Closer now, she could see he was sweating. His hands were smudged with earth. She saw it in the lines of his palms. There was color in his face, too, and his chest rose and fell rapidly. She'd caught him working.

He moved to a nearby spigot on the side of the barn

and cranked the handle. It shrieked in protest but a rush of water sprayed onto the dry ground at his feet.

He tossed his hat on the ground, leaned down and cupped his big hands under the water. He rubbed them together and dug under the nailbeds on each finger where dirt was caked. When his hands were clean, he lowered his head and splashed water onto his face. Spreading both hands, he scrubbed it.

As he rubbed his fingers through his thick, dark hair, she felt a long, hard tug in the danger zone behind her navel. She took several careful breaths as he spread water to the back of his neck.

He was freckled all over. She'd never noticed that before…when they were children together.

Eveline caught herself humming in agreement with those hands as he rubbed water over his sweat-soaked chest. She shook herself, taking careful steps back. What was she doing—ogling Wolfe of all people?

He turned the spigot, shutting off the water flow. She wished there was a neat little handle like that on her urges. He shook the water from his head, wicking the wet off his face with a swipe of his hand in lieu of a towel. When he straightened, his hair was a curly mass he pushed back from his brow, leaving beads of moisture spilling down his cheeks and neck. Rivulets ran down his shoulders and chest. They caught the light, making him look better than any Wrangler jeans commercial she'd ever seen.

She bent down and retrieved his hat from the dirt, more to find an excuse to look away than anything. Keeping her eyes studiously on what seemed like a safe point on his muscled throat, she handed it over.

He nodded once in thanks, then took it, holding it between his fascinating hands.

Seriously, why *had* she come here? she wondered desperately.

She pointed to the dog. "Your dog is really sweet."

Wolfe looked down at the animal. He crouched just as she had and began running his hands over its back and front in quick succession.

Eveline's mouth actually dried watching those hands move over the dog's ruff. The animal leaned into the scratch, tongue lolling out the side of its mouth. She couldn't blame it, could she?

Wolfe's hair was still thick on top, unlike so many other cowboys who'd worn hats throughout the years. It was dark in places but bronze in others with the sun shining on it. She found herself taking a few steps forward.

She stopped, curling her hand into a ball. She was *not* about to run her hand through this man's hair. That would not be in any way appropriate.

She thought about Rowdy and how lewd he'd been, how uncomfortable that had made her. She took a breath and gathered the purse against her hip toward her middle. "I'm sorry I showed up here without any warning. I talked to Rowdy about the car and he said I'd have to settle the tow bill with you personally."

Wolfe looked up at her. His eyes narrowed. He shook his head.

She pursed her lips. "I know you're not saying I don't owe you anything, Wolfe."

He lifted one of those bronze shoulders.

She blew out a laugh. "Come on. I woke you up in the middle of the night. You had to tow me to the Edge where my brother thinks you're still persona non grata."

He raised a brow and looked down at the dog at the mention of Everett.

She frowned at the pair of them. "Let me settle this bill. Please."

His hands stopped moving at the quaver in her voice. He stared across the distance between them, eyes a cloud of questions.

She swallowed. She had no control over her emotions. Not anymore. She might as well come to terms with it. Because she didn't want to break down—not in front of Wolfe, of all people. "Everyone in Fuego either treats me like a hussy or a princess. I don't care how they manage it—town hall meeting, confab—I need everyone to pick a medium. I'd like to be treated like I used to be, back before I was Eden Meadows. I need to be Eveline Eaton, Hammond's daughter. At least for the time being. So you'll let me pay for this tow. Or, so help me, I'm going to hug that dog you've got there and have me a good cry."

His loud stare had widened somewhat. He came to his feet slowly. For a second, she thought he would cross to her and her heart racked her ribs in a way that felt more melodramatic than the kind of cry she needed.

Silently, he placed the hat on his head. Then he whistled out the side of his mouth. The dog's snout pointed up at him. Wolfe whistled once more, then snapped his fingers.

The dog didn't hesitate. It broke into a run and came back to her.

Oh, hell, she thought. This was going to be a far bigger mess than she'd thought.

Chapter 5

She wound up on the deck he'd built outside the RV with a beer in her hand.

She got to watch that sunset, after all. Silently, but far from alone.

The dog had settled itself at her feet. She'd found out through a good deal of gesturing on Wolfe's part and guesswork on hers that his name was Storm. And the horse prancing around the paddock—the gorgeous white filly with smoke-colored freckles on its legs and hind—was Winter.

She didn't know what to watch—the way the colors bled from land to sky and sky to land or the way Winter pranced from one end of the paddock to the other, a postcard labeled young, wild and...

Free.

Eveline gathered a breath, tipping the bottle to her mouth. Wolfe had put a shirt on. That was well and good. Her pheromones had made a sudden and untimely appearance for the first time in...well, a long while. So long she'd forgotten she had them.

They were alive and they were well, and they'd gone crawling in the unlikely direction of the guy she'd practically grown up with. That T-shirt did little, however, to hide the fact that Ellis's best childhood buddy was jacked like a rogue superhero.

His arm strained against his sleeve as he lifted the bottle for a drink. She closed her eyes. She wasn't supposed to be watching him.

The pretty horse. The breathtaking view. *Aren't they enough, Eveline?*

"Get a grip," she murmured to herself. At the turn of his head, she buttoned up quickly. She eyed the contents of her bottle. She was an Eaton, born and bred, however far she'd strayed from New Mexico. She could normally handle her alcohol.

Her tolerance seemed to have gone out the window, thanks to what would seem to anyone else as an innocent interlude between a jean-clad man and a rusty water spigot.

The jean-clad man had gone back to staring into the distance, thankfully, his eyes narrowed against the hard line of the sun. "How do you get anything done around here?" she wondered out loud. "It's too pretty for work."

The line of his mouth softened slightly in answer.

"I'm going to have to get used to it," she said. At the tilt of his head and the surprised glint in his eye, she clarified, "Everett's talking about putting me to work at the Edge."

He pursed his lips, running his thumb absently through the perspiration of his beer bottle.

She looked away quickly. "Maybe it won't be so bad.

I liked working cattle, once upon a time. And he said I could send for my horse in New York."

He nodded, seeming to understand the relief she couldn't contain at that.

She felt herself moved to talk more. She found herself telling him more than she'd told Everett. "There was this auction. Show horses and ponies and the like. Her owner had clearly given up on her. Said she hadn't won a race in too many years to count. I looked at her and couldn't imagine anyone giving up on something so alive. The way she stamped her feet on the auction block. The way she swung her head at the pull of the lead. There were others like her. But there weren't. She was different. I knew it from the moment her eyes met mine. The whites disappeared. Her ears came forward. She...spoke to me. I bid a ridiculous amount of money—so ridiculous my accountant nearly came after me—and bought some acreage in Upstate New York just for her."

She saw his brows had disappeared under the rim of his hat. "I know. Probably the craziest thing I've done since leaving home to begin with. But... I don't know. I think sometimes we need crazy—to remind us we're alive, too. We get trapped in the day-to-day, the routine and the grind. We lose sight of what it feels to be free. *Really* free."

She fumbled into silence. She had to stop talking. He'd think she was talking gibberish if she told him how long it'd been since she'd felt free. She'd found wealth of her own, hadn't she? With wealth came enormous privilege.

Why hadn't she been able to stop chasing that feeling she only felt on the back of a horse?

She didn't understand it. How should she expect *him* to? Especially with the communication barrier.

She felt like she'd been talking nonstop since she got here. She pressed her lips together. *Stop, Eveline. This isn't a confessional.*

She caught herself looking at his hands again—his wrists. They were thick with muscle, just like the rest of him.

If this was confession, she had a few hundred Hail Marys to get through before she could think about wiping her slate clean where Wolfe was concerned.

She had so many questions she couldn't possibly ask him. Like why did he come back to Fuego? How did prison treat him? Not too grim, she found herself hoping.

Why had her father left him so much of the Edge?

She opened her mouth to start asking, then stopped when she saw him get to his feet. She rose to hers, too. "I've taken up too much of your time." She set the bottle on the small patio table between their two chairs. "I should probably be getting back, anyway."

He shook his head, tipping his bottle up to drain it before setting it next to hers. He held out his hand to her, and her lips parted in surprise as she eyed it. The calluses. The lines. She blinked several times, feeling flushed and tipsy again.

He lowered his hand when she couldn't take it. His eyes skimmed over her head and he tipped his head in a southerly direction.

Eveline followed him as he stepped off the deck and walked away from the RV. Holding her arms across her middle, she gave herself a good pinch. She felt so conflicted with him. How could she practically lust after someone she couldn't bring herself to touch?

Wolfe Coldero felt off-limits, for a lot of reasons. Maybe because he was Ellis's best friend. Maybe because he'd been to prison.

Those hands may be gorgeous, she thought, but they'd killed a man. And nobody in Fuego would ever forget it.

Not to mention, her hooking up with the town convict would land her in the kind of scandal her mother had introduced to their lives a long time ago.

The scandal had made her head for the hills and change her name from Eveline Eaton to Eden Meadows. Whenever her past had come up in interviews over the long years of her career, she'd lied and said she was from Dallas, because the thought of that gossip ever winding up on the front cover of the grocery store gossip rags had made her want to vomit.

She'd hidden nearly every part of who she was. She'd disappeared behind the alluring face of Eden Meadows, where she'd stayed, forgetting everything that had ever been good about her childhood, her family, Fuego... herself.

Wolfe led her into the stables and she tried to banish the unhappy thoughts. She tried disappearing behind a blank face. But she was so out of practice, she was alarmed to feel tears biting against the backs of her eyes again. Tipping her face into the shadows, she willed them and the unbearable loneliness away.

She didn't know he'd stopped in front of her until she ran headlong into the strong line of his back. "Oof!" she said, automatically.

He turned quickly, finger to his lips.

"Sorry," she mouthed.

He motioned her forward. She moved further into the stable, which she saw was still in progress. There were sawhorses and lumber stacked with various power tools on top of them.

From above, she heard an odd, keening cry.

She heard it low and wondered why it sounded familiar.

He led her to a ladder that had been left in place against the far wall. The noise was soft, a rhythmic shrieking that toggled some memory from far off in the past. *What is that?*

Wolfe gripped one side of the ladder and motioned her forward. When she hesitated, he pointed up.

She glanced down, glad she was in tennis shoes this time and not heels. She grabbed the rung level with her face and placed one foot on the bottom while he held the ladder steady. Slowly, one rung at a time, she climbed the ladder to the rafters. The wall in front of her still smelled like fresh wood. The rafters weren't too dusty. Despite it being an open barn, there weren't too many cobwebs either. Everything looked and smelled like new beginnings. Something about it excited her to no end. It reminded her of the construction of her own barn and stables in New York…

She took hold of the top rung, telling herself she shouldn't look down. Heights had never been her thing. Flying had only ever been achieved after a stiff drink or a Xanax. Unless she was in a saddle, she liked her feet planted on the ground…

"Don't look down," she whispered, closing her eyes briefly. She brought her feet up until she could peek into the rafters just above her head, grabbing the wall now for support.

The soft screeching noise grew louder. She craned her neck and saw the edge of a nest.

On a prayer, she brought her feet farther up, as high

as she dared, and grabbed the rafter on either side of the nest, bringing her head up to peer over the rim.

What met her eyes brought an awed murmur from her throat. "Aw," she whispered. "Look at you guys!"

Their eyes were closed, their tiny heads bald. They were gray with a scruffy coat of feathers and so small she could hold the three of them in one hand if she wanted to.

Owlets, she thought with a huge smile. Just like at the Edge all those years ago…

She didn't think about it. Her gaze tipped down to Wolfe far below. The years fell away. She saw a boy at the bottom of the ladder, inky dark hair and arms too long as he braced the ladder so she wouldn't fall…

She wanted to see the baby birds, desperately, just as her brothers had. Several of the hands' children had climbed the ladder to the rafters of the stables to see them while she'd stayed rooted to the floor, only able to listen and dream.

She hadn't been able to bring herself to climb that high. She'd started, several times, but never made it more than three rungs before rushing back down. The owls had lived in the rafters so long Eveline was sure they were old enough to take flight and leave forever.

She didn't see Wolfe come off the range after herding cattle. He hadn't been working long as a hand. He and Ellis had been learning the ropes. They always came back on their mounts at the end of the day, hungry and worn ragged, just to go out at dawn and do it again the next day.

She envied them that, too. Her only aspirations at this point in her life were horses and riding all day, every day.

He found her sobbing in an empty stall, her knees to

her chest, her arms around her legs. She looked up and saw him watching, his eyes wide with surprise under his black hat.

She couldn't help herself. She blubbered some more, telling him how Everett said she'd missed her chance, that the owl babies had flown off and she was too much of a coward to see them while she'd had the opportunity—how she was the only kid in Fuego who hadn't climbed up to see the owlets.

He grabbed her arm and pulled her up. Tugging, he pulled her to the ladder. She balked at the sight of it, but he held a finger to his mouth and pointed up.

She sniffled, rubbing a hand hard underneath her nose to choke back more tears.

And she heard them. Their soft screeching became more sure. She had been too busy crying to notice, convinced Everett was right.

Eveline looked at Wolfe, blinking in hope. "They're still there," she whispered in awe.

He nodded. Then he took her hand again and touched it to a rung of the ladder.

She shook her head. "I can't," she said when he insisted.

He closed his hand over hers. She remembered. It had been large then, too, to go with his lanky arms. He was all arms and legs. Still too thin, as Paloma liked to remind him when offering him seconds at every meal.

She couldn't look away from his insistent stare. She bit her lip and thought about the distance to the top. Too far.

He shifted, backing away while still keeping a tight hold on the edge of the ladder. He nodded her up.

She found herself gripping the rung in front of her with both hands. Her palms were sweating around the rough wood. She took a breath, thought of baby owls wrapped up tight in their nest.

She didn't look up or down as she climbed. It took forever to get to the top. She took her time, breathing carefully. Very carefully. If she panicked, she would fall, she knew. Nerves stirred at the base of her belly, but she breathed in and out in a steady cadence. She knew Wolfe was there, holding the base of the ladder. He hadn't left her high and dry like Everett would have...

She fumbled for the next rung and found that there wasn't one. Somehow, she'd reached the top. Looking around, she noticed the nest was tucked in a small recess in the stable wall. The cries were so close, she felt them.

She took one last step, boosting herself so her head was level with the nest. And there they were. Two perfectly round owl babies. Their eyes were open. She was fascinated by how their pupils took up more space than their yellow irises.

She beamed at them...then forgot not to look down.

She saw the distance to the floor and shrieked, hugging the ladder.

A whistle caught her attention. She glanced down, saw that Wolfe had the ladder. He tilted his chin up again. You're okay, kid, *he seemed to say.*

Eveline broke away from the memory. Her arms ached; she'd been holding herself up in the rafters for so long.

How long had she been looking at Wolfe—the adult version in what appeared to be the same black hat—down at the bottom of the ladder?

She took one last look at the owlets, memorizing their messy down. They'd be losing that soon. And those eye slits would open, revealing the striking yellow eyes she remembered.

Carefully considering where she should plant her weight, she lowered herself until she felt the top rung of the ladder again, grabbing it. If she shifted her weight back too far, would the ladder go?

Wolfe wouldn't let that happen.

She frowned at the assurance. Moments before, she hadn't been able to take his hand. She hadn't been able to touch him. Something had shifted. The memories had stirred up old feelings—of faith and trust. Things she'd forgotten.

She'd trusted him—as much or more than she'd trusted Everett and Ellis. Once, she'd trusted him so much she'd faced her greatest fear and climbed. Once, she'd put her life in his hands.

As she came down the ladder, she realized her palms weren't sweaty anymore. Her heart, though, was in her throat. She was level with him now. Letting go with one hand, she turned to find his eyes level with hers. Her feet were still almost a foot from the ground where she liked them. Still, she looked her fill.

Same eyes, she noted. Same eyes in a man's face.

Had she thanked him—back then? When she'd climbed back down to the stable floor, had she let him know what the gesture had meant to her?

She opened her mouth to thank him now. Words failed when he reached up and touched her face. Her breath hitched. A flush went up and down her body in an assaulting wave. *Oh, God...*

He brushed the top of her cheek in a featherlight caress. She felt her eyes closing. When she opened them, he was holding something between them. She focused and frowned. *An eyelash.* He'd been brushing away an eyelash…

She opened her mouth, then closed it. All that for an eyelash. She opened her mouth again to say thank you but couldn't bring the words up. She still felt everything…everything everywhere…

She found herself reaching up to the brim of his hat instead.

She took it off. His hair, still a mess from its run-in with the water spigot, caught the light behind him. All the bronze notes lit up. There were some strands of gray she saw now, surprised.

Prison time would do that to a man.

Her pulse quickened—not because she was afraid of him anymore.

No. There was no reason to fear him. She knew Wolfe Coldero was no more a cold-blooded killer than she was.

She reached up again to touch his face for no reason other than that she wanted to. The rim of his jaw was rough with unseen stubble. She touched the pad of her thumb to the point of his long chin.

She wanted to kiss him there.

His eyes darkened as they scanned her face. His hands still gripped both sides of the ladder which meant she was between them. Almost like an embrace.

She inhaled and breathed him in, that wild essence that was so unbelievably free. He smelled like the mesa after rain—the one he'd been found wandering as a young boy.

It had never left him—that wildness. After everything he'd been through, it still lived in him.

She wasn't breathing right, but she didn't care now. Floating on his scent and an impulse related in some way to her crazy, high-speed reentry into Fuego the night before, she slid her palms over the broad planes of his shoulders. They came to rest at the base of his neck.

He tensed but didn't back away. She teased that voice inside her that had wanted to run her hands through his thick mop, fingering the hair at the nape of his neck.

He still hadn't touched her. He was holding firm to the ladder behind her. His pupils had widened, however. She'd noticed that as his gaze tracked across her features. She noticed, too, that his breath had quickened.

She bit her lower lip and felt a long, low tug when his stare caressed her mouth. "Am I coming on too strong?" she whispered.

He didn't respond. He didn't even blink. It was almost as if he was afraid to move.

Not once had his gaze touched her scars. This close, they were all but glaring at him. He looked at her like she was the same person she'd been when she left. The person underneath the scars, the scandal…everything that had come to pass.

She was speeding toward something. Redlining. But she was in control—more in control and closer to the woman she really was than she'd been in a long time.

Despite the fact that he hadn't made a move toward her, she leaned in until her lips met the fine, firm line of his.

Chapter 6

The top of his head blew off. Wolfe was certain of it.

She was soft, as soft as he'd imagined her to be. Holy hell, Eveline Eaton was kissing him, Wolfe Coldero. Had she lost her goddamn mind—or had he? She smelled like gardenias—that sultry spring scent that promised summertime.

Okay, the world had turned upside down...or this was a cruel joke. Probably set up by Everett, or...

She tilted her head, her arms linking at the back of his neck. He felt her nails skim across his scalp.

Everett who? The man's existence was wiped along with everything else Wolfe had ever known, because Eveline was kissing him like it was allowed. Like he wasn't who he was—or she wasn't who she was. In this strange and wonderful new universe they found themselves in, she could kiss him. And he could kiss her back.

His hands lifted from the ladder, reaching up ready

to touch her. Her hair. Her shoulders. That face that had enchanted a nation…

His hands floated, unsure. She suckled tacitly at his bottom lip. His pulse flooded his ears and his blood did a quick hot dive toward his beltline. He was taut—too taut in places he shouldn't be.

Jesus God Almighty.

He made an involuntary noise in his throat—a noise that wasn't a whistle but a groan and the closest thing to speech he'd managed for two straight decades.

He still hadn't touched her. Couldn't.

Was she sure? She couldn't be sure. She was clearly lost, confused. Why else would she be kissing *him*?

I need you to be sure, he wanted—needed—to tell her. As much as it hurt—and it *did* hurt—he grabbed her by the arms, turning so her feet left the ladder. Gently, he set them on the floor. His head came down after hers for a second…more than a second…before he lifted his lips from hers and pressed them hard together.

Her eyes fluttered open, all green and lashes and sex. He almost made another sound but stopped himself. Realizing how hard he was gripping her arms, he immediately let go and took a step back. The ladder came up against his shoulder blades.

She stared at him, a hand raised halfway to her mouth. It would be warm. He knew it because his lips were on fire. The taste of her burned.

He closed his eyes, pictured fire and tried to remember how much it hurt—how it hurt others. He didn't want that for her. She'd been through enough, hadn't she? He shouldn't have let her linger. He shouldn't have let her…

Her throat moved on a swallow. She took a wise step away. "Sorry." Using the hand she'd left in midair, she brushed the hair away from her face. "I don't normally... This isn't who I am. I mean... I never make the first move."

First? Does she expect seconds? The thought did nothing to extinguish what she'd done to him.

"I'm sorry," she said breathlessly, pivoting on her heel in retreat.

She was gone now. He should be able to breathe.

It took a moment. Finally, he raked in an inhale. It wasn't steady in the least. Scrubbing his hands over his face, he made himself follow, picking up the hat she'd dropped on the ground.

By the time he rounded the corner of the barn, she'd broken into a run back to her truck. Twilight had settled over the land, a blue veil as soft as Eveline's lips.

Knowing what her lips were like would never leave him. Never. And for that he was profoundly screwed.

He put the hat on, pulling the brim low over his brow where his eyes could live in shadows.

When he saw her yank open the driver's door, he brought his fingers to his mouth and let out a piercing whistle.

It brought her to a halt. It took her a moment, but she turned.

As he closed the distance, he saw that her gaze didn't shy from his. She faced him and the new status quo she'd thrown down between them like some ill-fated gauntlet he was incapable of doing anything but tripping headlong over.

She lifted her arms in an empty gesture. "Did you know?"

He cocked his head in question, not daring to move forward. Distance. There should always be eight feet of distance between them from this moment on.

"Did you know—" she asked again "—that Dad left you a share of the Edge?"

Do what? He began to smile. Then he realized that nothing—not her coming here, staying, kissing him—had been in any way a joke.

"The reading was this morning," she elaborated. "Everett. Ellis. You. Me. The girls. All equal shareholders."

Well, she'd broken that down nicely, hadn't she? He wished she'd just hit him over the head with a two-by-four. Less shock, fewer consequences.

"Why would he do that?" she asked, sounding just as perplexed as he was. "Why would my father leave you a large part of his business empire?"

Wolfe couldn't feel his feet in his boots. He shifted them. Was there ringing in his ears?

"Did he owe you anything?" she asked. When Wolfe tilted his head, confused by the question, she elaborated, "*Anything?*"

He laced his hands together on the back of his head and stared at her, dumbfounded.

For a moment, she studied him. Reading his shock, she subsided, leaning back against the truck. She sighed. "Wow. It really was love. He loved you," she clarified. "As much as he loved any of us. You might even have deserved his love…more than some of the rest of us, at least."

He frowned. Did she really actually believe that? How could Hammond have loved Wolfe more than his own sons or daughter? He had to swallow the ball at the base of his throat—emotions he could identify and some he couldn't were lodging themselves there tight.

"It's good that you're surprised," she stated. "Everett's going to come after you, somehow. He's going to try to take back that twenty percent."

Wolfe pursed his lips. Right. Everett. He could only imagine how Big Brother had felt hearing the news this morning. He nodded, understanding that she was trying to give him a warning. He reached up, touching the front of his hat. He tipped it slightly.

She looked down the driveway, her route of escape, as she gripped the truck door, then looked back at him. "Don't let him take anything you want. It's not up to him. Daddy wanted this. He wanted us to be closer, somehow. He wanted us to be partners in this."

Closer. Partners. The words were heady in his mind.

"Just be ready," she advised. "Okay?"

He lifted a hand in acknowledgment, unable to manage much else.

She'd dropped two bombs in minutes—one verbal, the other…all too physical.

As she drove away, he wondered how he was going to survive the fallout of either.

Eveline stared at both of her brothers on the other side of the corner booth at Hickley's BBQ. Everett wore his practiced scowl. Didn't he know how pretty he'd be if he learned how to smile once in a while?

And Ellis. He smiled plenty. But since she'd come home, she'd yet to see the real thing. His eyes were still too sad, his brow too lined for a man his age.

Paloma had assured her a real smile was coming. Ellis's girls were coming to stay with him in Fuego for the weekend.

While Everett spread out in a comfortable slouch, taking up much of their side of the bench, Ellis's shoulders dropped in a pose that leant itself more toward wariness than relaxation.

Eveline tried not to catch either of their eyes. She

raised the plastic-wrapped menu. She felt like it was all over her face. *I was with Wolfe. I kissed Wolfe. I've been thinking nonstop about Wolfe.* So much so she'd read the entire menu twice over and she still got hung up on simple words like *tenderloin* and *rub*.

"What'll you have, Eveline?" Ellis asked.

She flinched. Her brothers were both looking at her.

Hell. They *could* see it. Couldn't they? They could see it as well as she could…

Wolfe's barn. Her between the ladder and him. His mouth under hers. His moan in her ears…

A quick flood of heat swamped her.

His name was all over her face, wasn't it? It was *written*—on her face!

"Eveline?"

She tried to swallow and failed. When was the last time someone had been this lit up inside Hickley's? The floors looked unwashed. Her pointed black flats had stuck to them slightly on the walk in. There were peanut shells under several nearby booths that hadn't been swept, even if the benches were empty.

Plus, did she *mention* her two big brothers? Eyeing her like the guilty vixen she was?

She'd kissed their new business partner. The town felon. The man whose name she'd learned several folks in Fuego didn't even like mentioning. *I* kissed *him.*

Why had she kissed him, exactly? Something to do with baby owls.

And freedom. A taste of wild.

Everett slapped his menu on the table. "Screw you. I'm ordering." He lifted his hand for the waitress.

"We'll order when we're ready," Ellis insisted. He eyed Eveline. "You okay?"

"Fine," she said tightly. She shifted, pulling the hair

from her neck and laying it carefully over one shoulder. She was sweating, for Christ's sake. "It's hot, I think."

"Feels fine," Everett muttered. "I'm hungry. We're not going anywhere else."

Eveline sighed at him, then looked to Ellis. "Nobody fed him today?"

"Paloma fed him plenty at lunch," Ellis reasoned.

"She could've fed me dinner," Everett reminded them. "She was serving pork tamales to the hands. I could be eating those right now—if *you* hadn't insisted we eat out."

Eveline's mouth twitched. "You're not cheating on her pork when you eat it somewhere else. You know that, right?"

He scowled. "Hers is better."

She rolled her eyes and looked back at her menu.

"You've read the damn thing five times," Everett told her. "Your choices aren't any better than the last time you read it."

She resisted the urge to throw her paper napkin–wrapped silverware at him. "Oh, my God, Everett! Can you get off my ass?"

"Can you pick something to eat?" he rebutted. "I'm starving!"

Ellis raised his voice over the two of them. "Hey, Nova!" With a friendly tilt of his chin, he invited the waitress to come take their order.

When she responded instantly, Everett eyed Ellis darkly.

"Are you ready?" Nova asked as she took a writing pad out of the front of her waist apron. She saw Eveline and stopped to stare. "Are you…really Eden Meadows?"

Everett groaned and dropped his head to his folded arms on the table.

Eveline ignored him and smiled at the girl. "Yes. And you're…"

"Nova," she said, extending the hand without the pad. "Nova Altaha. I'm sorry. But I love your pictures. Did you really walk the carpet at Paris Fashion Week?"

"I did," Eveline admitted. "Altaha. Are you Naleen Altaha's daughter?"

"Her oldest," Ellis said, watching his sister closely.

"Goodness," she said. "I went to school with your mother. She and I were close friends. How is she?"

"She's doing great," Nova said. "She's actually getting married again soon. Only a few weeks left before the wedding."

"That's wonderful news," Eveline said. "I hope I get to see her soon. I'd love to give her my best wishes."

"Oh, you can come over anytime," Nova invited. "You and Mom can catch up. And maybe you can tell me more about Fashion Week."

"I'd love that," Eveline said with a smile. "You look *just* like Naleen."

Everett lifted his head. "Yes, yes. She's a regular doppelgänger. Can I order now?"

Eveline sneered. Then she looked at Nova again. "Do you like him—the man who'll be your stepfather?"

"Oh, he's great!" Nova replied. "You may have gone to school with him, too."

"Terrence Gains," Ellis added.

"Terrence," Eveline said with a knowing smile. She could hear Everett's boot tapping on the floor. "I *do* know him."

Ellis smirked. "Didn't you and Terrence date for a little while?"

"Oh, just to piss Everett off." Eveline dropped her voice discreetly and leaned toward Nova. "He lost a shiny new belt buckle to Terrence in a bronco busting competition."

Everett's lip curled. "I hate everyone."

Nova giggled, taking a pen from her apron. "What can I get you three tonight?"

A few minutes later, Everett had a beer and an appetizer of jalapeño poppers. Nova had placed it in the center of the table, but he had grabbed it for himself and refused to share.

Ellis sipped from his bottle. Eveline turned hers to see all sides of the label. It was the same brand she'd drunk with Wolfe…or watched Wolfe drink on his deck several days ago. She waited until Everett's mouth was full before she spoke. "So…it *was* me who wanted to eat out."

He chewed, unable to give voice to his irritation without choking.

Ellis nodded, unfolding his napkin so he could make a coaster for his beer. "What'd you want to talk to us about?"

Everett swallowed. "I thought restaurants were for eating, not flapping your gums. God knows you and Paloma do plenty of that at home."

"We've been catching up," Eveline explained. "There *is* something I wanted to discuss with both of you." She took a breath, wrapping both hands around her bottle. "I'd like to go see Dad. I'd like to see where he…was laid to rest."

Everett frowned deeply. "Ellis and I were there five days ago. Not our fault you weren't."

"Everett," Ellis muttered. "Of course, we'll visit Dad. That's something we *should* do together."

She carefully broached what else was on her mind. "I'd also like to visit Coldero Ridge."

Everett's bottle clacked onto the table. "What?"

Ellis stared. "I'm sorry. You want…to go to Mom and Santiago's place?"

"Yes," she answered.

Everett shoved the appetizer plate away, half finished. "Damn it, Manhattan. Leave it to you to ruin my appetite."

"Why would you want to do that?" Ellis asked, confusion creasing the corners of his eyes and mouth. "There's not much there and nobody's lived there for years. Santiago's in a mental health facility upstate. He has been—since just after the trial."

"Nobody goes there," Everett said, looking unsettled. "Not even crazy teens looking for trouble."

"Why not?" Eveline asked. "Is there something wrong with the place?"

"Other than the fact that three people were murdered there?" Everett asked, droll.

"Why do you want to go?" Ellis asked her carefully.

She thought it through, as she had for some time. "Because… I don't have a lot of closure where Mom is concerned."

"She made it that way," Everett said. "Because she left. She left us to start a new life with other people. Another man. Other kids. She left us, Eveline. None of us have closure and we aren't meant to find it."

It was sad, she thought. But it might have been true. Still… "I feel like I never even came to terms with what happened to her and Angel. We had a sister."

"Half sister," Everett stated.

"Don't," Ellis interjected, more forcefully than Eveline had expected. He took a moment to look around, take control of himself and lower his voice. "Don't talk about Angel like that. She was just a kid. And she was kin to us."

They all fell into a moody silence. It took several moments for Eveline to gather up the courage to go on. "I just… I need to go. Maybe to reconnect. Maybe just to see where they lived—how they lived. To feel closer or…maybe to understand. I might never know. I'd like to go—and I'd like both of you to come with me."

"Hell, no," Everett said.

"Why not?" she asked. "Maybe there's something for you there, too. Some answers…or feelings you need to confront."

"I like my feelings where they're at," Everett informed her. "And she can't give me anything. She's *dead*, isn't she?"

"Shut up," Ellis said sharply.

"What did you say?" Everett asked him.

"I said *shut up*," Ellis said, meeting his brother's eye.

Eveline saw the aggression that passed between them and reached for both of them. "Stop. I didn't want this."

"It's you who brought it up," Everett accused her.

"And it's you who took it too far," Ellis told him, low.

"I'm not going," Everett said again. "End of discussion." He got up from the table and stepped out of the booth.

"Where are you going?" Eveline asked. "Your food's not even here yet."

Everett put his hat on. "I'm going to the taproom. Nobody there asks me stupid questions."

Eveline heaved a weary sigh as they watched him stalk out. "I knew that was a long shot."

"Kid…" Ellis shook his head. "I don't think I can go to Coldero Ridge either."

She looked to him, surprised. "Why not?"

"I don't think it's a good idea," he told her. "For me or you. There's nothing left. The house is gone. Whip Decker burnt it to the ground. Dad and I briefly talked about doing a memorial there for Mom and Angel but Santiago... He took ill and it didn't feel right, doing anything on his land without his say. All that's left is the caves, and you don't need to go there either. There's bound to be mountain lions."

She shuddered in spite of herself. Old childhood nightmares came flashing back. "Mountain lions."

"Yeah. Wolfe saw signs of them, on and off throughout the years of living there. With the place abandoned, I imagine they've moved right in."

"Don't make me go by myself," she begged.

Ellis pulled in a long breath and looked away. "I'm asking you not to go at all—with or without us. The land's taken the place back. As I see it, that shouldn't be changed."

Chapter 7

She went. Without either of her brothers' company. Without either of them knowing. She left Eaton Edge one morning, claiming she had to run an errand.

Both Ellis and Everett had ridden out early with the hands so she hadn't had to answer to anyone but Paloma about where she was going. Alone.

She'd never been to Coldero Ridge, but she remembered the way, where the land started to rise. The road turned and started to incline. The shoulder started to jut toward the sky until both sides sloped higher than the cab of the company truck Everett had reluctantly handed her the keys to the day after she'd borrowed Javier's for the joyride to Wolfe's place.

She'd started questioning her impulses. They had only gotten her in over her head since returning home. Racing her rental car had led to nearly killing herself. Escaping to Wolfe's had led to things she now had to lie awake at night thinking about, restless, hot and frustrated in ways she couldn't do anything about—at least, not alone.

As the road leveled off and the shoulders gave way to a wide clearing, she braked and slowly brought the truck to a stop. She put it in Park, her heart pounding for reasons she couldn't name.

She lifted her hands from the steering wheel. They were shaking.

It was an empty lot. What trouble could really find her here?

Choking back visions of mountain lions, she turned off the ignition and popped the handle to open the door. The air smelled like sulfur. It struck her off guard. Was it coming from the caves nearby?

She didn't know much about Coldero Ridge other than the fact that her mother, Josephine, had lived there with Santiago, had given birth to little Angel there and had passed away there.

As her feet touched the ground, Eveline reached across the driver's seat and grabbed the new hat she had bought. It wasn't bent out of shape like the one she'd found in her closet. She shut the door and squinted against the dust, lowering the hat to her head.

There were short, shrubby trees to either side of the clearing, offering some shade. The clearing was really a raised valley between two rock walls. The walls were overgrown with shrub growth and composed of red rock.

There weren't any signs of human life. That was her first impression. No tracks—vehicle, human or otherwise.

She shivered, eyeing the brush for movement. It was

her imagination, she was sure, but she felt eyes on her. Hungry eyes.

If anything happened to her, no one would know to look for her here. And no one would probably find her. That's what had happened to Whip Decker. At the trial, she'd learned that Wolfe had shot the man before rushing to help her mother and Angel escape the cabin…

Eveline walked through the tall grass until her toes bumped into something hard. She bent over double and saw the cracked concrete.

It was the foundation.

Her heart sped up as she straightened. She looked around, trying to gauge where the boundaries of the house had been—where her mother had been trapped in the last moments of her life.

She took careful breaths as she stepped onto the slab. This was where Wolfe grew up, under Santiago's care. Where he'd gone home for dinner every night from his work at the Edge. Where he'd slept as a child and young adult.

She held herself as her stomach churned. This was where he'd fought to save Jo and Angel. Decker had tied them up inside before barricading the doors and windows with nails and boards. He'd set the fire, pouring gasoline around the building's footprint.

When Wolfe arrived, Whip had been drinking his whiskey and watching it burn.

Decker must have heard them, the woman and child trapped in the house screaming in terror. And he'd stood back and drunk.

Why? Craziness didn't begin to cover it. It was too calculated for that. A land dispute that raged too long had finally leaned in Santiago's favor. Whip had lost the small plot his trailer had squatted on for twenty-nine years.

He'd come swinging, not for Santiago's knees but for his heart and soul. For the bedrock of his sanity.

Eveline held herself as she traced her steps across the cabin floor. Kitchen? Living room? Bedroom? A small one, perhaps. The lichen-covered rocks in the center, she found, weren't rocks at all. They were bricks from a crumpled chimney.

She laid her hand over them. They were warm from the sun.

Wolfe's lawyer had read from his written confession that Whip Decker had still been living after Wolfe shot him. While he bled out on the ground, Decker had laughed, watching Wolfe struggle to get past the boards and nails before it was too late.

Something inside had ignited.

Eveline remembered the mottled skin on Wolfe's arms—a memory that lived on his skin, forever a reminder that he'd been too late to save members of his family from a madman's cruelty.

Wolfe hadn't carried a phone at the time. He was too far out of range of the Edge to use the radio. He'd gone off for help, leaving Whip Decker to bleed out on the ground.

When authorities arrived some time later, there'd been nothing left but a blood spot on the ground—the logical theory being that the man had been dragged off by something bigger than himself.

No one found a trace. If not for the blood and his truck parked in the drive—the empty cans of gasoline—no one would've known he was there in the first place.

Except Wolfe.

Eveline looked off into the distance. There had been a structure near the red rock wall to the south. A barn, most likely. It, too, had fallen to ruin.

She closed her eyes and breathed deep. She smelled sulfur again, but fought for something else. Something that would remind her of Jo, the woman who had given birth to her brothers and her—who had cared for them and raised them, bathed them and cooked for them. Who had held them when they were sick.

Was it blatant impulse that had led her away? Had it happened on a whim, one she hadn't been able to take back or make right after?

Eveline could understand impulse.

She knew she was more like her mother than her father. She and her mother had both hurt Hammond—badly. They'd abandoned him, the Edge and their lives there for something…more? Or just something different?

Eveline had too many questions. Answers were too far out of her reach because they were gone now. Both of her parents were gone.

Everett's scathing words rang through her mind. *She can't give me any answers. She's dead, isn't she?*

She'd likely never know the answers she needed. Because in the case of both her mother and father, she was too late.

She'd run from all the things that had chased her out of Fuego for too long. Now she'd never know, would she? Who Jo had been—if they did share the same impulsive streak, the same capacity for leaving chaos in their wake.

The same blinders they put on when it came time to face what they'd done or apologize to those they'd hurt and left.

Eveline blinked, stunned when she felt tears rolling down her cheeks. Her eyes had been stinging for several minutes. She'd thought it was the smell or the dust stirred by the strong breeze. She reached up with both hands, pressing her palms to her cheeks. She pulled them back, saw them wet and cursed, wiping her face on her sleeve.

She felt the scars on her neck. They brought her back to the present. She'd come back, hadn't she? She'd nearly lost her life, too, to her impulses. And she'd come back to fix what was left of her family.

To recover what remained of her former self.

Her real self.

She gathered her composure. Maybe it was better that she was alone. Those eyes she felt on the back of her head...they weren't real. She was alone with her thoughts and her feelings.

It felt...oddly liberating.

The breeze strengthened, making her brace her feet. She studied the ground. She wished there was something here, something she could take away that had belonged to her mother, or Angel even. A connection—the one she'd come looking for.

She rounded what was left of the hearth. Something crunched under the toe of her boot. She stepped back, crouching...

She reached down into the grass, grabbed hold of something smooth, lifted it...

And screamed bloody murder.

Chapter 8

No sooner did Eveline see the bone fragment than she tossed it away. Her gorge rose as she backed away. She bent over double, her stomach cramping. The sulfur smell didn't help. She was going to be *sick*. Her breath heaving, she took backward steps away from the bricks.

Her heel snagged something solid, sending her off-balance. She grabbed for air but found herself falling and her rump hit the ground hard. The ground was loose, uneven. There was something there in the grass.

Her hands found something else smooth, hard, warm from the sun. She peered through the grass and screamed again.

More bones! They were everywhere!

She crawled backward, sobs raking across her throat, lurching off the edge of the foundation into more grass. She couldn't feel her knees and she wasn't sure her legs would work. But she'd be damned if she didn't make it back to the truck…

Her throat was raw from shouting, but there was saliva flooding her mouth.

She'd throw up. Then she'd go back to the truck and race back to the Edge.

Something grabbed her from behind. She screamed again, arms milling. She rounded, her hands ready to claw at whatever was there, and a hand came down on her mouth. She bared her teeth, biting down on a finger. The hold loosened and she nearly broke free...

Two hands clamped down on her arms. They shook her so hard her teeth rattled, then spun her roughly around. Ready to tear into the perpetrator, she raised both fists. She cried out, hoarse, and they froze when Wolfe's face filled her vision.

He grabbed hold of her face this time, firm. But he didn't hurt her. He held her still until it sank in—that she wasn't being attacked or dragged off like prey through the brush. She clamped her hands over the back of his, trying to bring her breathing back down.

Hyperventilating. She was hyperventilating. And she couldn't stop herself.

He touched his brow to hers, unable to offer words of comfort.

She could smell him now, through the shock and panic. She could smell the wildness of him over sulfur. She closed her eyes and hated how she shook like a tree under his hands. Even her teeth were clattering, her jaw locked so hard it ached.

His hands started to stroke. Warming her up. Trying to bring her back. First her face. Then her hair. He spread his fingers over the back of her head, cradling it gently. So gently. She saw his big shoulder and couldn't stop her face from rising up to meet it.

It took her several minutes to realize that her breath

was slowing. She could still feel her pulse in her ears but it wasn't hurting her eardrums anymore. The smell of sulfur had nearly been vanquished by his warm-washed scent. It cloaked his shirt. His skin. She drank it like the antidote it was.

She realized she had been clutching handfuls of his soft button-up shirt hard. She loosened her hands, spread her fingers. The joints were stiff.

She hurt everywhere. Everything ached. She could feel the impact now from falling on her derriere. She'd fallen harder than she'd thought, hard enough to bruise bone.

Bone.

She pulled away from him, her gaze flying to his. "I s-s-saw them."

His eyes narrowed on hers in question.

"B-bones," she said, pointing toward the footprint of the cabin. "Th-there. Everywhere. I-I *saw* them, Wolfe. I…h-held them."

His eyes raced over hers as he began to shake his head. Then he looked to the foundation and his face hardened.

God, what was he doing here? Was this the first time he'd been here since…

Her stomach clutched again. She pressed her fist to it. "Oh, God, Wolfe. What are you d-doing here?"

He held up a finger to stop her. Then he took a step toward the house.

She grabbed him. "No!" she said automatically. "D-don't. Please don't. Let's go. Let's just go. Okay?"

He held up his hand and moved away from her. She grabbed her elbows and took several steps back, unable to follow.

He approached the slab slowly and didn't stumble

upon it like she had initially. He knew exactly where it was. Where it started. Likely where it ended. Where each of its four corners lay. He roamed, as she had, over the parts of it she knew to be clear, then toward the place where the grass was bent out of shape. Where she'd fallen.

Something crunched under his boots. He paused, scraping his boot across the slab.

Her hands came to her mouth to hold back a scream as he crouched, reaching down. She turned away, too scared to ask herself why she covered her ears.

She knew why, she realized.

She didn't want to hear Wolfe's scream so she stayed as she was, her heart in her ears again. Minutes ticked by. She looked around the ground, knowing she would be sick now. There was a knot of bile at the back of her throat growing bigger by the second. She nearly choked.

His hand wrapped around her arm again. She turned, then stumbled back with a dismayed cry when she saw him holding something small and white. "Please!"

She jerked against the hold but he held her firm, unwilling to let her go. He thrust the item at her.

She threw her hands up to shield herself but stopped…because what he held was bone. A skull. But it was too long…too small to be human.

It dawned on her slowly, a small sprinkling of logic to fight the scream of panic inside her head. This had belonged to an animal. Had they all…belonged to an animal?

Her lips fumbled as she looked around him at the house. "Are they…are they all…?"

He nodded. His eyes fastened to hers, opening up for her to see the truth that was there.

It took a bit. But embarrassment began to trickle

in. She stepped back and he let her go this time. "I thought…" Unable to finish, she grimaced.

This time, he looked away. Then he glanced back at what had been the house.

She swallowed hard several times. "There were so many. I thought they were…" She shook herself. *Damn it.* She should've known. She'd been there, hadn't she? She'd stood between her brothers as her mother and Angel's remains had been buried in the same cemetery where Hammond, too, now rested.

"I'm such an idiot," she heaved. "Oh, God, I'm *such* an idiot. I'm sorry, Wolfe. So sorry."

His touch came to her shoulder. He rubbed, small circles this time until she could look him in the eye again. "I wasn't thinking," she said. It came out on a horrified whisper. "I think I'm losing my mind. First what I thought I saw the night I wrecked the car. Now this… What the hell is the matter with me?"

He reached up to cup her chin. To console. His touch was light, barely there.

Did he think she was going to break?

Maybe she already had.

She hated it. But she tossed the words out, knowing somewhere both Everett and Ellis would feel a lick of satisfaction. "I shouldn't have come here. I was *stupid* to come here." And she turned away from him and what remained of Coldero Ridge and walked back to the truck.

"What's this about?"

Wolfe met Ellis at his truck as he pulled in. He waved a hand for his friend to get out. As soon as Ellis did, Wolfe began to motion with his hands in the language only he and Ellis knew. *Did you bring it?*

Ellis got out of the truck, then shut the door. "The gun? Yeah, I brought it. But I don't see why—"

Grab it and come on, Wolfe motioned and set off for what was left of the cabin.

Behind him, he heard Ellis groan. But then he heard the back door of the truck open and shut, followed by footsteps trudging to catch up. "What's going on, Wolfe? Is this about what I asked you to do?"

Wolfe turned. Walking backward, he made words with his hands. It wasn't sign language as anyone else would know. He'd never learned to sign. Not properly. They'd both preferred this secret language between them. It was a comfort, knowing that there wasn't another person in the world other than Ellis who could read it. *Your sister was here.*

Ellis cursed a stream. "We told her not to come. Goddamn it, we both *told* her."

She found something, Wolfe motioned, then turned back as they came to the slab.

After he'd watched Eveline back the truck down the narrow drive to safety, Wolfe had made himself go back to the ghost of a house. He'd made himself look again. Search. Catalog. And wonder.

Ellis came abreast of him. "Jesus Christ."

His voice wavered. Wolfe scanned him carefully. Ellis's color had dropped and his jaw was taut. *You all right?* he signed. He hadn't forgotten that this was Ellis's first trip to Coldero Ridge since the fire.

Ellis didn't meet his eye. "About as good as you, I expect." He frowned at what was in front of them. "What's all this?"

Wolfe crouched. He'd made several piles. He lifted the skull from the first and passed it to Ellis.

His friend studied it, turning it over in his hands only once before guessing. "Fox."

Wolfe nodded. He placed the skull back on the first pile, then lifted the skull from the second.

Ellis's brows came down over his eyes. "That's dog or coyote."

Wolfe jerked his chin again in confirmation. He lifted another from the next pile. It was smaller. Much smaller.

"Snake," Ellis identified. To the following he said, "Feline. What the hell is all this?"

Wolfe propped his elbow on his knee as he knelt, looking out across the grass into the brush and red rocks pitted with hidden caves. Something had gone afoul here. He could feel it—something that went beyond fire and Whip Decker and memories too hard to revisit completely. Yet here he was. He began to sign an explanation—how he'd driven to Coldero Ridge at Ellis's instructions to check things. Just to check. Because Eveline's brothers knew her—enough to know she'd likely come here against their will. And Ellis had needed to know it was safe for her.

Wolfe came looking for mountain lions or rattlers. What he'd found was an Eaton truck at the crest of the drive, then Eveline herself in a state of hysteria he knew all too well.

It was what he'd felt the last time he was here. It was what had driven Santiago straight into a mental facility after Wolfe had been sentenced.

It was too much for one person. Wolfe thought he understood where Eveline's mind had gone. He didn't want to follow, but he made himself.

No, these weren't human fragments. That didn't

change the fact that they shouldn't have been found scattered in the same place.

Like a collection. Worse, trophies.

Ellis took several minutes to take the information in. Then he, too, roamed over the site, bending down to look into the small hollow at the front of the hearth. "You say you found most of them here?"

Wolfe nodded slowly when Ellis turned to look. He tried to separate his mind from the trauma of the past. It was like wandering onto a path that he damn well knew was riddled with mines.

Ellis straightened. He swung the rifle he'd carried from the truck up to his shoulder. "You're right. Let's have a look around."

They searched for the better part of an hour. The Ridge tumbled beyond the red rock cliffs and the homestead. It rose up and over shallow rises and snaked down into rabbit holes and hollows—the caves. Wolfe had lived there for years and hadn't explored all of them.

Some of them, Santiago had warned, weren't meant for people. They were too unstable. The sulfur alone would kill a man if he got trapped inside long enough.

They found no signs of life where they searched. "Should've brought Everett," Ellis commented as they headed back for the trucks. At Wolfe's speculating stare, he shrugged. "Not your biggest fan. I know. But he comes with a pack of hounds. We're going to need dogs if we're going to find anything that makes sense."

Wolfe thought about it. Then he nodded in agreement. He hadn't brought Storm. His sense of smell was unrivaled, but Wolfe couldn't have him venturing too close to a rattlesnake den because he couldn't see.

"How was Eveline when she left?"

Wolfe hesitated. Then he told the truth with his hands. *It took time to calm her down.*

"How'd you manage that?"

Did Wolfe have to spell it out? He liked the details where they were…inside his head, locked inside the twisted vault of his memories. They felt good there. They lit up the place. The feel of her skin. The softness of her hair. The shape of her in his arms.

"I'll talk to her," Ellis said, interrupting the sensory barrage. Good thing, too. The rush of blood had drained from Wolfe's head to his waist and his heart had done a sloppy turnover.

Ellis may be his friend. His oldest friend. His only friend. But he was still Eveline's brother.

If she hadn't kissed him…would all this have opened up inside him? Would he have to deal with this tangled twister of need every time he came into contact with her? Was there an end to it? Not likely with her living in Fuego…or him sharing a percentage of Eaton shares.

He and Ellis had spoken briefly about it. He'd sat in Lionel Bozeman's office for an uncomfortable half hour listening to the terms. He wasn't any more comfortable thinking about it than he'd been after Eveline had dropped the news unceremoniously at his feet.

There would be no peace. Not for the near future. Not with Eveline, nor her big raging brother coming after him with legal action, as it was rumored.

News of the Edge's split had spread far enough into town that Wolfe had had to deal with questions from everyone, from the manager at the Tractor Supply to Rowdy Conway. He wanted to shout it for everyone to hear—he didn't want any part of it, that he hadn't known, and still didn't know, what Hammond was thinking.

But he couldn't. The questions wouldn't stop coming. And life in Fuego was even more strained than it had been before.

At least no one knew about Eveline. Thank God nobody knew about Eveline, or he'd never hear the end of it. He'd be dead, more like, with Everett untethered. The guy was just looking for an excuse to end him.

"Do you hear that?"

Wolfe stopped to listen. The breeze strengthened and, underneath it, so did an odd clacking sound. They exchanged quick glances before moving toward a sharp decline to the left. It was too steep to walk down. Ellis broke down the rifle and slid to the base of the hill. Wolfe followed, letting his palm brush across the dirt.

The ground here was shaded by shrubby trees. As soon as Wolfe stood and dusted off his pants, Ellis pointed out the ruts in the undergrowth.

Wolfe studied the trail. It hadn't been made by a vehicle. The depression in the reeds made it look like a walking path. He knelt, brushing the grass aside.

"No tracks," Ellis observed.

Wolfe shook his head. It was difficult to tell what had done this. Animals weren't known to take the same path over and over, unless the terrain left them no alternative. The grass was dotted with trees, but the box canyon walls that rose around them yawned wide. He turned to study the hillside. Other than the ruts left by himself and Ellis, he couldn't discern any tracks or claw marks.

Ellis reassembled the rifle and nodded down the path. Wolfe let him lead the way.

The path stepped down several times before going off to the left, toward the canyon wall. Here the grass grew taller—tall enough Ellis used the rifle to brush it aside and peered through the opening. He held up a hand to motion Wolfe to stop.

Wolfe peered past his shoulder and narrowed his eyes. There was a small archway in the red rock, narrow enough to admit someone but only if they turned sideways.

The wind picked up again, whispering through the grass and stirring it so it floundered around them. The clacking sound reached a height.

Ellis moved toward the opening. Wolfe clapped a hand on his shoulder, bringing him up short. He made a motion with his hands when Ellis glanced back.

Mountain lion.

Ellis jerked his head in a nod. He flipped the safety on the rifle. Edging sideways, he had to squat slightly and tip his chin up to fit through the archway with the gun. Wolfe followed, his pulse tripping. The smell of sulfur, so strong near the caves, flooded his nostrils. They were downwind. Something else, however, made the hairs on the back of his neck rise. He'd had the eerie feeling before in the presence of mountain lions. Once, he'd happened upon one while riding fences in his days at Eaton Edge. The large male had been watching him at a distance.

The second time had been at Coldero Ridge. He'd been watching Angel play near the cabin from the porch. The hairs on the back of his neck had stood up suddenly and he'd known it was out there. He'd walked out to her and spotted the shadow of the mountain lion in the branches of the trees.

He'd felt it again, recently—the night Eveline had come to town and sworn she'd seen a strange creature in the road.

He palmed the butt of the large knife he kept sheathed

on his hip. As he entered the space inside the archway, he raised the blade an inch or two out, ready to confront whatever was on the other side.

The aperture was open to the sky. It was wide enough to fit the cabin's footing. One tree grew, its trunk thin and curved. It leaned on the wall, its limbs not quite tall enough to reach the opening overhead.

Wolfe shielded his hand against the angle of the sun as he surveyed the branches for lions.

What he saw made him still, his grip hardening on the handle of the knife.

"What in God's name..." Ellis's voice trailed off. The barrel of the gun was pointed up, but the scope fell away from his face and his mouth gaped.

It looked like one of those wind chimes people hung from the eaves of their houses. Maybe that had been the effect for whoever had hung the bones. They were different lengths, the largest being two feet, the smallest as long as Wolfe's hand. They'd been strung with twine and hung in a perfect circle in order by size. In the breeze, they clacked against each other in a chilling cacophony.

Wolfe had the presence of mind to look around the rest of the encampment. Snaking an arm out quickly, he grabbed Ellis in time to stop him from treading across the circle of rocks in the center.

Fire, he signed.

"An animal didn't do this," Ellis said as Wolfe bent down to press his hand to the blackened deadwood in the center.

It's cold, he signed.

Ellis sidestepped. He jerked his chin toward the corner. "Something on the wall over there."

Wolfe was on it. It was in shadow but he could see

faint tick marks ranging over the surface of red rock. He did some quick math. There were several hundred ticks that'd likely been drawn with another piece of rock. They were all faint, weathered by time.

"You ever hear Santiago talk about this place?" Ellis asked.

Wolfe shook his head. Santiago had never mentioned anything like this. And he would have, had he known about it.

"It's likely this was done by hunters," Ellis said. "Hiding out from gaming officials."

Wolfe didn't know about that. What kind of hunters did things like that? He eyed the "wind chimes." That and the piles of bones he and Eveline had found at the cabin...

Something, or someone, had been playing with their food at Coldero Ridge in the grimmest way possible, he suspected. Nothing about it sat well with him.

"Are you going to call this in?" Ellis asked.

Wolfe looked around at Ellis. *To whom?* he signed.

Ellis hesitated before adding, "Jones."

Wolfe would've laughed, but he didn't want to hear it echo off the walls of the hollow. Laughter didn't belong in a place like this, real or otherwise. *Why would I do that?* he wanted to know.

"He is the sheriff," Ellis said. "Somebody's been trespassing on Santiago's land. You're the closest thing to an heir he has."

It made sense. That didn't make the idea of facing off again with Sheriff Wendell Jones any more appealing. Instead of answering, he squeezed back underneath the archway and moved through the reeds until he reached the path to the hillside.

He heard Ellis moving through the brush behind him.

"Look, I'm not going to tell you what to do. I know Jones isn't your favorite person."

Or me his. Wolfe kept walking, refusing to pause long enough to sign it for Ellis.

"I don't want Eveline knowing what we found here."

That did stop Wolfe. After a moment, he turned around and moved his hands in a question.

Why not?

Ellis lifted his shoulders. "I think she's in a fragile state right now. She doesn't need anything piled on."

Wolfe pointed up the path toward the cabin.

"I know what she's seen already," Ellis acknowledged. "But I'd like to tell her it was mountain lions."

Lie?

"It'll set her mind at ease and keep her away from the place," Ellis said. "Everett and I never wanted her here to begin with."

You and your brother are making her decisions? Like she's fifteen again.

"She's not in the best frame of mind," Ellis repeated.

Wolfe's scowl deepened. It put a bad taste in his mouth.

"She says she's home to stay," Ellis admitted. With a long look around, he moved the rifle to his shoulder, hanging it by the strap before shifting his weight to his heels. "At least for a little while. I don't think she ever took the time to heal after her accident in New York. I'd like her to stay. Paloma does, too."

Wolfe took a moment before asking, *Everett?*

"He'll come around."

He better. Wolfe didn't raise his hands to sign it. Instead, he turned back to the path.

"Are you going to call Jones?"

Wolfe shrugged a shoulder roughly. It was the right

thing to do. It was what Santiago would have done—bad blood or no bad blood.

Wolfe would have to take some time before deciding to call the man who'd slapped him in cuffs and hauled him off to the jailhouse seven years ago.

Chapter 9

Three welcome faces came to Eaton Edge on Friday. Ellis's daughters, Isla and Ingrid, arrived first. Eveline saw Ellis beam for the first time since she'd arrived. She saw the worry and grief in his eyes eclipsed by joy. The laugh lines dug into his face as he knelt down to take them both into his arms on a running leap. "My ladies!" he said, standing with one on each shoulder. He boosted them up, craning his neck to press a kiss to each of their temples.

"Isn't that a sight?" Paloma murmured, hooking her arm through Eveline's.

"It is," Eveline said. She knew the girls had been born a year and a half apart, but they had matching, bouncing curls of white blond. They wore matching smocked dresses, as well, in whispering pink, white ruffle-trimmed socks and saddle shoes. "They look just like him," she said, stunned by the resemblance.

"And nothing like her," Paloma muttered, referring to Liberty. "Thank goodness."

Eveline bit her lip. Ellis's ex hadn't stuck around long enough to say hello to him. She'd knocked, exchanged a curt greeting with Eveline, adding, "Tell Ellis I'd like them home by four o'clock Sunday. They have a dentist appointment early Monday. Also tell him I'd prefer it if they didn't ride."

Ellis set them on their feet, straightened their clothes and knelt down, eyes shining to match theirs. "How 'bout we go get you two changed? We can ride out and be home in time for dinner."

"Yay!" they shrieked in unison, running back to the house.

He followed behind, the smile not fading from his face.

Eveline laid a hand on his arm. "I spoke to Liberty," she said, unhappy when she saw the hitch in his grin. "She said she didn't want them to ride."

He raised his eyes to the sky before bringing them back to her. "I didn't hear that, did I?" he asked.

She shared a secret smile with him. "I guess I forgot to deliver the message."

"'Preciate it, kid," he said, pinching her chin playfully.

Paloma sighed as she and Eveline followed him. She kept her voice low as he trotted ahead to catch up with his girls. "I wish he'd fight for more time with them. They make him so happy. And they bring laughter into this house, laughter we all need."

Eveline brought Paloma up short of entering the house. "What happened?" she wanted to know. "Why won't Liberty give an inch and why won't he fight her?

He doesn't love her anymore. I can see that. But he loves them."

"As much as any father ever loved his girls," Paloma agreed.

"So she must have something against him," Eveline guessed. She saw Paloma's quick grimace. "She does."

"I'd have thought you'd have heard the rumors in town," Paloma said with a sigh.

"Are you saying that the whole town knows?" Eveline asked, dizzy with the idea.

"She hadn't moved out of the house he bought for her before she started telling everyone she could find what he'd done," Paloma said gravely. "Or what she claims he did."

"What could Ellis have done that was that bad?" Eveline wondered, baffled by the mere idea of Ellis doing anything wrong.

Paloma took a furtive look around, uncomfortable. "I don't think it's my place to be airing your brother's dirty laundry."

"I'm going to find out eventually," Eveline reasoned, "if the whole town knows. Please, Paloma." She was desperate to know what hurt Ellis beyond his grief for their father.

Paloma eyed her uncertainly for several seconds. Then she firmed her grip on Eveline's hand, as if warming it—already consoling. "You understand I don't take to gossip. And I certainly don't believe a word of it."

Eveline nodded. "Of course not. It's Ellis."

"I know he's not perfect," Paloma admitted, "but God knows he's as fine a man as there's ever been."

"I've never known a better one," Eveline agreed.

"That won't make this easy to hear," Paloma warned. "Liberty swears up and down that he strayed."

Paloma looked so sad and resigned, it chilled Eveline to the bone. "No. It's not true." When Paloma said nothing, Eveline broke into a cold sweat. "Who does she say he slept with?"

"Luella Decker."

Eveline stared. "Whip Decker's daughter." She nearly burst out laughing. "Who could possibly take *that* seriously?"

"Don't you remember—before her daddy went crazy and killed your mama and Angel, long before—Ellis took a shine to that Luella."

"That was high school," Eveline said.

"He was gone over her," Paloma said. "Long before he went off to college and found Liberty Ferris."

"So Liberty thinks he's been carrying a torch for Lu Decker for fifteen years or more despite the fact that somewhere in the middle of it all her dad murdered our mother? She's crazy!"

"Maybe," Paloma granted. "She's got no proof. But his name is already mud where the wives of Fuego are concerned. Most of them took Liberty's side, even though she always acted like she was too good for the likes of this place. It was always a bone of contention between them—his loyalty to the Edge and his care of Hammond and her desire to go back to Taos and have him finish school so she could be a doctor's wife, not a wrangler's."

Eveline knew Ellis's dreams had led him outside of Fuego, too. He'd been well on his way of becoming Dr. Eaton when Hammond had had his first heart attack. "She didn't have to follow him here in the first place."

"You don't know the whole story then," Paloma guessed. When Eveline shook her head, Paloma tipped her head close and whispered, "She was pregnant with

Isla Jane when they got married. It was those babies holding them together. And it worked, for a time. Until she got it in her head that he and Luella Decker were having a thing on the side."

Eveline blinked several times. "Oh, Ellis," she murmured. "He shouldn't have to go through this."

"No, he shouldn't," Paloma said. "It breaks my heart, seeing him and his girls having to live through it."

"I still don't understand why he doesn't fight for more time with them," Eveline said.

Paloma reached for the door. "That's the mystery we've all been trying to get to the bottom of."

"Huh." Eveline beat her to it, swinging the door wide and letting Paloma walk in ahead of her.

"Maybe you'll be able to get the truth out of him."

"Maybe," Eveline murmured. "Thank you for telling me. I'd rather hear it from someone who loves him…"

Paloma nodded. "…than one of those gossipmongers in town. I agree. Here. I'll put on the coffee. You can have a splash of whiskey in it to help the whole sordid story go down."

It brought a small smile to Eveline's face. "A spoonful of sugar…" she chimed, settling herself on a stool at the counter.

Before either of them could indulge, Isla and Ingrid rushed in, clomping on two sets of brand-new boots. Isla's were baby blue. Ingrid's were fire-engine red. Gone were the starched dresses that had no business on a cattle ranch. They wore blue jeans and T-shirts and looked and smelled as fresh as wildflowers.

Eveline gathered them each into a long hug, sorry she'd missed watching them grow up this far. "Haven't they told you about Peter Pan?" she asked, kneeling down to their level. "You can stop all this growing up business if you believe."

Isla, who had inherited Ellis's serious streak, smiled and shook her head. "You're silly. There's no such thing as Lost *Girls*."

Eveline smiled back. "No, but you two are just cute enough to be fairies."

Ingrid was wide-eyed with imagination. "Ooo, I'd *love* to be a fairy!"

Eveline pulled her close for a hug. "And so you shall be."

Ingrid's vivid expression dimmed slowly as her eyes dropped to Eveline's neckline. She raised a hand to trace the scars there. "Do they hurt, Auntie Eveline?"

Isla hissed, "Ingrid! You shouldn't touch!"

"It's all right," Eveline said quickly, though her smile had fled, too. She patted the back of Ingrid's tiny hand. "And no. It doesn't hurt anymore."

"Daddy said we almost lost you."

Eveline blinked back surprised tears at the forlorn thread that had woven its way between the girls' brows. Their resemblance to Ellis was breathtaking. "I'm not going anywhere. And we'll have lots more time to spend together now."

"You're staying here?" Isla asked, a light coming into her eyes.

"Forever?" Ingrid echoed.

"I—"

"Can you come riding with us?" Ingrid asked, bouncing from one topic to another.

"Ingrid," Isla muttered, disapproving. "Let her finish."

Eveline beamed. "I would love to go riding with you."

"Yay!" Ingrid squealed.

Isla clapped her hands. "I ride Boon. Ingrid can't yet. She's too small to ride a full-grown horse."

"I ride Dander," Ingrid informed Eveline importantly. "The pretty pony."

"Though Mama doesn't like us to ride anymore," Isla said, her smile disappearing again.

Eveline couldn't have that. "Well, I know your daddy's got your back. You're safe, as long as you're with him."

Everett came into the kitchen, hollering, "What did I say about little people running in this house?"

Eveline scoffed. "You can't be serious…" She stopped as Everett roared, spreading his fingers into claws. The girls squealed and scattered, Isla between his legs, Ingrid toward the exit. He caught the latter, tossing her over his shoulder. "This one!" he shouted in triumph. "This one will be my dinner!"

"No, Uncle Everett," Ingrid giggled, throwing her arms around his neck. She snuggled into the long plane of his shoulder. "Don't eat me!"

Everett's snarl turned into a laugh that shocked Eveline to her toes. He ran his hand over Ingrid's back before setting her gently on her feet. "All right." He pointed at her with a mock stern expression. "But don't let me catch you gallivanting through this place again."

As Ellis came in to shepherd his girls out to the stables, Eveline stared at Everett.

He caught her look. His playful expression fled. "What're you looking at?"

"A big damn softie," she decided.

He sniffed. "I hear you snuck off to Coldero Ridge." That wiped the wonderment off her face.

"Did you find what you were looking for?"

She hated him for the dig. "I'd rather not talk about it."

He tutted at her. "Should've listened."

When he lingered, she asked, "What do you want?"

"Your horse arrived."

"My... Sienna?" She took a step toward him. "*When*?"

"Shortly before the girls did," he told her. "You'll introduce her to them."

"Of course, I will," she said, her smile returning as he turned to lope out again. "Is she—"

"In the round pen," he finished for her. "Looked like she needed to stretch her legs."

It was the best medicine. The girls. The horses. Sienna Shade. They had the weekend to acquaint everyone with each other.

A stall had been cleared in the stable prior to Sienna Shade's arrival. Eveline had cleared it herself. She'd even done the feed and hay run in anticipation, taking some of the load off of the grizzled stable manager, Griff—a man her father had hired twenty-some-odd years ago. Griff was a man of grunts and grumbles, but his expertise in all things working horse knew no bounds.

When she, Everett and Ellis were kids, he'd sent messages to the house every time there was a new foal. She remembered sitting up with them long into the night, waiting for a mare to foal. Griff, Javier...and Wolfe.

She couldn't forget Wolfe. His face was written on too many memories to count, enchanted or otherwise.

She didn't want to remember what had happened at Coldero Ridge. She'd embarrassed herself in front of him. Why was she always embarrassing herself in front of him? It was irritating.

So much so she'd decided she shouldn't see him again anytime soon.

It was better this way. She was convinced he preferred it this way, too.

Though she still lay awake at night with mixed-up thoughts of what mountain lions could do, what sulfur smelled like…and, by inevitable turn, what Wolfe's mouth felt like under her own. The texture of his hair under her fingertips. The weight and warmth of his arms around her…

She brought herself out of the daydream. She, Ellis and the girls had ridden out at noon to find their old picnic spot in the southern quarter. She bent over Sienna's withers, brushing a hand through her salt-and-pepper mane, trying to anchor herself to this moment. She'd needed to ride, to feel the freedom of being astride a moving horse—her horse.

"Up ahead," Ellis called.

Eveline looked off in the distance and found the small roofed structure. The hut had been there for decades, a watering hole for the horses and a shaded spot for the hands, should they need a rest.

It looked empty. As they rode up, however, Ellis—at the front of the pack—raised his hand.

"Whoa," Eveline said to Sienna, bringing the reins in. "Whoa, girl." She saw Isla and Ingrid bring their mounts to a walk. As Ellis rode ahead, Eveline turned Sienna so she and the horse were between the hut and the girls. Her throat was dry suddenly, especially when she saw Ellis reach for the sheath on his saddle where his rifle rode with him. She had horrible visions of mountain lions…or some bastardized version of them like she'd thought she'd seen on the highway outside Fuego.

She wet her lips. "It's okay," she said out loud—for

the girls and herself. "Your daddy's just making sure it's safe."

"Why wouldn't it be safe?" Ingrid asked, more curious than alarmed underneath her red cowgirl hat. It matched her boots perfectly.

"There might be rattlers, Ingrid," Isla said, only somewhat impatient. Eveline caught the slight quaver underneath the words. "That's why Daddy always brings his gun, remember?"

"Eveline!"

She turned at the sound of her name. Ellis was out of the saddle. The rifle was in his hand but the barrel was tipped down and his arm hung at his side. He motioned her forward, telling her to walk slowly.

"Stay here," Eveline cautioned the girls. "I'll be right back." She dismounted, flicking Sienna's reins over her head so she could walk her to Ellis's working horse, Shy. She tied her off on the hitching post and approached Ellis. "What is it?" she asked, apprehensive.

"It's not a mountain lion," he said, reading her well.

She tried not to sigh. "What then?" she asked.

"Pretty sure it's a horse," he said, beckoning her to walk around the side of the hut with him. He halted, pointing into the near distance. "See it?"

She raised a hand to shield her eyes even though she had her hat on, too. "It looks small for a horse."

"That's because it's thin," he judged, his eyes narrowed. "Too thin. There's something wrong with it. Look at the way it's favoring its right side."

She watched for a moment then exhaled weightily. "Oh, God. I think you're right." They stood watching it for a few minutes longer. Then she asked, "We need to get it back to the stables."

"To Griff," Ellis said with an agreeing nod. "There's a fair chance it's never seen a halter." He placed his hand on her shoulder. "Go grab the radio from my saddle. We'll call it in."

Chapter 10

The horse, a dun-colored filly with ears back and eyes peeled, refused to be corralled.

One of the hands had ridden with the girls back to the house and Paloma. Griff had made several attempts to tempt the horse with feed and sugar cubes to no success. The hands, Ellis and Eveline had been running and riding every which way to try to corral the filly to no avail. Despite her obvious injury, a bloody gash on her right foreleg, and the hard strain of ribs pressing against both of her sweat-soaked sides, she always managed to dance out of reach.

Everett had ridden up in his truck to try his luck at catching her. To his consternation, he'd failed, too. "Why doesn't she come for the feed?" he growled, pacing over the small space between Ellis and Griff. "She's frickin' starving."

"She's been starving for days," Griff guessed. "And that gash on her leg is swollen."

"Snakebite?" Ellis ventured, hands on his hips. Like a lot of the hands who had been chasing her, he'd stripped to the waist.

"Maybe," Griff grunted. He spat in the dirt. "Need to get her in. Need to check her. Once she keels over, there's no moving her."

"Reckon she has an owner?" Javier asked from his position on his mount. He too was shirtless and had hold of a lasso.

"Whoever the owner is, he should be shot," Everett snapped. "I've seen horses bad off, but nothing like this."

Eveline's mind was racing. It had flown back again, to the past where she so often lost it. She thought of another stray, one who had been found wandering the bounds of the Edge starving, bleeding and near death. Her breath shuddered out.

Her brothers glanced back at her. Ellis's mouth creased at the corners. "You all right, kid?"

Everett's gaze circled her features. "Look, if you're going to faint, do it over there." He pointed to the hut. "We've got enough on our plate without half the men running to catch you."

"I'm fine," she said, firmly.

Everett snorted, then walked off to gather the others. She waited until Griff joined them before saying, "Ellis, this isn't working."

"We have to keep trying, Eveline."

"We need something else. Someone else." She considered him. "Have you thought of him?"

"Who?" Ellis asked, only partly listening as the men started to position themselves again.

"Wolfe."

That brought Ellis's head around. He pivoted to face her. "Wolfe?"

"He has a way," she reminded him. "With animals. He always has."

"He does," Ellis granted. His eyes found Everett. "We can't ask him to come here."

"He's not afraid of Everett."

"No. But that won't stop Everett from making a scene."

She couldn't disagree with that. "We're running out of time. The sun's going down fast."

"I get that," he acknowledged. "Why don't you go back to the house? You can help Paloma distract the girls until I get back."

She knew Ellis didn't mean it to sound like a dismissal, but it stung anyway. She heard the terrified whinny of the filly as the hands closed in again. Her gut twisted. She cursed, unable to watch anymore.

She found Sienna Shade and Shy where they had left them, tied to the hitching post near the watering hole. The sun had slanted enough to the west for the hut to shade them. Feeling too raw on the inside, Eveline pressed her face into Sienna's neck. She breathed in the smell of horse. She inhaled carefully, until she felt more steady.

She hated feeling helpless. She hated not being able to do anything to help that poor animal.

Something pushed against her hip. She startled, then sighed in relief when she felt Shy's warm breath against her wrist. "You're sneaky," she said, raising her hand to the sweet diamond shape between his eyes.

He dipped his head again to nuzzle her hip. "Ah," she said, understanding. "You want something, don't you?" She reached into her pocket and pulled out a sugar cube she'd stowed there earlier while working with Griff in the stables. She held it on her upturned palm and smiled when Shy's rubbery lips and whiskers tickled it. She rubbed his nose. "I'm afraid that's it," she said when he nuzzled her again.

He tossed and shook his head but settled, turning his nose down to the ground again to graze.

Eveline eyed the saddlebag on his saddle. She edged closer, opening the flap and reaching in. She found Ellis's cell phone. It didn't have a lock, so she was able to access his messages easily. There were several recent texts from Liberty. They were terse missives about the girls and how they had to be home at a certain time.

She scanned through his inbox until she saw the name *Wolfe*. Her thumb hovered over it, uncertain.

She heard the whinny from the filly again, this one hoarse and plaintive.

She tapped Wolfe's name and started a new message.

It was near sundown when Wolfe finally made it out to the hut on Winter. He'd received the text from Ellis close to an hour before. It'd taken precious daylight to load Winter into the trailer and pull it to the Edge, then unload, saddle up and ride out to the southern quarter.

He found a knot of tired hands, half a dozen lathered horses, a weathered Griff and a very testy Everett congregated around the hut.

"What are you doing here?" Everett shouted, surprised. "Get the hell off our land, Coldero!"

Wolfe took his cell phone from his pocket and held it up for Ellis to see.

Ellis scanned the message. He shook his head. "I didn't send it."

"I did."

Wolfe looked around. His pulse braked hard, then racked itself up again. Eveline walked from under the hut roof to Winter's side. The horse sidestepped quickly.

Wolfe tutted to her, patting her neck. His filly was skittish, long after Wolfe had rescued her from an overcrowded stock yard and spent a long season gentling her.

Eveline stayed planted where she was. Her eyes met his. "Thank you for coming. The filly's just out there."

He looked around and spotted the horse some two hundred feet from their position. He laid his hands over the horn and leaned forward, gauging the animal's condition for himself.

"Will you help?" Eveline asked quietly. He heard the plea underneath the words. There was pain in her eyes he didn't like. His gaze inadvertently touched on her throat and the open collar of her white blouse. She'd unbuttoned it a ways. Her pearlescent skin was dewy with perspiration and the top edge of a lace-trimmed bra cup was visible. He lingered on the scars, like capillaries roving brokenly across her collarbone and lower.

As if he could deny her and her green eyes anything.

He dismounted, hearing Everett curse a blistering stream. As he fed the reins over Winter's head, he heard Ellis mutter, "What have you done?" To Eveline.

"The right thing," she said back. She turned to Wolfe and offered a ghost of a smile.

He clutched the reins tighter until the leather cracked against his calloused palm with the effort not to touch her.

"I want him gone!"

Eveline hissed at her brother for quiet as she crouched, watching Wolfe's progress with the filly. He was using feed in small batches on the ground, a kind of breadcrumb trail, waiting patiently for the horse to come closer. "He has a legal right to be here," Eveline reminded Everett.

"Shut your trap, Manhattan," Everett growled. "This doesn't concern you."

"But it does concern me," she informed him. "I have just as much a right as you and Ellis. If you think about it, the shareholders are stacked against you."

Everett glanced at Ellis, who shrugged in answer. "I don't see the harm in it," Ellis tried to tell him.

Everett took off his hat and started to pace in circles once more, kicking up dust. The hands had backed away at a safe distance so they didn't fall afoul of his temper.

A whistle brought their attention to Wolfe. He and Winter approached, one leading the other. He looked to Ellis and started using his hand in complicated motions.

"What?" Everett challenged. "You want to fight, you bastard?" He started unbuttoning the cuffs of his plaid shirt so he could roll up the sleeves. "I'll give you a fight."

"Pipe down, Everett. He's talking," Ellis told him.

Eveline watched the motions of Wolfe's hands, unable to understand what was being said. She hadn't seen the sign language unique to him in so long.

"Well?" Everett asked, impatient. "What does he want?"

Ellis stared at Wolfe, his expression unreadable. He shook his head, motioning back.

Wolfe jerked his head in a nod.

"You can't be serious," Ellis said out loud.

"What?" Eveline asked. "What is he saying, Ellis?"

"You're sure about this?" Ellis asked Wolfe, ignoring her. "Bozeman. We should talk to him first. See what he thinks…"

Wolfe shook his head at that and began to sign all over again.

Ellis groaned. Then he faced Everett. "He says…if

you let him catch and keep the horse, he'll hand over his shares."

"What?" Eveline exclaimed. "No!"

"Twenty percent for that nag?" Everett asked. "That's a fool's bargain."

Wolfe whistled again, motioning when he had their attention.

Ellis was quiet for a long moment after Wolfe was done talking. Eveline heard him curse under his breath. His eyes swung to her, measuring, and he translated slowly. "He wants his shares to be given to you."

"Me?" she asked. She looked to Wolfe. Both of her brothers were looking at her now, hard. "Why? Why would he do that?"

Another whistle, followed by the movements of Wolfe's hands.

"He says those are his terms," Ellis said. "Take them or leave them."

Everett looked to her, measuring, then to Wolfe. "Call Bozeman," he said simply. When Ellis didn't move, he shouted, "Now!"

Wolfe had already turned away to go back to catching the horse. Eveline started to follow him. A hand clapped down on her shoulder.

Everett frowned at her from the shadow of his hat. "One day, you'll explain to me what that was about."

"I don't know," she said with a shake of her head. "I… I don't want this…"

"Like it or not," Everett said, low, "you're about to be lead shareholder in Eaton Edge. If it means Coldero no longer has any weight around here, I aim to keep it that way."

Slowly…slowly… Wolfe coaxed the filly to take feed from him. It was near dark at that point and he breathed a long sigh. Keeping his movements slow, he introduced the bucket.

After more coaxing and some soothing, she dipped her head in and started to chew. Moments later, he had a lead rope around her. She nodded her head, eyes wheeling, tugging against the restraint. He made all the right noises, keeping very still, until she settled once more.

He led her to the Eatons. He didn't meet Eveline's eyes. Ellis wasn't smiling.

His brother, however, was grinning like a mother. "I'll be damned," he greeted. He held out a rope halter.

Wolfe held up his hand, refusing it. He had a feeling his new friend had never seen one. He saw Griff moving toward them and dipped his hat to him.

"Young Wolfe," he said. It was an old nickname. He held out a hand to shake.

The filly danced back, alarmed. Griff stopped and settled for a smile—or as close to a smile as Griff's grim mouth could manage. "Think she'll come with us?"

Wolfe eyed the horse. Her ears were still back. Looking to Ellis for translation, he signed.

"He says he'll lead her back on Winter," Ellis said.

"She'll need to be hosed down," Griff said, trying to get a better look at her injury. "Probably sedated before I can examine her."

Wolfe nodded. He knew there was no one better for horses than Griff Mackay.

"Let's saddle up, then, and head back," Everett ordered. The hands moved when he did, back to their trucks and their mounts.

Wolfe led the filly to Winter, gathering both the reins and the lead rope carefully before boosting himself into the saddle. It took more coaxing but the filly fell in next to Winter. The elder's calm example went a long way toward soothing the younger.

Wolfe lifted his head. In the twilight, he got his first look at Eveline on Sienna Shade. They suited each other well, he saw, warmth twining around his navel.

They rode back together, the three of them and the four horses. Eveline didn't speak to him or Ellis. He kept himself and Winter between the filly and the other horses. Because they kept it to a light trot so as not to cause her too much pain, inky black night had fallen before they came up to the lights and activity of the house and headquarters.

Instantly, the filly shied, forcing him and Winter to stop altogether. Griff came out to meet him and together, with apple slices and calming motions, they managed to get her into the round pen. Wolfe held her lead as Griff hosed her down, running his hands over her filthy coat.

Then Griff went to load a syringe for sedation.

Everett came out of the house. When he reached the fence, he said, "Bozeman's here."

Wolfe rubbed the filly's neck. He didn't want to put her under, but that leg needed to be treated and he didn't see any other way.

"Are you coming or not?" Everett needled.

Wolfe released a breath before tying her off to the fence. He whistled to Griff when he exited the stables.

The man nodded back. "She's in good hands."

Eveline was on the porch. She stood between Wolfe and the door. "I don't understand."

He tried to move by her but she brought him up short with a hand on his arm. "Wolfe, please. You don't have to do this."

He met her gaze. Under the lights, without her hat,

she looked vulnerable and soft. He caught himself looking at her lips a moment too long before he reached for
the door and entered the house.

It smelled the same. Twin pangs of longing and regret sank into his chest. He ran his hand over the rough
wood panels of the walls along the mudroom entry and
remembered to wipe his feet before he veered into the
kitchen, taking off his hat respectfully.

He half expected to see Hammond taking his evening coffee at the butcher block table. Disappointment
and grief snuck in on him.

Paloma heard him and turned from the stove where
she was stirring a big pot of what smelled like her old
corn chowder. Her eyes were like inkpots. She held out
her arms to him. "Wolfe. *Niño.* Come here."

He crossed to her without hesitation and took her
hands. Looking long at them, he gauged the bandage on
her finger, probably from mishandling a kitchen knife.
She'd always worked quickly at her counter, slicing and
dicing with the speed of a demon. Did anyone else notice her nails weren't filed down but chewed? Did anyone notice how much she took on herself?

Everett better treat her right, he thought with more
than a twinge of rage.

"I saw Santiago this week," she murmured.

His eyes snatched up to hers.

"He's okay," she said, stroking the back of his hands
with her thumbs. "He seems to be recovering nicely
from his cold." She gave him an ironic smile. "I think
he might've been disappointed I wasn't you."

He shook his head. How could anyone ever be disappointed with that?

"You'll see him next week?"

He nodded. They'd taken it in turns, their visits to

the mental health facility one county over. If he wasn't tied up with towing, he normally took Mondays to go— Tuesdays at the latest.

Paloma looked over his shoulder. "This household's turned upside down in one afternoon. What have you done, *niño*?"

He tilted his head in answer, not meeting her incisive stare.

She gripped his hands tighter. "Don't let him push you around. You have a place here, too, whether he sees it or not. I see it. Ellis sees it. Griff sees it. Half the hands do, too, I'm sure. Hammond wanted it this way. And Eveline…"

His eyes snatched back to her. He blinked, guilty.

She pressed her lips together, gleaning some understanding. "You're giving up everything…your place here—for her. I'm not saying she's not worth it. She's worth more than she sees in the mirror. But I am curious why."

He started to lift his shoulders, then stopped. He couldn't shrug it off, any of it. It was there. He was afraid that it was as plain as the boots on his feet.

Paloma raised her arms to his shoulders and pulled him in for a hug. He returned the embrace without question, pressing his cheek to her temple.

They stayed that way for a while, until Ellis entered and said his name. Paloma patted him on the back, wordlessly, as he turned away. He heard her sigh and made himself follow Ellis down the hallway to the door of the office. It was closed, but he could hear voices on the other side.

Before he could open the door, Ellis planted his hand on the knob. Wolfe's brows stitched together. He signed, *Not you, too.*

"You're about to make a deal with the devil," Ellis reminded him. "I love my brother. But when it comes to you, he's the devil."

I know what he is.

"Just…" Ellis took a careful breath. "…think about my dad and why he wanted this. It wasn't so you could give it all up."

It will make things easier, Wolfe signed. *He never wanted things to be hard.*

Ellis searched his face. "Jesus Christ. Can't you be selfish? Do something for yourself for once?"

Wolfe lowered his head. Then he raised his fist to knock.

It was opened immediately. Everett eyed him, from his head to his spurs. He opened the door to Hammond's office wider. With a wicked grin that made him look, indeed, like the devil, he said cheerily, "Let's see that John Hancock."

Chapter 11

Eveline sat in a fresh spread of hay, the filly's head cradled in her lap. She ran her fingers through its mane. It had been matted. After a bath and a brush, she was able to separate the strands. She found herself braiding it, like she'd once braided her pony's hair, the one her parents had gifted her when she turned six.

She watched the rise and fall of the horse's belly, counting the breaths as Griff worked on her injured foreleg. He'd determined that it was a snakebite. Thankfully, not a rattlesnake's. He'd stopped the bleeding, but the swelling was still cause for concern.

Wolfe's lady would have to spend a couple of nights at the Edge.

The filly's long breaths stirred the hair across her arm. She caught herself humming an old tune. "Shenandoah," she realized after a moment.

Griff grunted. "Don't think it'll need to be drained. Have to check again in the morning."

"She's going to make it," Eveline said quietly. Those ribs straining against the filly's side broke her heart. "Right?"

"If she keeps eating and drinking," Griff replied, running wise hands over the rest of the leg, "and she rests up. She's a fighter. All the best girls are." From under his bushy brows, he sent her a telling look.

She found her mouth curving into a smile she didn't feel. She went back to braiding and humming.

"Young Wolfe," Griff said suddenly.

Eveline jolted and looked up to see Wolfe standing at the gate, one boot propped on the lowest rail. He nodded to her.

She nodded back. He'd been watching. *For how long?* she wondered. "She's going to be okay," she said, fetching the smile back to reassure him as much as herself.

He scanned her then the horse in turn, leaving her feeling warm and flustered and confused.

"Your business up at the big house concluded?" Griff asked.

To that, Wolfe frowned. He gave another nod.

Eveline wanted to curse, loudly. Instead, she patted the horse's cheek and focused on the play of white through her dun coat. She still couldn't understand what had happened between him and her brother—the agreement that they had reached.

"We'll be keeping her for a day or two at least," Griff explained. "She'll need to get her strength back and I'd like to keep an eye on her leg."

Wolfe nodded to this, too. He paused only a moment before gripping the top of the gate and climbing over.

Eveline clutched the filly's head tighter. She had to make herself relax as he crouched next to Griff to see what he'd done with his old-fashioned poultice and ban-

dage. There was a lot of muttering from Griff and more
nodding from Wolfe. She watched his hand skate the
same path Griff's had taken over the filly's leg. He
brushed circles over her shrunken belly.

Licking her lips, Eveline went back to her humming,
leaning down to rest her cheek against the horse's neck.
She wondered what he would name her. Summer? The
perfect equivalent to his Winter.

She wondered if he would regret this—regret giving
up all the shares her father had left him.

She heard the rustle of hay. Wolfe and Griff were on
their feet. They shook hands. Griff opened the gate to
walk him out. "Come by anytime," Griff told him. "The
horses like you much better than the other wolves."

A small grin played at Wolfe's mouth. He met her
gaze, held it. Then he touched the brim of his hat and
walked off.

She scowled. *That was it?*

She shifted gingerly out from under the filly's head
and scrambled to her feet. She brushed by Griff. "I'll
be back." Then she went after him.

She didn't manage to catch Wolfe until he was on
the other side of the house, walking in a quick, steady
gait to his truck. "Wait," she called out.

He came to a stop. He glanced back, saw her, then
decided to keep going.

She did blow out a curse. "Wolfe, please! I just want
to know why. Why did you do it? I don't want it. Not
badly enough for you to give it up."

He reached his truck and made for the driver's side.
Ellis had already loaded up Winter for him. He checked
on her through the small window in the horse trailer,
then checked the latch on the back.

"You can't just leave," she said, grabbing hold. His

muscles jumped at her touch. She held fast, however. Why wouldn't he look at her now? "I need to know."

He shrugged in a helpless gesture. She saw it bleeding over his face. Whatever he had to say was trapped inside him.

"I'll get Ellis," she said, shifting her feet to go back to the house.

He cupped his hand and cradled her elbow in a barely-there touch that brought gooseflesh all over her skin. She froze as he stepped closer. Her feet were planted, but she wavered over them like prairie grass. She saw him eyeing her mouth. Her heart drummed against her breastbone. Bringing her hand up to his chest, she suddenly wanted nothing to do with either one of her brothers.

She didn't want anyone—anything—between her and Wolfe. She just wanted to know him. His mind. His body. His soul.

He tilted his head by a fraction, dipping his head to her level.

She closed her eyes, gripping his shirt as she'd done before.

His mouth brushed against the center of her brow. His hand had risen to her throat. It spread, long fingers coming to rest against broken skin. She jerked automatically, not wanting him to feel the damaged texture. He held her steady, gentling her with the caress of his thumb back and forth across the line of her collarbone.

She swallowed hard. Frustrated, she blinked hot tears from her eyes. "One day you'll find a way to tell me," she asserted, "why you did what you did today."

His touch skimmed across her shoulder. He lifted his hand to her cheek.

The tenderness was unbearable. Couldn't he see it was melting her down to the core?

Shaking her head, she whispered, "You have to stop, Wolfe. You have to stop being so wonderful."

When he didn't move away, she grabbed his wrist and followed the crushing impulse to turn her lips into the sensitive inside of his wrist—the place he'd been burned trying to save her mother and sister. How could anyone…*anyone* think he was a bad person? How had she for even a moment thought that she couldn't trust him?

She did what she'd promised herself she wouldn't do. Because she'd made the first move, because he'd been unsure, she'd sworn she wouldn't kiss him again. Unable to stop herself, she raised both hands to the back of his head and pulled his mouth down to hers to steal a kiss anyway—here in the dark, where they were alone and safe.

She kissed the hell out of him. And, for the first time, he kissed her back, palms roving free and firm up and down her spine. They spread across her ribs and planted themselves on either side of her waist.

Her nails dug into his collar when his tongue flicked across hers. Her body rose like a wave, bringing her up against the hard, strong line of his. It was her that made a noise this time—a long, keening moan at his quick suckle on her bottom lip. Then, with her mouth open, again on the tip of her tongue.

She bit down on his lip, breaking away before she could hurt him. "Sweet Lord," she cried out. She was still locked against him. If she stepped back, she'd sink like a noodle to the ground. Pausing to catch her breath, she held on to him, glad he was there to buffer her—glad he hadn't pushed her away or let her go like last time. "For…for someone who's never said a word, your mouth is frickin' dangerous."

He loosened a sigh that wasn't a sigh. It was a breathy laugh, she realized. And it delighted her as much as the wolfish grin that had taken over the lower half of his face.

She planned to kiss him again. Now. Later. Just *again*. But the sound of footsteps had them both shifting to their heels.

Ellis came around the truck, catching them both in retreat. "Christ," he cursed, turning right back around and pacing away. "I *knew* it." Hands on his hips, he turned back to them, looking anywhere else. "You're lucky it was me who came to check on you, Eveline, and not Everett."

"I'm fine," she started to say.

Ellis went on, "We just got him to cool off where you're concerned," he said, pointing accusingly at Wolfe. "Now you go and do this?"

"It isn't the first time," Eveline found herself saying.

Both the men stared at her. Ellis blew out a whistling breath. "You just got here. When did you..." He held up a hand, stopping himself. "Never mind. I don't need to know. I don't *want* to know."

Wolfe's hands started moving, communicating.

"You wouldn't need to apologize if you'd known where to keep your hands to begin with," Ellis all but growled at him. "When I said do something selfish, this wasn't what I had in mind."

Eveline laid a protective hand on Wolfe. "Don't come after him. It was me who came onto him."

"What the hell, Eveline?" Ellis said miserably.

Wolfe shifted from one foot to the other, uncomfortable. She closed her mouth.

She didn't want to share what was here between

them. With anyone. Not even Ellis, who shared so much history and understanding with Wolfe already.

He began signing again.

After a moment, Ellis grimaced. Instead of talking in front of Eveline, he used signals, too, in reply.

Eveline watched the exchange wearily before Wolfe got into his truck, then started it up. He exchanged one, long look with her before he put the truck in gear and drove off into the night.

"What did he say?" she asked.

"Wouldn't you like to know?" Ellis muttered.

"I would," she said. "In fact… I want you to teach me."

"Teach you what?"

"How to do that," she said, pointing to his hands. "How to talk to him."

"You do talk to him," Ellis said. "You've talked to him plenty from what I gather. More than you talk to the rest of us."

"Ellis," she said, patient. She had to be patient. Ellis responded better to patience. "Teach me."

"I would," he said, "if I didn't think it'd bring us all a world of trouble. Let's leave it at that."

"You think if you don't teach me I'm going to stay away from him?" she challenged.

Ellis raised his face to the sky. He gathered a long breath and pushed it out. "Tell me why you went after him. After everything our families have been through, why did you choose him?"

"I didn't," she admitted. "It was just there. Like it'd been there all along or something."

Ellis looked tired. Very tired.

She went on. "I went to his place outside of town. To pay for the tow. And, yes, I talked to him. He makes it easy—to talk to him. And I needed to know why Dad made him a shareholder." She swallowed the lump in her throat. "You know already why he did."

Ellis nodded. "Because he loved him, too."

"Yes," Eveline breathed. "Like his own."

"If Santiago hadn't adopted him," Ellis said, "Dad would have. I'm fairly certain the only reason he didn't beat Santiago to it was because of—"

"Everett," she finished.

"Everett," Ellis agreed. "He would have made Wolfe's life and the rest of ours a living hell."

"He does that anyway."

"Everett has issues," Ellis excused.

Eveline rolled her eyes. "That's the understatement of a lifetime."

Ellis was quiet for a while. Then he said, "I can't believe I'm telling you this. But Wolfe told me why he gave up his shares."

Eveline waited, not daring to breathe. She had wanted, *needed* to know. It was why she'd chased the man out to his truck to begin with.

"He said you have a place now," Ellis explained. "You told him, apparently, you didn't feel like you belonged anywhere."

"Why is that so hard to believe?" she asked. "This isn't the first time I've felt trapped between two worlds. Two lives."

"I believe it," he said, quiet now. "The fact that you told him…before any of us. Even Paloma. That's what confounds me."

"You talk to him," she pointed out, defensive. "Why shouldn't I?"

"You have a place here, too," he wanted her to know.

"Shares or no shares. I'm not sure how you ever felt that you didn't."

"I gave it up," she reminded him.

"It doesn't work like that," he said firmly. "We are the Edge. The Edge is us. There's nothing that could change that, kid. Nothing."

A part of her wanted to believe it. "Oh, Ellis. What has Fuego ever been to us but a place of heartbreak, betrayal and scandal?" He looked askance at her and she held out her hands. "Tell me I'm wrong. You gave up *everything* to come back here. A residency. Your dreams. The future you *wanted*."

"What do you know about what I want?"

"Are you happy?" she asked. "Are you happy here, after everything? Is this where you saw yourself at thirty-five? Divorced. Stuck by Everett's side, per Dad's wishes. Not to mention…"

His eyes narrowed when she trailed off. "What?"

"The rumors," she said. She treaded carefully. She didn't want to hurt him, but it had to be said. "About you. And Lu Decker."

His jaw clenched. He looked grim in the lights from the house. "Ask me," he said.

"What?" she asked.

"Ask me if it's true," he said, his voice guttural.

"I don't want to," she told him.

"Why not?" he tossed back. "Because you think you know the answer?"

"No," she replied. "Because it's your business. Not mine. Not the gossips in town. Not anyone's but yours." When he only frowned at her, she sighed. "My point is…neither of us thought we'd wind up back here."

He raised a brow but didn't argue. He looked around at the company trucks crowding the parking lot, then at the stars scattered far into the distance. "It's like that point on a compass," he said slowly. "Always drawing us back. I stopped fighting it. There's nothing wrong with coming home, Eveline. Starting over. Hell, everybody deserves a second chance. Even us."

For the second time in a short while, she found tears building behind her eyes.

She did feel that pull. To the land. To her brothers. To other things—things she couldn't yet admit out loud. Her voice broke. "I don't know what I want." She shoveled in a shaky, tumultuous breath. "I've been afraid to want for so long... I'm afraid to want anything anymore."

"Because when you do," he said, knowingly, "you feel guilty about it or it seems wrong somehow."

"Yes!" she exclaimed. "Exactly."

They knew each other better now. "Your place is here," he said, gentle. He took several steps toward her. "Hey." His arm came around her shoulders. "It's here. Like mine. The rest of it... You have to trust it to fall into place."

"That's a lot of faith," she whispered. "Even for you."

"The girls are happy here."

"You should fight," she told him. "You should fight for them. For yourself. We can help you. I can help."

His smile fell away. He patted her on the back. "Don't worry about it."

"Ellis."

He started to walk back to the house. Then he stopped. "Be careful with Wolfe."

She scowled. "You're really not going to show me how to talk to him, are you?"

He thought about it. Then he decided. "He has signals for all of us. Dad's was..." Ellis tapped his fist against his shoulder. "Santiago's is..." He pressed his hand to his brow. "Mom's was…" He tapped his other shoulder twice. "Paloma…" He pressed the side of his forefinger to the bridge of his nose. "Everett…"

Eveline found she could grin when Ellis showed her the borderline rude gesture for their brother. "What about me?" she asked when Ellis paused significantly.

"You've always been this," Ellis said heavily before tracing a circle around his face, starting and ending at the peak of his brow.

Her pulse missed a beat. "Always?" she murmured.

Ellis jerked his head in a nod. "I don't know. I always got some sense that he cared about you…maybe more than he should. Even in the beginning."

"We were kids."

"Didn't stop you from thinking you were going to marry Javy," Ellis reminded her.

She released a laugh. "I hate that you know that."

"Everybody knows that, Eveline," he stated. "There are no secrets in Fuego. Remember that now." With that, he turned and went back to the house finally.

No secrets. At least not for those who talked.

But she knew someone who didn't. And he'd just given up his stake in the Edge so she'd feel more like she had a place to belong to.

Eveline stared up at the stars for a long time. Then she heard the chilling *yip-yip-yip* of coyotes in the distance and let it chase her inside.

Chapter 12

She had to get over her fears. She slept well until moments before waking, when dreams turned to terror, tossing her into the back seat of the car that had flipped into oncoming traffic in New York or the driver's seat with an animal's reflective eyes making her jerk the wheel off the road outside Fuego.

Eveline had driven some since returning to Fuego—the night she had visited Wolfe at his place and to do a run or two into town for clothes, feed or other supplies for the horses. She'd driven ten under the speed limit, hands gripping the wheel at ten and two and sweating to boot, telling herself she was okay.

But she wasn't okay.

She refused to ride in the passenger seat of Everett's truck anymore. Ellis was a much better driver, even with the obvious debris of fatherhood everywhere—empty Juicy Juice containers, applesauce packets and cracker crumbs. But she'd grown too accustomed to being chauffeured by him, Javier or Paloma. There wasn't a decent therapist in Fuego she could talk to about her driving issues.

The only way she knew how to overcome them was by tackling her fears head-on. At least, that's what she told herself as she attached one of the Eaton Edge horse trailers to the back of her company truck.

If she was going out for a morning jaunt, she was going to take her horse with her. Sienna Shade went willfully into the trailer, which made Eveline feel a little bit better.

"Where should we come looking for you?" Everett asked distractedly as he stared at the screen of his phone and leaned against the wall of the stables. "You know, in case you turn into a head case again."

She glared at him as she secured the door to the trailer and wished with all her might that Ellis hadn't told him about her visit to Coldero Ridge and what had happened there. "I'm not a head case."

"Sure," he said, noncommittal.

She went around to the driver's door. "I'll be at the state park."

He raised his face from the phone. His eyes were lost behind a dark pair of aviator shades and his hat was pulled low over his brow. His jaw worked lazily around a big wad of gum and his mouth was permanently etched with disapproval. "You can't ride all the way to the arch without a guide."

"The hell I can't," she replied, opening the door.

He pushed off the wall. "Wait a minute. That's forty-five minutes to an hour. Both ways. There's no way you remember which way to go."

"If you're worried about me," she taunted, "come with me."

"Take somebody else with you. Ellis."

"Ellis is in the western quadrant today," she said.

"Javy."

"Javy is taking care of his wife and kids," she said. "Stomach flu. Explain to me how I know your men better than you do right now."

Everett grumbled. Then he swore an oath. "Hang on a damn minute."

Before Eveline knew it, he had Crazy Alice loaded and they were ready to ride out. "I'm driving," he told her.

"No way!" she said, making a dive for the driver's seat. Thankfully, she beat him to it.

He sneered all the way to the state park.

Her heart was tripping so she tried the radio. Settling on a station with Dolly Parton, she did her best to roll her shoulders back and relax in the driver's seat. "You can just take the day off?" she wondered.

"No," he said, not turning his head to look at her. "But damned if I'm going to watch you go asking for trouble."

She felt her shoulders ease. "You *do* worry about me. Don't you?"

"I'm head of the family now, Eveline. I've got to worry about everything and everybody."

"Who worries about you?"

"Nobody gives a damn about me."

"That's bull."

"What?" he snapped.

"I said that's some BS, *hermano*," she stated clearly.

His frown deepened, if possible.

She took her eyes off the road long enough to glance at him. "Oh, my God."

"What?"

"It *is* true."

"What?"

"If you frown enough, your face will get stuck like that," she said, pointing at him. "And I know the real reason you wanted to come with me today. Paloma threatened to haul you off to church this morning."

His mouth folded into a worn line. "She's got me and Ellis taking frickin' turns escorting her to the ten o'clock service. Ellis went last week."

"And you stood her up this week," Eveline concluded.

"You don't have to say it like *that*."

"I've never seen a man load a horse that fast."

"All right." Everett turned around to face her fully. "So I stood her up. And she'll make me pay. You just wait."

"I really can't," she said wryly.

"But I ain't going to church," he claimed. "She makes me sit in the front row and I swear to Christ Reverend Claymore preaches right at me when he's going on about sin. Christa McMurtry, the baker's girl, is always pawing at me after the service, which makes it worse because the reverend sees. He always sees. Then there's the mayor and his wife."

"What's wrong with the mayor?" she asked.

"He's True Claymore. That's what. Did you know that his wife, Annette took Dad to court over a land dispute? They served him the papers when he was in the hospital after his first heart attack."

"What?"

"At his wake, she offered Paloma a housekeeping job at The RC Resort."

"Unbelievable!" Eveline said with a shake of her head.

"What makes it even worse is that Annette is Liberty's biggest supporter in town," Everett went on.

"She's the one who told everyone Ellis was rolling around with Lu Decker."

"But Ellis still goes to church," Eveline said slowly.

"Because he's a saint," Everett griped. "A freaking saint. And not a person in Fuego sees it anymore because of Annette Claymore and her pearl-clutching hens."

Eveline stared out the front window, stunned. "Remind *me* not to go to church." She saw the turn for the state park ahead and put on her blinker. "There's beer in that bag back there."

Everett glanced into the back seat. "For real?"

"I'll give you one if you can prove you still know how to smile," she said.

He narrowed his eyes. As she pulled into the empty parking lot and chose a spot in front of a line of saguaro cacti, he pursed his lips, considering.

They rode hard over the plain, bent low over the horses' necks. Sienna Shade and Crazy Alice had fallen into stride, seeming to know what their owners needed—a hard ride toward that horizon line that seemed to reach for the ends of the earth.

It'd rained recently. She could smell it as much as the horses. She could smell New Mexico. Home. She ached, just ached for all that was and all that had been. The division of the two was too much in some areas and not enough in others. Home wasn't a fixed point. It might remain in the same place, but the world burned and churned around it, so much so that little truly remained of what was.

They didn't slow the horses until they reached the stunning rock archway that signaled the break for the picnic area. Together, she and Everett walked Sienna Shade and Crazy Alice the rest of the way.

Eveline raised her face to the cloud-studded sky. She had ridden Sienna plenty over the last week at the Edge, but she hadn't unleashed her. She hadn't ridden as she once had—wild, fast and free. She didn't know a wide, satisfied smile had spread across her cheeks until she was startled to see the same stretched across Everett's.

For the first time in forever, she saw Everett as he once had been—the drag-racing Everett, the one who'd told the worst bedtime stories imaginable—but who, by turn, had beaten boys for patting her ass at school. The one who had retreated so far into himself after their mother left—but who had quit high school early so their father never had to be alone.

There was so much about Everett she didn't understand—and vice versa. But this she did. This was the narrow course of middle ground they shared.

When they dismounted and tied their mounts to the hitching post in the shade of the arch, she carried her saddlebags to the picnic tables in the shadow of the grove. The first thing she reached for after opening the flap was a bottle of beer. She cranked the cap with her fist, then handed it over to him.

He took it, nudging his hat back from his brow. Turning the bottle up, he drank deep.

She cracked one for herself and drank, too. Coming up for air before he did, she eased her hips back onto the wooden tabletop. "I wanted to come out here myself."

He lowered the bottle, smacked his lips. It was now only a third of the way full. "How many of these did you pack?"

"Enough," she said, "to get well enough plastered

it'd make our Eaton blood proud. But only if my plan failed."

He frowned. And wasn't it a shame his smile had fled so quickly? "What plan?"

"To get over my fears," she admitted. "I've been having a hard time in cars."

"How long's that been going on?"

"A year."

He emptied his bottle, then gestured to hers. "Don't make me drink alone."

She raised the bottle to her mouth, because it was an order she didn't mind taking.

He took a seat on the tabletop next to her and slouched over his knees, holding the empty beer with both hands. "Paloma says you've been having bad dreams. I figured it was still mountain lions and skin-walkers."

She thought of the animal that had crossed her headlights. She shook her head. "Not exactly."

"Is that why you came back?" he asked pointedly. "Because your mind's jacked?"

"It's one of the reasons."

He lifted his shoulder. "Well, I'm no headshrinker. You know that."

A rueful smile turned one corner of her mouth in an upward direction. The idea of Everett as a shrink… It was amusing.

"But your damn demons aren't going to stop chasing you," he continued, vanishing the mirth in a single sentence. "Doesn't matter where you run off to."

She met his hard stare. She blinked several times. "I guess you're right," she said carefully.

His brows emerged from the edge of his sunglasses. "Did that hurt coming out?"

"More than you could possibly imagine."

He surprised the hell out of her by barking a laugh as hard as his gaze. He slapped her knee good-naturedly, shook his head and reached for the saddlebag. "Give me another."

She reached into the bag and dug out another beer for him. Watching him closely, she waited until he'd opened it and taken another long drink before she said what she needed to say. "You're really not mad, are you?" she asked. "That I'm a forty percent shareholder now."

He snorted as he dropped the bottle to the table with a clack. "Wherever Dad is, he's laughing. And that's okay by me." He caught her gaze and frowned again. "Don't get all weepy on me. I'm still not calling you boss."

"Of course not," she said sensibly. "What do I know about running a cattle ranch anymore?"

"Griff brags on your work with the horses," he said. "And he doesn't brag much on anyone so I have to pay attention."

Eveline gave a soft smile. "He does, huh?"

"I don't know how long you're staying this time," he said, "and I'm not fool enough to believe you're not leaving again when you get the itch to. You're like her. You leave."

Eveline's lips parted. They felt numb. "You think… I'm like Mom?"

"Explain how you're different," he challenged.

Leave it to him to ruin a good moment. "She left behind a husband and three children. I left after high school graduation to pursue the life that I wanted, just like Ellis."

"And yet the two of you ended up right back where you started," he said. He finished off the beer and stood to stretch his legs again. "Funny how that works."

"I'm not Mom."

Everett turned back to her, crossing his arms over his chest. "If you say so."

"I'll work," she vowed. "I'll work until you're the one admitting I'm right."

He gave her a sour smile. "That'll be the day."

She threw the last volley between them. "You need to stop hating on Wolfe Coldero."

The smile fled. "I'll feel how I want to feel."

"He knew you didn't want him to have a part of the Edge," she told him. "And he gave it up."

"He knows what's good for him."

"He's a good man," she rebutted. "You'd see it like Ellis and I do if you dropped your stupid grudge against him."

"You know why you and Ellis always get burned, Manhattan? Because you're suckers."

She jumped to her feet. "Not *everyone's* out to hurt us, Everett!"

"'Kay," he said sarcastically, pivoting and walking back to the horses.

She checked the urge to throw the glass bottle down on the ground so that it broke into a million little jagged pieces. Just when she thought she could get through to him, he shut her and everybody else out again.

Needing to get farther away from him for a spell, she walked in the opposite direction, through the grove of trees at the base of arch, across the dappled ground until she broke free of the shade and stood in the hot sun again on the other side.

She planted her hands on her hips and glared at the landscape.

You're like her.

She snarled, pulling her hat off so she could drag her

hands through her hair. *Goddamn Everett.* He fought dirty, always hitting where he knew it would hurt the most. Why did she even try with him? Never mind her father thinking that he and Wolfe could get along smoothly. What had made him think that she and Everett could?

She stilled her pacing when she heard the close rumble to the south. Raising a hand to her brow, she squinted against the midday light. Storm clouds gathered, stern brows stacking quickly with the promise of upheaval. She made a half step to go back to Everett and the horses but stopped when something caught her eye.

At first, she'd thought it was stationary, but now she saw that it was moving. A long, reedy shape, curved over slightly as it moved slowly across the ground in the distance toward a tumble of boulders.

It was dragging something.

Reaching into her back pocket, she pulled out her cell phone. Lifting it, she unlocked the screen and tapped the camera icon. She feathered her fingers across the screen, zooming in and bringing the figure into focus.

She nearly dropped the phone altogether.

The head was that of a predator…but it stood on two legs. Its back and arms were furred, its legs bare. The thing it was dragging was a limp pronghorn. It was dragging it by the antlers.

The stories came back to her. Maybe because Everett had brought them up. Maybe because she couldn't stop thinking about the animal—the *thing*—she'd hit in the road. But her mind skipped right past mountain lion this time and landed sickly on skin-walker.

"Everett!" she screamed. And again, louder and more desperate. *"Everett!"*

Chapter 13

Wolfe always passed the parking lot for the state park on his way into Fuego and back. He rarely stopped, especially on busy towing days like today. The two police vehicles and Eaton Edge trucks caught his attention, however. He mashed on the brake and turned in.

He saw the horses, Sienna Shade and Crazy Alice. He saw them seconds before he saw Eveline, Ellis and Everett standing close with the sheriff and one of his deputies, Kaya Altaha, Naleen Altaha's sister. Wolfe parked the wrecker, then opened the door and climbed out. He moved across the blacktop to the noise of raised voices.

One raised voice in particular—Wolfe's strides lengthened as he skirted a police SUV and found Eveline at the center of a cluster. Her hat was gone. Her hair looked like it had had her fingers running through it over and over, and her eyes... They wheeled like a spooked mare's.

"I don't care what you say I saw!" she shouted at Everett. "I know what I saw!" She held up a cell phone. "I have a picture!"

"That isn't much of a picture, Ms. Meadows," Sheriff Wendell Jones reasoned in his good-old-boy voice. "Er, Ms. Eaton. It's too blurry to make heads or tails of anything."

"Look, see?" she said, pointing to the screen. "There's those boulders there. That's the animal. And this is the pronghorn it was dragging."

"Ms. Eaton," Jones said carefully. "I can take that photo into evidence, but no one's going to be able to identify anything from it."

The deputy, Altaha, was swiftly taking notes. "And you say you couldn't see the animal with the naked eye? You had to zoom in with the phone to get a clear...er... ish picture?"

"Yes," Eveline admitted. "But even if the picture's blurry, I remember what it looked like."

Jones looked to Everett for help. "You didn't see anything?"

"No," Everett said. "By the time I got to her, she was in hysterics. I couldn't see anything from the picture, either, so I rode out to have a look-see."

Ellis studied him. "And you didn't find anything?"

"I found a trail," Everett said. "Not so much footprints, but like something had been dragged, like she said. But nothing else. Not even the stench of something dead."

"Did you ride with him, Ms. Meadows...or Eaton?" Jones asked.

"She was in hysterics," Everett repeated pointedly. "I was lucky to get her to saddle up and ride back here to meet you."

"I *know* what I saw," Eveline reasoned, slowly. "Why else would I have been so upset?"

"I don't know," Everett said with a grimace. "Wasn't it you who told me you've been going through a bad time lately? She did this at Coldero Ridge, too, didn't she?" he asked his brother.

Ellis looked away when Eveline looked to him, pleading. "I wasn't the one who saw her upset." He glanced sideways at Wolfe.

Eveline turned with the others, but she was the only one to twitch noticeably when she saw him standing there. "Wolfe…"

Her eyes pleaded with him. *Tell them I'm not crazy*, they screamed at him. He fell back on a shrug, unable to communicate what she needed him to.

Jones eyed him warily. "I'd be interested to know what happened at Santiago's old place. No one's supposed to be loitering there. No one."

Wolfe curbed the need to offer Jones a rude gesture. He caught Ellis's look, however. A curse blew through his mind. He hadn't called Jones after they'd found what they had together at Coldero Ridge.

The people of Fuego County may have faith and trust in their elected sheriff, but Wolfe certainly did not.

Eveline's lips weren't the color they should have been. Her face was flushed red, but her lips were almost white. He checked the urge to step to her, comfort her as he had at Coldero Ridge.

Ellis cleared his throat. "The reason she was upset at Coldero Ridge is because she found something there. Right, Eveline?"

Eveline looked to him, shaking her head. "I don't think…" She shook her head more firmly, locking her arms over her chest.

Ellis took pity on her, laying a hand on her shoulder. "Why don't you go wait in the truck?"

"What, so you menfolk can discuss my hysterics without me hearing?" She noticed the deputy, Altaha, who was a foot and a half shorter than any man gathered with long, thick hair banded at the nape of her neck. "Sorry."

Altaha raised a brow. "I think we need to hear what you found at Coldero Ridge."

"There were bones," Ellis said carefully. "Piles of them, particularly in the old hearth of the cabin. Wolfe and I went through them. They were animals, different species. Different sizes. But the way they'd been left there… It looked less like the way a predator stores its catch or disposes of it. It seemed more purposeful than that…like a collection."

"Animals don't act like that," Altaha noted. "Not any animal around here, anyway."

"No," Ellis agreed. He met Wolfe's eyes and shifted his feet when Wolfe didn't blink. "We looked the place over. We found some compressed grass—a trail, we figured—and followed it to an opening in the rock wall. Inside, we found more bones hanging from a tree. They'd been strung up with twine in a perfect circle. They clacked against each other like wind chimes. There was evidence of a fire, long cold. And markings on the wall."

"What kind of markings?" Jones asked. He turned halfway to Altaha to make sure she was taking notes.

Ellis looked again to Wolfe, who reluctantly raised his hands and began to motion slowly. Ellis translated. "A record of some kind. Wolfe thinks they were tallies."

"Huh," Jones grunted. He narrowed his eyes on Wolfe. "And you didn't bring this to me because…"

Jones stared at Wolfe. Wolfe stared at Jones. The

stare down went on long enough for Everett to roll his eyes and pace away.

It was Eveline who intervened. "I asked Wolfe not to tell."

They all rounded on her, the four men and the one deputy. Her pale mouth fumbled, opening and closing before she set her chin. "I didn't want anyone to know—about me breaking down like that." She shifted her feet, uncomfortable. "I didn't want word to get around. People might think I'm...crazy."

Altaha stared long across her nose at Eveline. "Weren't you the one who called us this afternoon?"

Eveline hardly missed a beat. "Yes." In a quick dart, her gaze flew to Wolfe before dropping to the ground at Jones's feet. "Coldero Ridge isn't far from here. I thought...whatever left the bones there may have been running around out here." Wolfe heard the click of her throat as she swallowed. "I may have seen it once before..."

"What?" Everett exclaimed.

"When?" Ellis asked.

"The night I came to Fuego," Eveline said, explaining quickly now. Her hands moved as she talked. Her nerves were up. "It was late. I was alone on the highway in my rental and something jumped out in the road—"

"Can you describe it?" Altaha asked, her pen bumping across the page of her notebook.

"It was so fast," Eveline said, squinting to remember. "But when I first saw it, it was on all fours. Then my headlights hit it and it stood up on two and—"

Everett stopped her. "I'm sorry. *Do what*?"

"I know it sounds unreal," Eveline said but was interrupted again by her brother.

"Was it Big Foot, Manhattan?" he asked. "Maybe a gorilla—escaped from the zoo?"

Wolfe moved toward her, hating the amused light in Everett's eyes. He was poking fun at her trauma in front of the sheriff and his deputy. Wolfe's hand balled into a fist at his side.

Eveline scowled. "Don't be a bully."

"This sounds like one of those stories Ellis and I used to tell you before bed," Everett said. "But you're not a little girl anymore, Eveline. You're a grown-ass woman—one who may need to see a head doctor sometime soon."

"Everett," Ellis said in warning. "Let's hear her out."

Eveline told the rest of it, quietly. Everett had snatched what little confidence she had, so her voice was near a whisper. She described something furred with a large head and a snout. The description hadn't changed much since she'd given it to Wolfe the night he picked her up in the wrecker on the roadside.

"And nobody was around who can corroborate what you saw?" Jones asked.

Eveline paused, bit her lip and shook her head. "No."

"And you think this is the same animal you saw today?" Altaha asked.

"Maybe," she said. "It was at a distance. But it was there. Everett may not have seen it, too, but there was a trail. There was something out there that shouldn't be. You have to know that."

Everett drawled, still amused, "Saddle up the horses, sheriff. We've got a hunting posse to assemble."

"Cut it out," Ellis snapped at him.

"I'm taking my horse home," Everett said. "That all right with you?"

Jones nodded. "I don't see any reason to keep you."

Everett placed his hat on his head and tipped it to him and Altaha. "Pleasure." He ribbed Eveline, who swatted him in return. "I'll take the horses. You hitch a ride with Ellis. Jumpy people don't need to be driving."

They waited until he was gone before Jones turned to Eveline and dipped his chin. "Do you think you're of sound mind, Ms. Eaton?"

She looked stricken. "Yes," she said strongly. *"I'm not crazy."* She swung her eyes to Ellis. "You believe that. Right?"

Ellis searched her face. Then he said, "I admit something strange is going on around Fuego. If you say you've seen this thing twice… I can't ignore that."

"You didn't say it," she said under her breath. She sounded betrayed.

Before Ellis could reply, Altaha tucked her pad and pen away in her pocket and placed her hands on her gun belt. "If you say you're of sound mind, there's no reason we have to disagree with you. Right, Sheriff?"

Jones cleared his throat. "Do you have anything else you'd like to add for the record?"

Eveline shook her head.

"All right," Jones said. "It's too late to send a party out to investigate the area tonight. But will you meet us here tomorrow morning so you can show us the place where you saw it?"

Eveline nodded. "Yes."

"We ride early," Jones warned. "Six at the latest."

"I'll be here," she promised.

"Good," Jones said. He pulled in a breath. "See you tomorrow." He nodded to Ellis in departure, then eyed Wolfe. "We'll need to see what you found at Santiago's. Tomorrow afternoon you'll show us?"

It was worded like a question, but it wasn't, really.

Wolfe lifted his chin. If it would help Eveline make her case, there wasn't anything he could do but say yes.

They waited until the officers left in their squad car. Eveline pressed her hands over her face. "That was a disaster."

"It's all right," Ellis said, still trying to soothe. "If Jones didn't believe you, he wouldn't be going back to search the area tomorrow."

"He won't find anything!" Eveline shouted, throwing out her arms. "Everett didn't find anything convincing. There was a storm out there. What little was there will likely be gone before sunrise."

Wolfe stood miserably aside. She looked helpless.

If he were anyone else, he could have helped her. He could have told Jones she was credible. He could have backed up her claims in a strong verbal sense. The sheriff seemed to see silence as suspicious. He always had. Wolfe was sure it was part of the reason why Jones had cuffed him the day he'd watched the cabin at Coldero Ridge go up in flames. Because he hadn't been able to *say* what he'd seen, regardless of the fact that he'd been burned and he'd still been in a fair bit of shock.

"Come on," Ellis said, touching her elbow. "I'll get you back home."

"No."

Ellis frowned. "Everett took your truck. I don't think you want to stay here."

"I never said I was staying here."

Wolfe stood up a little straighter when she slid her gaze up to his. He stilled, however, when Ellis looked at him, too, and he saw his friend's own suspicion.

Ellis's jaw hardened. "I don't think that's the best idea."

"I don't want to see Everett," she reasoned. "I'm

going to need a while before I can face him again, or anyone else at the Edge once word gets around that I'm crazy."

"Nobody thinks you're crazy," Ellis told her.

"No?" she challenged. Her chin rose as she squared off with him. "You believe what I saw out there and on the road into Fuego is real?"

Ellis searched her face. He tried to take her arm again. She took it away. He blew out a breath. "Eveline…"

"I'm hysterical, right?" she said in a dangerous voice. "In a bad place. I'm the little female you menfolk need to circle the wagons around until I learn to calm down."

"Don't do this," he said. "I'm on your side."

"Then I'll see you here tomorrow morning," she said and began walking to Wolfe.

When she bypassed him and crossed to his wrecker, Wolfe faced Ellis, man-to-man.

Ellis shook his head. "You believe her?"

Wolfe narrowed his eyes on his friend. *You don't?* he signed.

"I think she sees what she wants to see," Ellis said. "Or what her trauma tells her to see."

He could remember the pool of blood left by Decker in front of the cabin at the Ridge. He could remember being the only witness to what the man did to Jo and Angel, not being able to communicate what he'd seen.

You believed me then, he signed carefully. *Why can't you believe her now?*

"Whip Decker was a man," Ellis explained. "What he did was horrendous, but he was never what you'd call *good*. What she says she's seen isn't a man. It doesn't even sound real."

She says it's real, Wolfe signed. *So it's real.*

"Send her home," Ellis said. "Send her home before Everett gets word of this."

Wolfe took a step back. *She'll come home when she's ready.*

He heard Ellis curse as Wolfe turned away and followed Eveline to the wrecker.

"They all think I've lost my mind," Eveline said as Wolfe turned the wrecker down the lane to his tract of land. "Even Ellis."

Disappointment burned her blood. Disillusionment was a bitter taste in her mouth. She'd come home knowing she would face their sense of betrayal, however strong it was. She hadn't known she could be betrayed by them as well. "I know what I saw," she repeated to herself as the wrecker bumped through a rut and she bounced a bit in the seat.

She almost didn't want to look at him, afraid she would see doubt on his face, too. Maybe she could survive her family's ridicule. But Wolfe's?

Something closed over her hand. Something hot, hard and strong.

Glancing down, she saw that it was his hand.

She blinked several times before she could raise her eyes to his. He was wearing his hat low over his brow, his eyes drilled into the dirt lane in front of him. But he was holding her hand in a firm grip that told her everything she needed to know about what he believed.

Emotions pushed up into her throat. She swallowed several times, trying to choke them back. There was so much there. Too much. Unable to say anything, she turned her palm up to his. Their fingers didn't intertwine. His touch lightened and grazed over the surface of her fingers, moving slowly back and forth in a tacit, tender dance. The friction of his calluses made her skin feel uber-sensitive.

Underneath, she felt charged. That reckless bent she'd been battling made her want to hold and keep him.

Keep him.

You can't keep something wild, her father had told her often. He'd looked sad, too, when he said it—so much so that she'd known he was thinking of her mother. *Wild things don't survive cages.*

Back then, it'd been a fox kit that had been separated from its mother.

She knew from her father's experience that wild things broke your heart. That's why they were best left alone.

But she could no more take her hand out from under Wolfe's than she could walk away at this point.

She was too far gone and she needed to know… How far was he?

He turned off the lane into his driveway. The barn came into view. He'd painted, she saw. It was a nice desert red. The RV and deck were where they'd been before, along with the paddock with Winter and the filly from Eaton Edge grazing inside it. She looked beyond it all at the slab of what would be Wolfe's house and her lips parted in surprise. "You've been building."

He'd started framing. He'd built walls and stood them up. She could see the shape the house would take. Simple lines. Straightforward floor plan. Nice and open. Would there be windows everywhere? There should be with that view.

She heard a chorus of barks and looked around to see Storm racing off the flat, shrubby plain to greet them.

"It looks great," she said. "Have you had any help?"

He shook his head.

Loyal Readers
FREE BOOKS Voucher

We're giving away THOUSANDS of FREE BOOKS

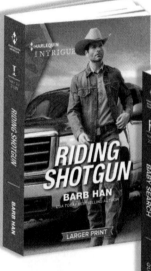

See Details Inside

Get up to 4
FREE FABULOUS BOOKS
You Love!

To thank you for being a loyal reader we'd like to send you up to 4 FREE BOOKS, absolutely free when you try the Harlequin Reader Service.

Just write "YES" on the Loyal Reader Voucher and we'll send you 2 free books from each series you choose and a Free Mystery Gift, altogether worth over $20.

Try **Harlequin® Romantic Suspense** and get 2 books featuring heart-racing page-turners with unexpected plot twists and irresistible chemistry that will keep you guessing to the very end.

Try **Harlequin Intrigue® Larger-Print** and get 2 books featuring action-packed stories that will keep you on the edge of your seat. Solve the crime and deliver justice at all costs

Or **TRY BOTH** and get 2 books from each series!

Your free books are completely free, even the shipping! If you continue with your subscription, you can look forward to curated monthly shipments of brand-new books from your selected series, always at a discount off the cover price! Plus you can cancel any time.

So don't miss out, return your Loyal Readers Voucher today to get your Free books.

Pam Powers

LOYAL READER
FREE BOOKS VOUCHER

YES! I Love Reading, please send me up to 4 FREE BOOKS and a Free Mystery Gift from the series I select.

Just write in "YES" on the dotted line below then return this card today and we'll send your free books & gift asap!

➡ **YES** ⬅

Which do you prefer?

☐ **Harlequin® Romantic Suspense**	☐ **Harlequin Intrigue® Larger-Print**	☐ **BOTH**
240/340 HDL GRRX	199/399 HDL GRRX	240/340 & 199/399 HDL GRSM

FIRST NAME   LAST NAME

ADDRESS

APT.#   CITY

STATE/PROV.   ZIP/POSTAL CODE

EMAIL ☐ Please check this box if you would like to receive newsletters and promotional emails from Harlequin Enterprises ULC and its affiliates. You can unsubscribe anytime.

HI/HRS-622-LR_MMM22

HARLEQUIN® Reader Service —**Here's how it works:**

Accepting your 2 free books and free gift (gift valued at approximately $10.00 retail) places you under no obligation to buy anything. You may keep the books and gift and return the shipping statement marked "cancel." If you do not cancel, approximately one month later we'll send you more books from the series you've chosen, and bill you at our low, subscribers-only discount price. Harlequin® Romantic Suspense books consist of 4 books each month and cost just $5.49 each in the U.S. or $6.24 each in Canada, a savings of at least 12% off the cover price. Harlequin Intrigue® Larger-Print books consist of 6 books each month and cost just $6.49 each in the U.S. or $6.99 each in Canada, a savings of at least 13% off the cover price. It's quite a bargain! Shipping and handling is just 50¢ per book in the U.S. and $1.25 per book in Canada*. You may return any shipment at our expense and cancel at any time by contacting customer service — or you may continue to receive monthly shipments at our low, subscribers-only discount price plus shipping and handling.

▼ If offer card is missing write to: Harlequin Reader Service, P.O. Box 1341, Buffalo, NY 14240-8531 or visit www.ReaderService.com ▼

BUSINESS REPLY MAIL
FIRST-CLASS MAIL   PERMIT NO. 717   BUFFALO, NY

POSTAGE WILL BE PAID BY ADDRESSEE

HARLEQUIN READER SERVICE
PO BOX 1341
BUFFALO NY 14240-8571

NO POSTAGE
NECESSARY
IF MAILED
IN THE
UNITED STATES

"Just you?" She found a smile. "Did you wear a tool belt?"

His smile eclipsed hers. His hazel eyes warmed as he turned them to hers. She liked how the outer corners were soft with lines. They didn't used to be. In her old industry, lines were imperfections. Lines had been chased by enough creams and serums to fill a barrel. She'd hocked them in magazines and commercials, billboards and boutique marquees. Lines on Wolfe... They were sexy. Just like everything else about him. She'd yet to find anything that wasn't sexy about the man he'd become.

Her pulse flipped out. They'd been smiling at each other for a while—so long the truck cab had grown warm. He'd shut off the engine minutes ago and neither of them had moved.

She could take off his hat again, run her fingers through his hair the way she liked. His gaze spanned from her left eye to her right...then dropped to her mouth. She bit her lower lip, wishing he would.

Storm's racket reached her ears again. He'd planted himself underneath Wolfe's door, rife with rapid-fire reports of anticipation. He reached for the handle and opened the door. The noise increased as he slid out of the driver's seat and made the leap for the ground.

Eveline eyed the empty driver's seat, the hand he'd held curling into a protective fist. She frowned at her knuckles. Her stare swept over the dash and fell on the RV. There were blackout curtains over all the windows. To keep the heat out—and the secrets in. Would some of those secrets be hers? Nerves built underneath her sternum until she felt heavy with them.

There was a benefit to living in an industry that took you at face value. She hadn't made connections that were anything more than that. She hadn't let anyone in. Colleagues, friends, lovers… No one. People didn't need to know her. They'd have learned too quickly—that she wasn't Eden Meadows at all.

She'd always been Eveline.

It was a lonely life but a safe one. She'd never been hurt. Some people would argue that her profession was a heartbreaking one, but she'd never let professional disappointments or letdowns bring her low. She'd skimmed the surface of hurt like a hawk kiting on invisible air currents.

Maybe that was why the wreck had nearly destroyed her. After, she'd grown reacquainted with her own heart all too fast.

She'd missed it, she realized. It hadn't taken long to understand that she needed who she had been. She'd missed *knowing* who she was. She'd gotten tired of lying about what she wanted. More, what she needed.

Coming home had been wrought with more complications than she knew what to do with: her father's death. Her brothers' feelings. Her mother's ghost. Whatever the hell was living on the outskirts of Fuego that only she could see.

And Wolfe.

She knew what she wanted and it was hard to rise above a decade of habits—making excuses, pushing her needs aside to avoid complications…

She jumped when her door suddenly opened. Wolfe was on the ground. His hat was in his hands. Storm was at his heels, tongue lolling in a wide, happy grin that was contagious—contagious enough there was a wide one stretched taut across Wolfe's face, too.

It dimmed when he saw her.

She couldn't imagine what was on her face. It was

difficult to know what she still knew how to hide and
what she couldn't.

He lifted his tan, hard hand, waiting.

She licked her lips. She couldn't go back to the Edge.
And there was nowhere else in the world she'd rather
be than right here with him.

She reached out and let him pull her down to the
ground.

Chapter 14

Wolfe sensed something troubling Eveline other than what she'd seen at the state park—something to do with being here, alone with him. So he avoided the RV, leading her to the paddock instead.

Winter snorted a greeting. Ducking down between the slats of the gate, he eyed the other filly as he patted Winter on the chest. His new girl hadn't moved from the far end of the paddock. She was still wary of him, and he'd been working with her every day. Gaining in inches was progress. He'd once only been able to trust in inches. It had taken time—to put his faith in anything. Anyone.

He may not remember much about his past before Fuego beyond pain and trauma. But he could remember how hard Santiago and Hammond and Paloma had worked…how patient they'd been with his wariness…

He approached the new filly slowly. Her ears went back. He reached out his hand, bending at the waist to get a look at her bad leg. The bandage had held. She hadn't rubbed it off. It was dry, too. No fluids had bled through. The swelling had gone away over the last few days, thanks to Griff's poultices.

She'd been eating well, and drinking. She seemed to enjoy Winter's companionship. She wanted to live. He knew that much. She wanted to run again. He could see it in the evenings when he came to the gate to watch her, the way she stared at the horizon line…trying to bring the indigo shadows there closer.

She'd run again, and maybe he'd have her saddled by then. Maybe not. But he'd make sure she galloped again across the plain, the wind in her mane.

He straightened when he heard the rattle of the feed bucket. Behind him, Winter nickered. Wolfe looked around to find Eveline coming out of the barn with a bucket hanging from each arm. She met him at the gate. Wordlessly, she handed the first over, and he took it. He couldn't tell her—that he'd seen the same hungry look in her eyes as the new filly's. He'd seen her drink that vista. She was a wild thing, too, who had kept herself away too long. Her soul was just as starved for the land and the wind and the freedom that came with both.

He came across the gate again so the new filly would feel comfortable enough to come to her bucket and eat. He and Eveline both watched her shrunken stomach round as she did.

Eveline propped her chin on the hands she'd laid across the top of the gate. "Have you given her a name yet?" she asked quietly.

He began to lift his hands and stopped. It was difficult to communicate something intangible. Falling back on what little he knew of American Sign Language, he made his fingers into the shapes of the letters.

Her eyes softened. "Faith?"

He nodded slowly.

"That's perfect," she breathed. She smiled as she went back to watching the horses.

He watched her. Her cheeks were still stained with color. It passed down her neck, the side without the scars, and slipped away under her collar. He could smell her. It was enough of a hit to get him buzzed. He thought about passing his hand over the glossy surface of her hair but stopped. She was still jumpy, probably.

While the horses finished chowing, he refilled their water trough. He did a quick check on their stalls to be sure they were ready and no snakes had decided to cozy up in the hay while he was gone.

He grabbed a lead rope from the tack on the wall and went back to the paddock gate. He unlatched it and stepped inside.

Winter was ready. She let Wolfe loop the rope loosely around her neck and lead her into the barn. She went into her stall willingly and Wolfe closed it. He looked out to the paddock where Eveline was still watching Faith, her boots perched on the lowest rung.

He smiled a little because it made him think of Hammond's little girl. She'd haunted the stables at the Edge, always chasing Griff's shadow with long hair and questions flying around her. She'd had questions about Wolfe, too, when he'd come, questions for him he'd been furious he couldn't answer. She'd learned to cool her curiosity with patience, like Ellis—a feat for a young girl. She'd learned to be watchful, to read him in her own way. The understanding hadn't been as close as Ellis's. But it'd been there.

She didn't know what that meant—what it still meant, all these years later.

He walked back to the paddock gate. When he opened it again, he motioned for her to follow.

Her eyes rounded. She shook her head in refusal. "No. I don't want to spook her."

He curled his fingers for hers again, insisting.

She released a long breath, glancing at Faith, before taking his hand.

Holding it fast in his, he positioned himself in front of her, tugging until she was snug against the line of his back. He cupped the back of her hand, moving gradually toward Faith. He dug a treat out of his pocket and placed it in her palm, turning it toward the sky in an offering.

Faith's ears went back, then sideways. They twitched. He tutted to her, the noises he knew she was growing accustomed to. He stilled, wanting her to come to him as she had once before.

Farther. A little farther this time.

Neither he nor Eveline moved as they waited. He could feel Eveline's pulse through the back of his shirt. It was a battle charge.

Faith took a few moments to look by turns uninterested, then uncertain, and uninterested again. Finally, her hooves shuffled. She put her body behind her. Her head high, she came to him as he'd approached her. Slowly.

He breathed easily, knowing she was reading him, wanting her to sense his calm, just as she did with Winter. She'd watched man and horse riding. He'd seen her weighing how he was with the other filly...

Her nose lowered to Eveline's hand. The whiskers brushed across the heel of it. He felt more than heard Eveline's gasp of delight. He felt her pulse harden against his backbone.

Faith's mouth worked around the treat. She didn't

dance backward as she had yesterday. Wolfe took this as a very good sign and decided to try their luck further...

He guided Eveline's hand up to the filly's neck. Wolfe could feel the horse's warmth through Eveline's palm. He could feel vibrations of excitement running through Eveline's arm and torso. Using her, he petted Faith's neck, rocking Eveline with each stroke.

Faith finally broke free. Her tail was high, but her ears hadn't turned. That was a good sign, too. *Progress*, he noted, pleased, as he backed away carefully as not to get their feet tangled.

Color was high in Eveline's cheeks again, but this time it was an overjoyed flush. "You," she said as he shut the gate with him on one side and her on the other. "You really do work miracles."

He took the lead rope he'd hung on the fence. He attached the lead to the halter Griff had put on Faith before sending her home with Wolfe, then led her out of the paddock. Eveline opened the gate for them.

When Faith was safely inside the barn, he eyed the two stalls on the other side. Normally, he stabled Winter and Faith on one side of the barn overnight before switching them to the paddock for the day if the weather was fine. He'd muck out the other side before leaving for work, placing a nice bed of hay down so it was ready for them that night, and then he had little to do but brush Winter down after an evening ride and offer feed and water before tucking in for the night.

Eveline took one of the pitchforks off the wall. "Need some help?" she asked.

He raised a brow in question as she handed him one.

"It's not much of a date," she admitted, "but I'm down."

He watched as she set herself to work on the stall

closest to the door. Amused, he wondered if anyone in New York had seen her like this: hair mussed from a long day of riding. Face flushed with effort and the dregs of emotion.

He didn't imagine anyone who'd seen her in glossy magazine ads would believe Eden Meadows had ever shoveled manure. Yet here she was in his barn, the long line of her spine bent over the task.

He wanted this Eden—this Eveline, the one who lost it over a lost horse. The one who drank the horizon with her eyes. The one who went toe-to-toe with her big brother—with the goddamn sheriff to boot. He wanted her so bad it took everything he had not to take the pitchfork from her, toss it aside and pull her down in a fresh bed of hay.

The low knell of thunder drew his attention. He glanced out the open doors and saw the thunderhead building to the west. They'd have to hurry if they didn't want to get drenched.

Trying to calm the Texas twister he got caught in more and more with his feelings around her, Wolfe dragged the wheelbarrow closer, positioned it between both stalls and began shoveling alongside her.

Chapter 15

They got caught in the rain. Wolfe hurried to close the barn doors. He pointed across the yard to Storm.

From under the umbrella of her hat, Eveline saw the dog crouched underneath the wrecker. She could hear him barking again. She raced across the yard, calling to him.

It wasn't until she reached the truck that the dog launched itself at her, straight into her arms. He drew his front legs over her shoulder and turned his wet nose against her throat. Eveline staggered, laughing as she turned and found Wolfe. "Did you lose this?" she shouted over the downpour.

He took Storm's weight, cradling him in his arms like an infant. He nodded for her to go ahead up the steps to the RV.

She didn't argue. She pulled back the screen door at the top of the stairs and held it open for the two of them before letting it slam. Wolfe set Storm down before closing the door of the RV to keep the wet out.

She swept her hat off and with it the rain that had pooled around its brim. Storm chose that moment to shake. Thousands of tiny water droplets misted her and Wolfe and everything around them.

Eveline giggled as she glanced up at Wolfe. His shirt was plastered to his torso. His hat was as soggy as hers when he took it off and tossed it to the sink in the kitchenette. He took hers as well, setting it down. A grin played at the corners of his mouth as he eyed her appearance. It seized, however, when his gaze took a dip over her front.

She glanced down, then quickly looked away. Her white lace bralette was visible through her white shirt and there was no padding. In the cool of the air-conditioned RV, she could feel her nipples drawing up to hard points. His attention didn't help.

Before she could cross her arms over her chest, he turned away, going quickly up a small set of steps. He opened a narrow door, reached in and pulled out a stack of towels.

"Thank you," she breathed as he handed her one. She patted her face and neck, watching him do the same. Then she looked away. Seeing him wet made her remember the day she'd first come to his property—when he'd soaked himself at the spigot outside. And that definitely wasn't doing anything to solve her nipple debacle.

She looked around. Everything struck her as male. The air itself was spiced with his scent. She dried her hair and eyed the leather sectional against the long wall with windows above. There were blueprints and a tool belt on the tabletop. A plate and cup were stacked on the drying mat next to the kitchen sink. There was another set of boots—these more worn and muddier than the ones on his feet—on a mat near the door. In the corner, a broom and mop leaned against the wall.

There was no art. No trinkets. No throw blankets or pillows. Intrigued, she saw a braided rope on the sectional—a halter, hand-braided. Everything looked clean and sparse, broken only by the water and streaks of mud they'd tracked in and sprigs of Storm's coat in the corners of the floor.

Eveline realized suddenly how filthy she was by comparison. She'd mucked a stall, held a wet dog and run through the mud. She saw the grime she'd rubbed off her arms on the towel. "Here," she said, trying to toe off one boot. She reached down to pull the first one off.

She pulled too hard and lost her balance, tipping toward the wall. But his arm was there. It came around her in a lightning move and stopped her from falling.

She took a steadying breath, but his wet shirt clung to hers. She could feel the heat of him under the flannel and felt the opposite of cold. "Whoops," she said, making no move to untangle them.

He used one hand on each of her shoulders to place her back against the wall.

Her heart drummed. She felt her nostrils flare, but she wasn't breathing, not adequately, because all of a sudden she felt light-headed. Going very, very still, she watched as he knelt down in the small space between her and the door. As rain drummed on the metal roof, he took off one of her boots.

She let him tug, leaning against the wall. It made a wet plopping sound as it finally broke loose, nearly tumbling him to his backside. She pressed her lips hard together to choke back a nervous laugh. Letting her hair curtain her face, she watched as he took her other boot. She liked watching his teeth work his bottom lip. She liked the colors of his face. The tops of his cheeks were dark—browned by the sun—almost red but not quite. Everything else was tan in color except for the slight dent beneath his lower lip, which was pale. It reminded her of the mountains outside of Fuego, their variegated hues.

He had generous lips. His lashes were wet and black. They were thick. There was a rain drop caught in them.

The boot slid free. He grabbed both walls when the release sent him back against the door. His smile reached for hers. She loved how the color of his eyes was undefined like so much of the rest of him: his past. His thoughts. His feelings.

She looked down at his lap because she thought it would be better than feeling naked and flushed again in front of his eyes. It was a mistake, of course, as his jeans formed to him even better when wet. They clung to long thighs thick with muscle. Like a true cowboy, they were dirty, especially below the knees.

She thought about taking off his boots the way he had taken off hers. But he beat her to it, working them loose. Then he lined them all up on the drying mat. His boots. Her boots. His boots.

She ran her hand over her face. It wasn't wet anymore. Uncertain what to do, she stayed pinned against the wall, unable to move.

She had a feeling she was standing on a cliff looking down into the cavern below.

Apparently, she was one of those crazed adrenaline junkies who contemplated jumping. It was only good sense that held her back from taking the leap—at him.

The coming together would feel so right. Despite her better judgment, she knew that it would. Colliding with

him, her own feelings, their attraction—their connection… It would light this wet night on fire.

Had this always been inevitable? she wondered. Were
they always meant to wind up here? Together, inexo-
rably. The inertia made her catch her breath. She staggered under it. Undoubtedly, she was scared…of what
was, what could be—what it would mean.

If she spent the night in Wolfe's bed, it wouldn't just
be the one time. No. One night would not be enough,
no matter how explosive.

Wolfe had raised himself to his feet. Again, he went
up the small set of steps and opened the narrow door.
This time, he disappeared altogether behind it.

She heard the sound of water hitting a shower wall.
When he opened the door again, it was to motion her up.

She followed. The bathroom was tiny. They fit inside
but just barely. The edge of the sink pressed against her
back as he turned away from the small linen cupboard
with another towel. His front buffered hers. Her skin
felt alive with sensation beneath the shirt that felt barely
there anymore. For one delicious moment, he eyed her
mouth in a way that nearly sent her up to her toes.

He bowed his head and maneuvered himself to the
door, closing it behind him.

She stayed frozen a beat. Two. Then on a wash of
breath, she closed her eyes and uttered, "Oh, give me
strength."

She undressed, placing her wet things in the sink.
Shivering, she ducked under the shower spray and slid
the glass shower door into place. She used his soap,
scrubbing until the mud and grime were gone. Scrubbing until his smell was all over her. Then she yanked
the tab all the way to cold and stood, teeth clenched,
absorbing the onslaught.

Thinking sensibly was key here. She was raw from this afternoon, from what she alone had seen in the desert. From the betrayal of her kin. From the sheriff's scrutiny. And from needs—thick and tangled needs that would surely drown her if she didn't keep her wits about her.

She hadn't wanted this. This isn't what she had come home for. She'd needed *home*, a sense of place. She'd needed family and some semblance of who she was so she could heal. Had she found those things? Was there a chance she was confusing any of that with what she felt for Wolfe?

Damn Ellis for not teaching her how to ask Wolfe the things she needed to ask—to help him communicate the answers back. How could either of them be sure when they couldn't do that?

She shut off the water and stood, shivering. Then she made herself get out and dry off.

As she was drying her hair, she noticed her sopping wet clothes draining in the sink.

Well, she hadn't thought that through, had she?

There was no putting them back on, not now that she was clean. She eyed the door she knew led back down the steps to the living/kitchen area. But there was another door, a pocket door that slid into the wall.

On the other side, she found the place where Wolfe slept.

The bed was wider than she'd have thought. It was made, neatly. The comforter was unassuming, neither patterned nor textured. Small, nondescript sconces built into the wall above the bed were turned low.

There was a T-shirt on the bed, folded.

She looked around, realizing that there was no other laundry in sight. He'd set the shirt out—for her.

At least *someone* was thinking.

Still shivering, Eveline picked the shirt up and pulled it over her head. It fell on her, overlong and loose. She smiled a bit at the bagginess of it. Then she sat on the bed because she didn't know what else to do.

There was more braided rope hanging from the sconces—other halters in various states of completion. Some were plain rope braid. Others were colorful—bright blue intermixed with earthy brown—red and black—burnt orange and evergreen.

Here she found some trinkets, though they were sparse. A watch—an old one, the gold band scratched and the face beginning to cloud beneath the glass. A memory toggled as she frowned at the numbers just visible still beneath. She remembered this watch.

It was Santiago's, she recalled. She remembered him wearing it. It had seemed an oddly flashy piece for a weathered wrangler. Santiago had never struck her as the flashy sort.

There was a five by seven photo she saw on the nightstand. Unframed. She started to reach for it, then stopped. Santiago, she recognized—a smiling Santiago, which was striking enough. He'd never smiled much, not that she'd seen.

In his arms, a small girl, also smiling. She had his dark eyes and hair the color of fresh hay.

Angel.

Eveline's hand came to her mouth. She held it there for some time, staring at the innocent face.

The girl had looked nothing like Jo. Nothing like Eveline or Ellis or Everett. She'd been Santiago's child, through and through. And yet…

Eveline's insides ached. That sweet face. That sweet

girl. The sister she'd never known. None of them had. Except Wolfe.

There was a knock on the door to the bathroom, from the hallway beyond.

It took her a moment to find her voice. "In here," she called. "The shower's open."

Wolfe must have hesitated because it was several seconds later that she heard the bathroom door open, close, then the shower turn on again on the other side of the pocket door that had slid closed behind her when she entered the bedroom. She heard the sound of the shower door sliding along the track.

The past was alive here, as alive as it had ever been. There would always be the past between them, along with everybody else. Ellis with his "it's trouble for everyone" warning. Everett had more beef with Wolfe than any other living soul. Half of Fuego still thought he was a stone-cold killer.

She made herself look away from the picture of Santiago and Angel and moved away, restless. There was a long window at the foot of the bed and space enough there between it and the bed to pace.

Why did she want him? Because it was forbidden?

No. It was more. She had a feeling if she walked away, she'd regret it. Always. Like she regretted not coming back sooner to be with her father. Like she regretted ever thinking she could be indispensable to an industry that had tossed her out like a stray cat. Like she regretted not knowing her mother. Or Angel.

She had so much regret. Too much regret.

A heart could only carry so much.

The pocket door slid open behind her. She turned toward it, surprised when he stepped through, towel wrapped around his hips. She hadn't heard the shower shut off. And here she'd thought these walls were thin.

His eyes seized on her and he stayed put as the door slid shut behind him. The hair was slicked back from his brow.

She didn't look away from him this time. She looked her fill. The lines of him were familiar and yet they weren't. She might have seen him shirtless once, but she hadn't touched. Her hands itched to touch all that sun-browned skin and the ridges of muscles, tapering to his waist. He was perfect in his burn marks and calluses. The towel was slung low, almost precariously. She could see a line of hair just above it.

She felt weak and heavy with need.

Storm slipped between his legs and he jumped. The dog's wet hair was sleek and clean. Eveline realized Wolfe had washed him, too, in the shower. Panting lazily, the dog came around the bed, rubbing against the comforter's edge. He began to rub himself against Eveline's legs again, leaving tufts of loose hair behind.

Wolfe snapped his fingers to stop him.

"He's okay," she told him, smiling. "It feels kind of nice, actually." When Wolfe still didn't move, she nodded to the door. "Do you want me to go so you can get dressed?"

He shook his head quickly. His feet seemed to come unglued from the carpet. He veered around the bed, passing through the small space to a door on the other side that must have been the closet.

Storm turned his body lengthways. Wolfe nearly tripped, grabbing the wall over Eveline's head.

She put her arms around him, low on his waist. "I got you," she murmured when his face tipped downward.

His pupils looked huge and she could hear him

breathing. His chest rose up and down in rapid sequence.

She placed one hand on the center of his chest. "Easy, cowboy," she whispered. "It's okay." She wanted to press her face into the line of his throat when she saw him swallow hard. "We're okay. Aren't we?"

He jerked a quick nod. Still, he didn't move.

She could see him and all his secrets. They were written on him. He was just as spooked as she was—at the inertia of what happened when they came together. Would it lead to catastrophe—or everything they'd ever wanted?

Eveline's lips trembled together. She parted them. "Sometimes…sometimes I'm afraid I'm more my mother's daughter than I thought."

His brows came down. He shook his head, then lifted his hand from the wall to touch her face. It fell and he shook his head again, pushing himself away completely.

She watched him go. When he disappeared, she cursed. She cursed herself. She cursed Ellis for not giving her the tools she needed to talk to him.

Swiping the hair away from her face, she followed him. Her clothes were gone from the bathroom sink. She went down the small set of steps and found him beyond the kitchenette where a small hatch opened to a stackable washer and dryer. He was placing their clothes in the low washer.

Her things looked delicate in his hands.

There was nothing about this that wasn't delicate. Delicate like a grenade.

"I look like her," she blurted. Unable to wind the words back in, she went on, "Even if I don't talk like her or walk like her. That last one's on purpose. I schooled it out of me. Told myself it was for the runway. I realized along the way it was something else. I changed everything. Who I was. What I was. I even lied about where I was really from so no one would ever tie me back to her or what she did to my father. My brothers. Me."

She released a tumultuous sigh. "I understand myself better now. Why I ran away. Why I lied about Fuego and her for so long. It's hard because she died so suddenly. There's no closure. Any grief I've ever felt is so tangled up in resentment and betrayal I don't know if they'll ever be resolved. But I want… I need for you to know I'm not her."

He'd turned. He had one hand on the dryer and the other on his hip. His brow was low, but there was no sympathy on his face. He started to move his hands together, the way he would with Ellis to communicate. He stopped, knowing she wouldn't understand.

Eveline felt at a loss. For a second, she felt completely lost.

He pressed his lips together before he squared his jaw and faced her fully. And he mouthed words as he never had before. *I know.*

Her heart started to hammer again. She could only look at him and how far he was willing to push himself for her sake. He nodded, driving the message home.

Her breath came ragged now. "I envy that relationship you had with her in the later years. And I'm grateful—*so* grateful you were willing to go into the fire to save them." She took a step toward him. "I would've shot Whip Decker, too. I would have made him turn and face me. I'd have shot him in the heart for robbing us all blind."

He stared at her, his eyes too full to read.

She tried not to stare. Couldn't stop. He was too fine a thing not to look at. "I'm a hot mess. My family's a mess. Jesus, this whole freaking town's a mess. You had some guts coming back here."

He pointed to her as if to say, *You, too.*

"Why do we do it?" she wondered out loud. "Why do we go home when it'd be easier to start somewhere fresh?" She thought about it. "Is it because…it's where what's meant for us has been…all along?"

There was too much on his face still.

She shook her head. "I'm running my mouth. And I used to be so good at keeping to myself."

He closed the washer door, started the timer. When the machine hummed to life, he walked to her.

"I can go," she said, managing nothing more than a whisper as he closed the distance. "I'll call Ellis. Have him come pick me up."

He touched her mouth, his fingers barely brushing her lips. It caused her to miss a breath. Under his shirt, she felt naked with him once more. Something about this man made her feel bare, barer than she'd ever been. "E-Ellis showed me what your sign for me is."

His chin lifted slightly. Then he lowered his hand to her brow. From there, he traced the shape of her face, slowly, tacitly.

Her eyes were closed now. "He told me…you've had a yen for me. Maybe since we were kids." She raised her hand to his forearm, where she could feel the mottled skin. "How did I miss that?" she asked, bewildered.

He kissed her below the jawline. She tilted her head back so he could get to more of those places that made her knees feel like jelly. "They wouldn't have liked it then, either. Would they?" She opened her eyes to find that he was smiling.

She kissed his smiling mouth. Banding her arms around his neck, she pulled him in tight. Tilting her head, she opened her mouth and he gave. He gave as good as he got, taking it up a notch.

He bent at the knees without breaking the kiss and hooked an arm under her knees. Boosting her into his arms, he somehow navigated the small space between the table and kitchenette, past the door, up the flight of steps and ducked into the bedroom.

Her shirt was riding up but she didn't care. It may as well not have been there. The heat of him had seared it off. When he set her on the bed, she began to pull him with her.

He held up a hand. Then he pulled open the drawer of the nightstand and pulled out a small packet.

She smiled, amused, when he turned away to put on the condom. When he turned back to her, she grabbed him by the knot at the front of his towel. It loosened. Neither of them stopped it from falling away to the floor.

She gasped as his hands came under her and he scooped her into his lap. Placing her hands on his shoulders for balance, she went up on her knees so her face was above his. She nipped the edge of his nose just enough to make him hiss. Grinning, she sifted her fingers through his hair.

He hummed deep in his throat, head falling back as her nails breezed across his scalp. The noise made her need grow claws. They sank in, piercing until the sweet hot ache in her center mushroomed.

She readjusted, settling over his lap. His hands were under her still, kneading her bottom under her shirt. She felt the strong point of his arousal and pressed against it.

His hands spanned up the back of the shirt, sweeping over her spine. He grabbed the back of her shoulders, bringing his arousal and hers firmly together, demonstrating exactly where he wanted it to be.

Okay, she thought, far beyond the point of questions. She began to reach for the hem of her shirt. He beat her to it, yanking it up. She raised her arms and he tugged it off, away, pulling her closer still.

Skin to skin, mouth to mouth, she could hardly breathe. There was so much here. If she thought about it, she'd think there was too much again.

But she didn't think, any more than she could question. His mouth was on her throat again and open to the web of scars. A cry bubbled up her throat before she could stop it. This time, though, she didn't attempt to turn his attention away from the damage. He traced it across her collarbone, over the point of her shoulder until the voice inside her that wanted the ugly marks to magically disappear had ceased.

His knuckles skimmed over the crests of her cheeks as his mouth came back to hers.

His mouth was dangerous, she thought again. He may have never spoken a word in his life. But damn, he knew how to use it. He kissed her and touched her until diamond points of pleasure coiled sinuously in her womb and waiting any longer for him to drive his point home felt inexplicable.

"Hurry," she said, reaching for him.

He held her back. That wicked, wicked smile graced his mouth again and her excitement spiraled out from the center, like fireworks on the Fourth of July.

Sweet Lord, she thought. She was done for.

Done in by his secret smile.

He wrapped her up tight in his arms and began to tilt her toward the pillows. She let him roll over her. On a thrilling wave of impulse, she kept the momentum going until she was above him and his head was in the pillows.

She ranged over him, knees on either side of his hips, hands going up against his until his were above his head.

He didn't fight. As she teased his lips, he closed his eyes and lifted his chin, accepting the slow play of her mouth.

She wove patterns and pictures across his shoulders and chest. She took her fingertips over his sternum, which he'd broken at one point, she recalled. Kicked by a horse. It stuck out farther than it should, just enough for her fingers to catch on it.

He let her touch skate across the surface of his belly, shivering in an involuntary wave. She noted that he was gripping the pillowcase above his head and his other hand had fisted until it was white-knuckled at the point of his brow.

She wanted to spoil him with her touch, to the point where he was gasping. But she was already too eager to know what it was to be joined with him. She reared up. They both reached for his erection. Her hand closed over him at the base. She looked at him, then. His eyes appeared black in the play of low light. His jaw had hardened, his lips seamed taut and his nostrils flared. He gave a slight nod.

She guided him in until she was full. She ground to a halt because her eyes rolled back and a noise escaped her, long and low.

His palms cupped the back of her hips. They stayed there as he took them up over the first wave, then the next. She cried out again, losing hold of herself.

When he flipped their positions, she didn't stop him. She turned her knees outward and absorbed as he rose and fell over her. Holding on. Just holding on. Clamping her mouth shut because she was afraid of what would come spilling out if she left it open.

His hand came up to grip her chin. She opened her eyes in reaction. He hadn't stopped. But he held her, watched her. She realized she'd started to pant through her nose as the pleasure reached terminal velocity.

This was when she splintered, in little rifts. Then it felt like she split in two. Her heels dug into the bed and her toes curled so hard under she wondered how they didn't break off altogether. She opened her mouth but all that escaped was a stunned whisper.

He'd stopped, which she realized gradually as she came down off the high. He was still watching. And her hand was balled so tight in his hair, she knew it pained him. He held still, so still.

She relinquished the hold. "I'm s-sorry," she said.

His mouth tipped up slowly at the corners. That wicked, wolfish grin again.

She shook her head. "Oh," she murmured. "You really shouldn't do that."

He lifted a single brow.

She sighed over him. "*Because.*" She brought his mouth down to hers to tangle until she wasn't the only one who was breathless. She traced the long line of his spine from top to bottom. "It makes me want to drive you crazy," she finished and brought her center up against his.

The smile tapered. He turned his face into her throat as she brought her hips up again. He'd let go of her chin to place his hands under the small of her back, guiding her up to meet him once and again until they'd fallen back into the fine cadence of lovemaking.

She held him, because she needed to hold him over the next peak. She wanted him over the flame, as he'd held her over it. He delighted her by making that noise she'd heard before—when she'd kissed him the first time at the bottom of the ladder. It drew itself out as his body seized under her hands. He breathed hot against the hair above her ear and he spent himself entirely.

She absorbed the full weight of him, closing her eyes. Aftershocks shot, sparkly, sweet and devastating, through every nerve in her body.

She held him—held them both—in the moment because letting go felt too costly.

Chapter 16

She didn't dream. The bliss of deep, uninterrupted slumber cradled her lovingly, so lovingly she felt she'd slept the day away.

Confused, she tried to get her bearings. It was dark, and she was alone. She sat up suddenly in Wolfe's bed, the sheet falling to her waist. The space next to her was still warm, she felt when she pressed her hand to it. The only light filtered through the slight parting between the pocket door and the jamb.

Storm was outside. She could hear him barking. He'd been sleeping on the bed with them when she and Wolfe had stopped rocking it. She'd dozed off to the sound of the man's long, deep breaths rising and falling under her cheek and the soft snores of the canine.

She found the switch near the nightstand and flipped it. The sconce above the bed flickered on, and she tossed her legs over the side of the bed, blinking as she tried to orient herself. The night wasn't over? When the sound of Storm's barking increased, she pulled the lost T-shirt over her head. Was something wrong?

Going through the pocket door, she retraced her steps through the bathroom, then out onto the small set of steps to the kitchen/living room area. Guided by the soft stovetop light, she crossed to the laundry closet. She opened it, expecting to find her clothes and his in the washer.

They were in the dryer instead. When she opened the door and reached in to pull out her jeans, she was happy to find them warm.

She dressed, slowly. She was sensitive, achy in places. But she still moved carefully, enjoying the loose feelings in her joints, the dregs of pleasure that blinked to life every time her legs came together. Pressing the heel of her hand over her navel, she tried to hold it all in—all the sparkly, translucent ghosts of sensation she didn't want to let go of. Not just yet.

Walking carefully, she eventually found him on the deck, facing the night. He was wearing clean jeans but his back was bare. In the far east, she gleaned the virgin stain of a new day breaking. To the west, though, everything was nameless black. The moon had sunk from the sky, chased by the threat of day. Only the stars remained.

She went to him, raising her face to the sky. She sighed, twining her arms around his middle as she brought her front to his back. "I forgot how many stars you can see here," she whispered, so as not to break the night's hush.

Her hand came to rest over his sternum. He raised his to it and covered it, holding it there.

They stayed that way, listening to the night. It took

several moments for Eveline to realize that Storm was no longer barking. "It's quiet," she muttered.

For the first time, she realized how tense Wolfe was. "Why is it so quiet?" she asked, uncertain.

He stayed very still. Was he even breathing? "Wolfe?" she whispered.

Eveline jumped out of her skin at the sound of barking from the direction of the barn. Almost simultaneously, the horses started to whinny.

Wolfe moved fast, off the deck.

Her fear was huge. It was living and writhing. The coward she was, she reached the door and put herself on the other side of it. Desperate, unsure, she yanked open the kitchen cupboard drawers. In one, she found a flashlight. In another, a steak knife.

She held one in each hand as she went to the door again. She listened.

It was quiet once more. No dog barking. No horses whinnying.

Wolfe was taking too long.

She switched on the flashlight and cautiously swung the screen door out. She went out on the deck, trying to see through the shadows. She beamed the light forward but it didn't reach as far as she needed it to. "Wolfe?" she called.

Why was he taking so long?

Breathing unsteadily, she followed the flashlight beam, moving off the deck. She walked toward the barn. "Wolfe," she called again. "Answer me, damn it."

She walked until the red wall of the barn fell under the light. She reached out to touch it. She began to follow it around to the west-facing doors.

She stopped when a foul stench touched her nostrils. She heard footsteps—quick ones. Someone heavy was coming toward her. Before she could raise her light in their direction, a shape came out of the dark.

Big and furred. Wide and matted. Glassy, flashing eyes.

She screamed.

It came at her on all fours. But just before it reached her, it went up on two legs as she'd seen it do before. It charged and she was frozen, her blood ice. The weight of it knocked her back against the wall, and the flashlight and the knife went flying.

Fear was an ugly, greasy thing and its tentacles were wrapped so tight around Wolfe's lungs he couldn't breathe.

Eveline lay on the ground on the side of barn. She was bleeding from the temple. Her eyes were closed and she was dead still.

He dropped to his knees in a rush. Storm was there, whining sharply. The dog could smell something. Wolfe had followed him around the paddock, then in the barn and out again. It was then they'd heard her scream—a scream that had curdled Wolfe's blood.

He took her face in his hands. She didn't respond. Wolfe whistled. Nothing. His heart racking hard against his ribs, he caressed her cheek. The cut on her head was bleeding freely into her hair. He reached into his pocket and was relieved to find a bandana there. He folded it and pressed it to the wound.

Her lashes fluttered. Her chest rose, fell away and rose again.

Wolfe patted her cheek, first softly, then insistent.

She blinked her eyes open. They rolled once, then fixed on him. She moaned.

He held up a hand for her to see. The light was coming up in the east now, enough for them to see each other a little more clearly. *Still.* He needed her to be still. *Very still.*

She winced until her eyes closed again. "Wha…what happened?"

He wished he knew. When Storm's whine reached fever pitch, he looked around carefully, shining the beam in the direction Storm was looking.

Eveline did still, sensing what he did: something was still out there. "Wolfe…did it…did I…"

He pressed a finger to her lips and shook his head. It traced the seam of her lips. She still looked pale and he still felt panicked.

What it had done to see her…passed out on the ground… He didn't think he'd ever recover from that.

She lifted her hand to the bandana. "Am I…bleeding?"

He nodded. Cautious, he pulled the bandana back. The blood was slowing, but it wasn't done. He wanted to bite off a curse. It was trapped inside him along with too much else. He needed to get her to a doctor.

"I think…" She touched her hand to the back of his. "I think I'm okay. It only hurts a little."

Nope, he thought, shaking his head. *No, you lie still.*

"Wolfe, I'm okay," she repeated. She began to sit up despite his urging. Holding the top of her head, she grimaced and wavered a bit as she did so. "*Ah.* Did something *hit* me?"

You don't remember?

"I can't remember," she said, echoing his thoughts. She eyed him, suddenly alarmed. "Are you all right? Did you see anything?"

He shook his head again. *No. But you did.* Why else would she have screamed?

The light strengthened in the east. He could see the barnyard and paddock now, the silhouettes of the RV and wrecker—even the bones of the would-be house in the distance. He peered into every corner of the yard, into the brush, trying to find what had hurt her.

He wished for a gun.

It was the first time since he'd used one to end another's life.

It struck him. She wasn't safe here. She never had been. Carefully, he tucked his arm under her shoulders and the other under her knees and lifted her gently. He whistled to Storm and took her back to the RV.

Ellis showed up at Wolfe's, dust kicking up behind his tires as he came speeding up the lane. From the RV, she watched him take a rifle out of his truck, and together he and Wolfe had a look around.

"No tracks," Ellis said as he came up the steps twenty minutes later. He opened the screen. "If there was an animal, it would have left tracks."

"You didn't find anything?" Eveline asked, incredulous.

Wolfe shook his head. He pointed to his feet.

Ellis concurred with a nod. "Boot prints and bare foot tracks. He said you were running round in bare feet."

She glanced down at her feet. They were dirty. She'd have to wash them again. Her head ached so much she didn't stand to meet her brother when he came to gauge her condition. He hovered over her wound, making his doctoring noises.

"Something did a number on you," Ellis judged. The words were even but there were storms in his eyes. "You don't remember anything?"

"Only that we were chasing something through the

dark," Eveline said, trying to reach back into the blank tunnels of her mind. "I remember grabbing a knife and flashlight…then, not much from that point."

Ellis took the first aid kit Wolfe offered him. "You said you smelled something?" he asked Wolfe as he opened the tin box and riffled through the contents.

Wolfe nodded. His hands moved in explanation.

Eveline's mind started to work. A smell. A stench. Foul and unkempt. It had hit her nose…right before…

She gave a cry that made both men still. Clapping a hand over her mouth, she closed her eyes as the assault of visions hit her. "It…it came out of the dark. It smelled so bad. It was walking on fours. It looked at me." She remembered the stare, the dead stare, most of all. "It looked *into* me. And it charged."

She'd seen it go up on two legs, right at the end there. Thin, bald legs that had been in sharp contrast to its furred head and shoulders.

"What else do you remember?" Ellis asked firmly.

A hand closed over her shoulder. Wolfe's.

"Did you see what it was?" Ellis asked. "You must have, if it hit you. What kind of animal?"

She licked her lips. "I…" She thought of the creature in the flashlight beam. It had smelled like something foul, something worse than the smell cattle or bison put off. Glassy eyes. Jaw hanging askew. She hadn't noticed how odd that was because she'd been so focused on its eyes and fangs. But now that she thought about it, it wasn't normal—the way the animal's jaw had hung open and wobbled as it moved toward her. "It doesn't make sense."

"If you can't tell us what it was at close range," Ellis reasoned, "how do you expect Jones or Everett to add merit to your story?"

"You really think I'm still pretending?" she asked, offended.

"Not pretending," he said with a shake of his head.

"Imagining, then."

"You've been through a lot," he said.

"Yes." She curbed the need to scream it at him. "I have. But that doesn't make me psychotic."

"Again, nobody said—"

Wolfe whistled to get Ellis's attention. He began to sign with his hands.

Ellis frowned from him to Eveline. "How big was it—the thing that attacked you?"

She thought it through. Narrowing her eyes, she pressed a hand over her pounding temples. "When I saw it before, I always thought it was big. Taller than me, at least. But when it stood up… I don't think it was. It just looks bigger because its top is stockier than its bottom." She remembered the thin legs in contrast to its furred, matted head.

Wolfe was signing again. Ellis translated. "Was it on four legs this time—or two?"

She looked at Wolfe, because there was belief on his face. She wanted to sink into that belief. It was warm, like bath water. "Four at first. Then when it came at me, it was on two."

Ellis blew a long, winding breath out through his nose as if fighting for patience. "How did it knock you out? Did it swipe or run into you?"

"Ran into me," she said. She fingered the space on the back of her head that was sore, too. It had definitely connected with the barn wall. "But that wasn't what knocked me out. Something hit me hard in the face. I didn't see what…or I don't remember what did."

Ellis's forehead was deeply furrowed. His brows were

low. He stood studying her with his hands on his hips. "It isn't a scratch. There's no claw or bite marks. Best I can tell, it's an impact wound. Something definitely hit you. I've only seen wounds like this from thrown rocks. Or the butt of a gun."

"But that doesn't make sense," she said. "It wasn't exactly packing, Ellis."

"Tell me what about this does make sense," he rebutted. When she only scowled, placing the ice bag Wolfe had given her earlier back on her head, he asked Wolfe, "Do you have any game cameras around?" At the shake of Wolfe's head, he cursed. "And you saw nothing."

Wolfe signed. Ellis shook his head. "No concussion, as far as I can tell. I can stitch it up myself if she'll allow me."

"She'll allow it," Eveline bit off, still bitter and disappointed in him.

"You're not going to be able to meet Jones in an hour," he noted.

She let the bag of ice fall and tried to stand. Her legs worked fine even if her head swam slightly. "I can and I will."

"He'll need to know what happened," Ellis said.

She thought she heard a noise from Wolfe. He shifted his weight, restless at the thought of the sheriff.

Understanding dawned. Telling Sheriff Jones meant admitting where she had spent the night. And expecting the man or his deputy to be discreet about who she had been with was foolhardy at best. She met Wolfe's grim stare. She didn't want anyone to know any more than he did—not because she was embarrassed and not just because scandal of any kind made her want to run away.

She wanted just this. Her and Wolfe. Just them—

wrapped together in the bubble of secrecy for a little while longer.

Ellis addressed Wolfe. "What do you want to do?"

Wolfe eyed Eveline. He lifted his chin, as if determining something for himself. He started to sign.

When Ellis was silent, Eveline asked, "What?" Her brother didn't respond. She balled her fist into a knot and slugged him in the shoulder. *"What is it?"*

He hissed at the jab, pressing his hand to it. "You're not going to like it. But he's right."

"About what?" she demanded. "Ellis!" she shouted when again he didn't respond.

"He doesn't want you here anymore," he blurted.

Eveline took the jab. It sank like a stone. *"What?"* she asked, rounding on Wolfe.

Wolfe was frowning at Ellis now, too. He signed quickly.

"I said that wrong," Ellis granted. "I'm sorry. But, in essence, you can't stay here again."

"Why the hell not?" she asked the both of them. She felt bruised in more places than her temples. "Don't *I* get to make that choice?"

Wolfe was signing again. Ellis explained, "If that creature, whatever it is, comes back, Wolfe's a felon. He can't own a firearm. He *can't protect you.*" When Wolfe kept going, Ellis locked his jaw for a moment, then continued, as if unwilling to. "He wants you. With him. But he can't take the risk of something like this happening again while those of us at the Edge have the protection you need."

She stared at Wolfe. "I'm not leaving you."

"Come on," Ellis said, taking her by the arm. "I'll get you cleaned up and then we can go meet Jones."

"I'm not leaving!" She shrugged out of his grasp and

closed the space between her and Wolfe. He was tense when she wrapped her arms around his waist. "I'm fine, okay? See? I'm right here."

Worlds opened up inside his eyes, but he didn't touch her. His jaw was taut and his mouth stern. His gaze trekked across her brow and lingered on the gash. He shook his head and stepped out of the circle of her embrace.

She felt Ellis's hand on her arm again. "He'll meet us at the state park," he said, "for the hunting party. Come on now. You're bleeding. I need to close the wound for you. And you're going to need Sienna for the ride."

Eveline stared at Wolfe, but he kept himself closed off—long enough for her to realize she wasn't going to convince him. At the tug of Ellis's hand, she let him pull her away to the door.

Chapter 17

By the time they returned to the Edge from the hunting party, Eveline was plum dead exhausted. Her feet dragged on the floor as Ellis led her inside. She felt heavy—so heavy and heartsick all she wanted was to crash into bed fully clothed and sleep for the next forty-eight hours.

They'd found nothing, just as she knew they would. She'd had to fess up to Sheriff Jones and Deputy Altaha about what had happened to her this morning—and *where* it had happened.

So on top of being viewed as a crazy person, her choices were being scrutinized by strangers who were very unlikely to keep their mouths shut about it.

Wolfe had been with the hunting party and he hadn't looked her in the eye. Not even once.

Yes, sleeping for two days, maybe three, sounded perfect.

Before she could turn to go up the stairs, however,

Ellis steered her into the hallway to the kitchen. "Uh uh," she said, resisting. "I'm done."

"You need something to eat," Ellis advised. "I need to check your stitches. And you need this."

She frowned when he hit a switch beneath the stairs. A quiet motor whirred to life and a panel began to slide sideways to reveal a hidden cupboard she'd never seen before. "Um, when…" she began but stopped. Her jaw dropped as rows of firearms slowly revealed themselves. "Skip when. Tell me why."

"Everett requested," Ellis said. "Dad approved."

"Dad didn't like guns unless they're for hunting," she reminded him. Not everything here was for hunting.

"Yep," Ellis agreed, grabbing a pistol from the shelf. "But you forget. Whip Decker changed everything. He came after our own."

She flinched when he pulled the chamber out of a pistol and checked it. He handled the gun well.

"Everett and I don't agree on much," Ellis commented. "But we do agree that no one and nothing's going to do that again without us having something to say about it. Something comes after my family, I'm coming after it."

Eveline watched him choose another pistol and check it, too, before selecting ammo. "You always said he did the right thing," she said carefully.

"Who?" Ellis asked, distracted.

"Wolfe," she answered. "That day. With Decker."

He nodded, loading the pistol. "Tell me you would have done different."

She shook her head, unable to deny it. She shook it again when he handed her one of the pistols, butt first. "I don't have a permit."

"New Mexico's open carry," he explained. "You don't need a permit or a license."

"I'm too jumpy," she refused. "And seriously out of practice."

"When was the last time you went shooting?" he asked.

"Probably the last time Dad took me hunting."

"There's a shooting range," he revealed. He reached around and tucked the other pistol in the beltline of his jeans at the small of his back. "We'll visit—later, after you've eaten, slept and sharpened up. I still want you to have this."

Eveline reluctantly took the weight of the pistol. It felt cold and uncomfortable in her hands. She thought of the night before—Wolfe disappearing into the night with nothing but his bare fists. "If Wolfe can't protect me," she said slowly, "then he can't protect himself, either. Can he?"

Ellis ducked around her to the kitchen.

She trailed him. "*Don't* ignore me."

"I'm not ignoring you!" he insisted, turning back to her. "Wolfe can take care of himself. He always has."

"You said that if someone comes after your family, you come after them. Wolfe is like a brother to you. Or he used to be."

"He's not leaving his land," Ellis told her. "Neither can he violate the law. Not if he doesn't want to go back to jail."

"I don't want him to be alone," she blurted.

"I don't know what you want me to do about that, Eveline," Ellis said, throwing out his arms. "Would you have him come *here*?" He held up his hand as she opened her mouth to answer. "Don't. I know what you're going to say. And it's a bad idea. You're better off here.

He's better off there, and that's all there is to it. We're going to have enough problems on our hands when Everett finds out about the two of you."

Feeling frustrated, helpless and more tired than she'd ever been, Eveline didn't argue further. She turned away from her brother, because if she was going to spend the next few days recovering in bed, she was going to need sustenance first.

"Girl, you've got your brother worked up about something," Paloma said as she met Eveline in her bedroom close to an hour later. In her arms was a laundry basket full of clean, folded clothes.

"You didn't have to do my laundry," Eveline told her. She took the basket and set it on the floor next to the bed. "I'm not like them. I can do my own."

"I enjoy seeing a woman's things in this house," Paloma said as she lifted a pearl-snapped blouse from the top of the pile. "So pretty," she murmured, running her hand over the silk collar.

Eveline managed a small smile. "I'll have to get you one."

Paloma raised a brow. "I'm too old for finery."

"You're never too old for finery," Eveline said, pulling off her boot. She felt a pinch just above her sternum, remembering how Wolfe had done this for her the night before. Right before they…

Paloma studied her as she let the boot thunk to the floor and didn't reach for the other. She pressed the blouse to her bosom and reached out with the other hand to stroke her cheek. "I'll draw you a bath."

"Pretty sure I'd drown at this point," Eveline warned.

"You'll feel better," Paloma said, going to the closet

to hang the blouse. "All those aches and pains… They need a good soak."

Eveline didn't argue when Paloma veered into the bathroom. She heard the tap running in the tub and closed her eyes. A soak wasn't going to cure everything, she knew. But she couldn't go to bed this dirty.

She made herself get up, take off her other boot and follow Paloma into the bathroom. The woman was already adding Epsom salts to the pool of water. "These'll help," she promised. "Help put everything to rights."

Eveline felt tears behind her eyes. They hardened. She'd wanted sleep. If she went to sleep, she wouldn't have to do this until later. Covering her face, she buried it in the back of Paloma's shirt.

"Oh, Miss Evie," Paloma clucked when a sob surfaced. "Come here, *niña*." She turned and enveloped Eveline in a warm hug.

Paloma rocked, soothed and murmured until Eveline felt the tears start to dry. She lifted her head finally to the light and scrubbed the wet from her cheeks. "I'm sorry. I don't know what's wrong with me."

"You do know," Paloma ventured. "Ellis told me where you'd been all night."

Eveline thought about avoiding her gaze. But she couldn't, because there was no condemnation there. "It doesn't matter. Apparently, I'm not going back. He can't protect me, even though Ellis says he's fine protecting himself."

"He wants you there," Paloma assured her, taking her by the shoulders. "That man gave up the shares Hammond gave him. There's nothing he would deny you at this point."

"Except a place at his side," Eveline said miserably.

"If Wolfe thinks you're better off here, then you're

better off here," Paloma said. She stroked her hands up and down Eveline's arms. "And you're not planning on leaving anytime soon. Right?"

Eveline felt her probing for information. She accepted it. "I don't plan on leaving," she answered truthfully. "Not now."

Paloma beamed, framing Eveline's face in her hands. "Then there's plenty of time for you to be together, after this business that's got you involved with the sheriff is over."

Eveline nodded—not because she believed, but because she was tired and she could smell the bath's essential oils and they soothed.

"Come on," Paloma said, urging her toward the tub. "I'll take your things. You ease yourself on in there and let the water do its work."

The water did some magic, Eveline had to admit after soaking for a while. She kept her face above the surface, careful of the stitches. Paloma had read the pain on her face and brought up aspirin for her to take. The pain was just starting to dim, along with everything else.

Paloma had taken to scrubbing the bathroom counter, like a mother who wanted to be within arm's reach while her child sat in the water. Her hands busy, she said conversationally, "Home's where lost souls go, you know. To look for the missing pieces."

Eveline's lips parted. She thought about how she'd come home to Fuego—how Wolfe had, despite everything.

"It's a sweet thing when two lost souls find one another." Paloma smiled to herself as she wiped the mirror clean with a microfiber cloth. "Such a sweet thing."

Eveline studied her several seconds before she said

what was on her mind. "Is that what happened before—with my mother and your brother?"

Paloma stopped working. Her hands lowered to her sides and her smile faded as she stared at Eveline. "You better not be thinking this is history repeating itself."

"What's different?" she asked. "A Coldero man and an Eaton woman." She raised her hands from the water and frowned at how pruny they were already. "A forbidden romance, one liable to shake Fuego to its foundations and tear two families apart. Only this time it's worse because it's happened before. Who would risk that again?"

"Two people who love each other," Paloma answered simply as she went back to scrubbing.

Eveline lowered her hands. "Now, I never said anything about love."

"Didn't you," Paloma replied, knowing.

Eveline let that sink in. It made all the aches and pains inside her fire up again. "There's nothing wise about that."

"Love isn't wise, *niña*," Paloma said. "It may be patient. And kind. But damned if it doesn't make people do the wildest things."

Hearing Paloma curse startled a short laugh out of Eveline. Curiously, she asked, "Is that what you told them when they ran away with each other all those years ago?"

"They didn't ask," Paloma revealed, head down. She scratched at the counter's surface with her thumbnail.

Eveline took a careful breath. "If they had…?"

Paloma stopped working again, gripping the counter's edge with both hands. "If they had asked me… I might have advised against it."

"Really?" Eveline said.

"She had children at home," Paloma said, planting her hand on her hip. "I'd have thought Santiago would have had enough sense to leave that well enough alone. He knows the importance of family. But, like I said, love is *not* wise. He asked her to come away with him, and she did."

"Do you think…she ever regretted leaving?" Eveline asked.

"She regretted leaving you," Paloma said. "She regretted hurting you. And her boys. Everett never spoke to her again. She regretted that a great deal."

"But not leaving," Eveline said. "Not choosing a life with Santiago."

"Joy and sorrow come hand in hand," Paloma reasoned. "She had joy, especially when Angel came. That was a surprise. She thought she wouldn't bear another child. And then she did. But she never forgot Everett, Ellis or you. And she saw what she did to your father. His health. That's not what she wanted for him."

"I don't think you get to choose the consequences," Eveline said. "You can choose to leave. You can choose to live your own life. But you don't get to choose what happens to those you leave behind. She may have been better off, but we weren't."

"She was proud of you," Paloma said with a wistful expression. "So proud of how far her girl flew toward the sun."

"And got burned in the process," Eveline said, brushing her fingers over her scars.

"If you hadn't been," Paloma said, "would you not have still been lost—even up there in the clouds?"

The water was growing cool. Eveline closed her eyes. "Tell me how you're so wise," she said. "Because you've never let a man talk you into leaving?"

Paloma chuckled deeply. "If that were true, I wouldn't be doing your brothers' laundry now would I?" She sobered quickly. "If you're unsure of anything, Miss Evie, know this—both your mother and your dear old daddy loved Wolfe Coldero very, very much. If they were here right now, there's not much they would say to discourage you from choosing that path if you wanted it badly enough." She reached out to pat Eveline's shoulder. "You think on that, hmm? I'll get you something to wear."

Eveline reached up to grab Paloma's wrist. "You're all the mother a girl could wish for. You do know that? Don't you?"

Paloma blinked several times. "Oh, *dulce niña.* You and those consternating boys are the only children I ever wished for." She bent down to touch a kiss to the peak of Eveline's brow. "It's been so good, having you all together these last weeks. If you decide to stay on permanently, you'll get no argument from me."

Eveline nodded, feeling the bite of tears again. And here she'd thought she was all cried out. "Do you think I'm crazy like they do?"

"They don't think you're crazy," Paloma said, lowering her head and her voice and widening her eyes. "They're afraid. It doesn't matter how old or tough they get—in hard times, everybody still believes in the bogeyman. Especially since the bogeyman normally hides in plain sight."

Chapter 18

Everett strode into the stables at Eaton Edge, looking somewhat worse for wear than he had at breakfast that morning. He was covered in mud from the knees down and looked like he was asking for an excuse to bite someone's head off. "Ellis!" he shouted, making a jumpy colt two stalls over wheel its eyes and whinny.

Ellis, who'd been saddling Shy in anticipation of bringing in heifer pairs, exchanged a look with Eveline, who was mucking stalls. It was a glance laden with apprehension.

Someone told him, Eveline thought. *About me and Wolfe.* It had been less than forty-eight hours since she'd reported what she'd seen at Wolfe's place to Sheriff Jones.

Ellis patted Shy, then tugged on the reins so the horse's body was between Everett and Eveline. "Yeah?" he replied.

"Maybe you could explain to me," Everett said, his

voice raised to the rafters, "who stepped up the weapon presence with the hands?"

Eveline leaned on her pitchfork in relief. She'd prepared for the moment Everett found out about her and Wolfe's would-be relationship. But the idea of it going undetected for a while longer wasn't something she was going to turn her nose up at.

"I gave that order," Ellis said as he adjusted the rifle sheath on his saddle.

"Why—and why wasn't I consulted?" Everett asked.

"Because Eveline says there's a dangerous predator about," Ellis reasoned.

"Oh, Christ," Everett cursed. "You don't honestly believe—"

Ellis interrupted him. "If Eveline says she saw something, we ought to listen."

Everett peered around the horse and found Eveline. "This have anything to do with your little head injury?"

Eveline had denied telling Everett about the bandage on her forehead, maybe because explaining what had happened to her would involve admitting *where* it had happened to her. She'd only been too happy when both Ellis and Paloma had played along, at least for the time being. She caught Ellis's look. He gave her a nod. She swallowed and said, "Yes."

"Why am I just now finding out about this, too?" Everett asked.

"Why should I have told you the truth when you find it so hard to believe anything I say?" Eveline asked him.

He pursed his lips and she knew she had him. "Did you get a good look at the thing this time?"

She frowned. "Yes. Though I doubt if I described it to you, you'd believe me any more than you already do."

"You have to admit, that's fair," Ellis said to him.

"Fine," Everett returned, testy.

She raised a brow at his appearance. "Did you sit down in a cow patty again today?"

He spat on the ground. "You missed a spot," he rebutted.

"You're an ass," she replied, turning back to her chore.

He must've seen the gun stuffed into the waistband of her jeans because he added, "Don't shoot the hands. Last thing I need's the paperwork."

She heard him trudging away. "His concern is touching," she noted.

Ellis had no response as he cinched the strap under Shy's belly.

She heard the sound of footsteps returning and scowled. "If that's him, tell him to get back. I'm armed and dangerous."

"You can barely hit the target at the shooting range," Ellis reminded her.

"But I do hit it," she muttered, shoveling.

"Mr. Eaton," a pleasant voice called.

Ellis's head snatched up. "Why, Deputy Altaha. You're a sight for sore eyes."

Kaya Altaha was in full uniform, not excluding her weapon belt, but she smiled a soft smile for him. "Don't you start," she advised. "I don't take to flattery."

Ellis tilted his head, spanning his arm over Shy's saddle. "Sure," he said.

She knocked a fist into his middle.

Ellis crumpled with laughing respect, his hand over his stomach. "You were always too much for a man to take."

"Careful you don't let anyone else hear you talk like that," she said. "Word on the street is you're a serial cheater. Not that I buy it," she added quickly when his easy expression dimmed. She sighed at his sad eyes. "Oh, come on, Eaton. If I had a dollar for every time I saw that wife of yours flirting with Walker Sullivan at the rodeo, I'd be living more than a small-town deputy's life."

Ellis tipped his hat to her, studiously keeping his mouth shut. "Ma'am."

She scowled at him. Then she turned her attention to Eveline. "How's the head injury?"

"It's fine," Eveline said, wiping sweat from her neck with a handkerchief. "Thank you, Deputy."

"Are your brothers always this irritating?" she asked, curious.

Eveline eyed Ellis as he prepared to saddle up. "This one doesn't give me too much trouble," she revealed. "The other one…"

"I've never come up against Everett's sharp points," Altaha said, sweeping off her hat. "I think he knows I'll cuff him faster than he can say, 'Boo.'"

"Maybe he's wiser than any of us believe," Eveline suggested.

"I bring interesting news," Altaha told them both. She gave Ellis a once-over. "…if a bit complicated, where you're concerned."

"Oh?" Ellis asked, feeding the reins through his hands. "What's it about?"

"Not your wife," she said, reading him well. "Haven't seen her in a while, actually."

"She's taken to living in Taos," he said, "with the girls."

She stared at him for a full half minute. "You're just going to take that—and all the rest of the crap she's been shoveling in your direction?"

"She'll come around," he said noncommittally.

"I thought you were an Eaton," she challenged. "Don't you people fight to the bone to hold on to what's yours?"

He stared back. A slow smile began to weave its way across his features. "I've always liked you, Deputy."

"And I've always hated seeing a good man brought low," she remarked.

Eveline smiled, too. It was nice knowing that Ellis had someone other than those at the Edge on his side. "What's this news about?" she wondered out loud.

Altaha braced her hands on her hips. "It's about your missing animal. I went back through our records. We occasionally get reports of strange animals here and about—mostly tourists who don't know a bull elk from a rattlesnake. But I did find something from seven years back. Not long after the tragedy at Coldero Ridge. There was a sighting, out near Ollero Creek. It matched your details of the animal almost exactly."

"Really?" Eveline said. "Seven years ago?"

"Yes," Altaha said.

Ellis was back to frowning. "Ollero Creek. That's where…"

Altaha met his eyes. She nodded.

Ellis tipped his chin up and was silent, too.

"What's wrong with Ollero Creek?" Eveline asked, narrowing her eyes.

"Nothing's wrong with it," Ellis murmured.

Altaha decided to throw her a bone. "It's where Luella Decker resides."

Eveline's eyes widened as she looked from the deputy to her brother. "Is that who reported the sighting?"

"It is," Altaha said. "The sheriff didn't think much of it. But I thought you had a right to know. My instincts tell me you're no more crazy, Ms. Eaton, than your brother is a cheater. And I'm rarely wrong where they're concerned."

"Thank you," Eveline said, honestly.

Altaha placed her hat back on her head. "I hope I see your family at my sister's wedding. It's next Saturday at The RC Resort."

"I believe we're invited," Ellis commented. "I'll double-check with Paloma."

"Bring her, too," Altaha said. "Her company's better than most."

Eveline watched Ellis carefully as he drove her out to Ollero Creek. He'd been strangely reticent since Deputy Altaha's visit to the Edge. "You didn't have to come with me."

Eveline looked out over the hilly landscape. In the distance, she could see cliffs. They seemed to beam with their own light under the sun's rays. "But she *will* talk to you?" she asked softly.

Ellis remained silent on that point. The cab of the truck was too quiet. He hadn't put on the radio. Only the tires' whir against the pavement broke the silence. "Did you tell Everett where we were going?" she asked.

"Sure," he said. "He was all for it."

She squinted at him. "Wow. You're a really bad liar." That made the corner of his mouth twitch. It vanished quickly. She touched his arm. "Ellis. Are you all right?"

"I'll keep, kid," he assured her without taking his eyes off the road. He turned off the highway, then made a right on a dirt road.

He knew where he was going, she realized. He hadn't asked anyone for directions. He hadn't checked the GPS once. Eveline pressed her lips together, watching the land change from rocky to flat plain. "How long has she lived out here?"

"More than ten years," Ellis said. "She, uh, disappeared for a while there. After high school."

Eveline couldn't help it. She studied his profile. "After you dated?"

He gave a short nod.

"Where do you think she went?"

"She's never told anyone."

"Not even you?"

"Most especially not me."

"Have you two spoken at all?" Eveline wondered. "Since you dated?"

"Why the third degree, Eveline?"

"Because if she hasn't spoken to you since whatever happened between you two at the end of high school," Eveline considered, "she's no more likely to talk to you than me."

"We've spoken," he admitted. "But not since Liberty told everyone she and I…"

Eveline gleaned the rest. "I see. Was it at least friendly…before the rumors started?"

"You could say that."

She sighed. She hated the subterfuge. "Ellis… I'm not going to believe you cheated on Liberty with Luella Decker. Nothing can make me believe that. But you do seem raw where Luella is concerned."

"So?" he prompted, making another turn on a graveled road that wasn't quite so pitted.

"So you don't still have feelings for Luella," she said, framing it not as a question because the answer was too ridiculous to consider. "Not after everything her father did to our family."

"She had nothing to do with that," he told her.

Her lips parted. "Ellis..."

"There's nothing between Lu and me," he explained. "Nothing."

Why did he sound more resigned than defensive? "That's not what I asked," she whispered. She cursed. All signs pointed to Luella Decker not talking to either of them. "If she's not going to talk to me...and she's unlikely to want to listen to you...what are we doing here, Ellis?"

"I asked Wolfe to come."

"Wolfe?" Eveline asked, shocked. "Why?"

"Because he and Lu get along fine," Ellis said. "They're both outsiders. They've both been alienated from the 'good people' of Fuego. Outliers tend to stick together."

"So Wolfe and Luella Decker are friends?" Eveline asked cautiously.

"Something like that," he said neutrally.

"Jesus Christ, Ellis!" she shrieked. "Can't you give me a straight answer about anything?"

"I don't know what you're asking," he claimed.

"I'd like to know what's between Wolfe and your ex-girlfriend," she insisted. "I think I have that right."

"If that's your way of asking if they're involved, then no," Ellis explained, lifting his hands off the wheel. "We were all friends, in school. We spent a lot of time together senior year. If Wolfe ever wanted anything to happen between him and Lu, it never did."

She realized why. "Because it would have hurt you. And you're practically brothers."

"He looks out for her," Ellis said. "She's got no one in this town. Someone needs to look out for her. She's never wanted that person to be me. So he does."

"Okay," she said, nodding. "Okay."

"Are *you* going to be okay?" Ellis asked pointedly. "Seeing him again?"

She saw the house at the end of the drive. It was three stories, a bit rickety in places. There was a waterwheel in front of it, but the riverbed had dried and cracked long ago. There was nothing left of Ollero Creek other than Luella Decker's house and the small barn and workshop on the outskirts.

Wolfe's truck was parked outside it.

She released a breath that wasn't at all steady. "Oh, help," she said under her breath.

Chapter 19

Wolfe heard Ellis's truck pull into Lu's place. He went down the steps from the front porch to greet him. As soon as Ellis's door opened, he signed, *She's not answering the door.*

His hands flailed to a stop when the passenger door opened and Eveline stepped out, too. His heart did several funny flips in a row.

She still had a bandage on her temple, though she had plenty of color in her face again—the night she'd left his place she'd looked so pale, she could've been translucent. He felt something twist around his navel, that same, sick feeling he'd felt when he'd found her unconscious outside his barn.

He found himself taking two, long, jerky strides toward her.

"Whoa," Ellis said, holding out a restraining hand.

Eveline ignored her brother and came the rest of the way to Wolfe.

He caught her in his arms, pressing his face into her shoulder. He breathed hard over the next several bouts, then slow, deep and careful to pull in as much of her gardenia fragrance as possible.

If she held him any harder, she'd be on the other side of him. Her hand went under his hat, into the hair on the back of his head. She might've looked healthy, but she wasn't steady in his arms. She quaked and he rocked, turning his nose into her hair.

"I don't like this," she said, muffled against his collar.

He rocked her more, tracing her shoulders, the length of her spine. He had to make sure she was whole.

He wished she was still his—with everything in him.

His grip fell on cold steel at the small of her back. *A gun?*

She tensed. "Ellis wanted me to start packing. He's been teaching me how to use it again." Pulling back enough for her to see him, she splayed her fingers across his cheek. Her thumb caressed his stubbled upper lip. "I'm going to get so good at it you won't have to worry about protecting me. I'll protect us both."

A smile crawled across his mouth, warming it from corner to corner. It faded quickly when he lingered over the bandage, bringing his touch up to trace its outer edge.

"Don't worry," she whispered. Her big green eyes filled. The lashes swept down to hold back the dam. "Ellis fixed me up."

He touched the tip of his nose to the center of her brow. Then he lifted his lips to the spot and kissed it.

Ellis cleared his throat. "Still here."

Eveline didn't let go. Wolfe brushed his fingers through her hair once, then again, before he extricated himself, taking a reluctant step back.

She jabbed her finger at Ellis as they moved as one

around the side of Lu's house. "If I'm staying at the Edge, you're going to teach me how to use my hands to talk to this man."

"Oh, you two talk," Ellis said. "And not in any way anyone can understand but the two of you."

Wolfe's hand brushed against hers. He couldn't help himself. He took it firmly in his and *held*.

"Check the barn," Ellis told them. "I'll look in on the workshop."

Several chickens scattered as Wolfe and Eveline trekked across the yard to the lean-to barn. They heard the sounds of a horse and the snorting of pigs.

There was a roan in the stall. He had to stop her from lifting her hand to touch its cheek. He shook his head. Sheridan, like Winter, wasn't the least bit friendly toward anyone but his owner. He'd been known to bite.

Wolfe jerked his chin to the other side of the barn where there was a sow and three piglets.

Eveline grinned. "It'd be sweet, if I didn't sense they're all going to be bacon one day."

Wolfe couldn't tell her that Lu, too, was partial to the piglets—the runt, especially.

Eveline pressed her cheek to his sleeve. "If we didn't have to find Luella Decker so bad, I'd say this was the perfect place to make out."

When she reached up for his collar, he brought his mouth down to hers without hesitation. He meant to dance and dapple, but he plunged straight in. Cupping the back of her neck, he bent it back as he turned her to face him, navel to navel. When her tongue sought his, he answered in kind.

He remembered what it was to be inside her. He remembered, though it cost him to do so. He remembered how her absence in his bed the last few nights had caused him to lose sleep. They had to catch this thing. They had to catch it so he could get her back. So he could have her again—every way he'd imagined and then some.

He went back on his heels, cursing every which way inside his head. He palmed her shoulders, holding her apart from him.

If he stared at her long enough, he'd forget why they couldn't be together. He'd forget everything entirely.

He was in love with her. He'd been alone with that over the last few days. Better or worse, he loved Eveline Eaton. And he intended to find some way of telling her on his own when the time was right. Until then, they had an animal to hunt down. And they weren't going to do that without talking to Lu Decker first.

"Wolfe!" Ellis called from across the yard.

He took Eveline's hand again and they walked outside. They came up short, however, when they saw Ellis in front of the workshop, both hands raised. There was a grimace on his face. "She doesn't think I'm welcome," he said grimly.

He turned, just enough. Eveline gasped because Lu Decker was behind him. She had the barrel of a rifle aimed at his low back. She tilted her head to see around him. "What makes you think this particular posse would be welcome at *mi casa*?" Lu called to Wolfe.

Wolfe let go of Eveline's hand. He moved both of his hands quickly. *Put down the gun, Lu. You're not going to shoot him.*

"Give me one reason I shouldn't," she challenged. There were two long braids down both her shoulders. The color of her hair was mixed—mostly red with streaks of golden blond and others burnished brown. She wore a bloody white butcher's apron, freckles on her cheeks and a pronounced scowl.

She'd been sweet once. She'd been innocent. She'd loved his friend more than a heart could love. But she'd gone hard over the years. Life had made her that way.

Wolfe signed, *Because we both care about him.*

"You don't know me as well as you think you do," she said. She cocked her weapon.

"Son of a bitch," Ellis muttered. Sweat was starting to run down his face.

Wolfe treaded carefully. *We just want to talk. You reported something to the sheriff's office a while back. An animal sighting. Do you remember?*

Lu squinted at him. "That's what you came out here for?"

He nodded. *She's seen something that matches the same description.*

The gun barrel lowered in the direction of Ellis's knees and not on purpose. Lu was looking hard at Eveline. "That was a long time ago. I don't remember."

"I think you might," Ellis ventured.

"Excuse me, do you want buckshot in your ass?" Lu asked him pointedly.

"Please," Eveline said, then stepped forward. She stopped when Wolfe's hand came down on her shoulder.

Lu saw the protective move. She rolled her eyes as the barrel came the rest of the way to the ground. "There's only one thing the matter with you, Wolfe. It's that you've never known better than to leave these people to their own. When it matters, they protect their own—and nobody else." She put the safety on the rifle and disappeared into her workshop.

"Lu," Ellis murmured.

"Shut up," Luella said as she picked up a long boning knife and went back to carving up the dead deer on the top of the worktable in front of her.

Eveline fought not to cover her mouth with her hand. She could smell blood and raw meat. Her gorge worked against her throat and her stomach churned.

She must've made a noise because Lu peered at her, the knife pausing. "I think the skinny bitch is going to faint."

"I'm fine," she said when Wolfe's side buffered against hers. His arm came around her, regardless. She didn't fight it. Making her voice steadier than she felt, she said to Luella, "I know you don't want us here."

"Twiggy's smarter than she looks," Luella drawled, separating meat from bone with deadly precision.

Eveline tried not to dwell on the fact that Luella understood the sign language she had thought only Ellis and Wolfe knew. How much *had* they all hung out in high school? "I've seen this animal three times. The first time I thought I was crazy. The second I saw it at too far a distance. But then, a few nights ago, it attacked me."

Lu stilled. "It *attacked* you?"

"Yes," Eveline said, thinking quickly. "In your report, you said that you saw it walking across your land on four legs. Then when it saw you watching, it went up on two?"

Lu's eyes fixed on the bandage on Eveline's forehead. She didn't say anything but her mouth opened.

"And you said," Eveline continued, licking her lips, "that it was furred on top with fangs and claws, but it was furless on the bottom."

Luella looked away gradually, her gaze falling on her work. She didn't use the knife again. Her hands hovered in the air. "That doesn't sound like anything, does it? Just a nightmare."

Ellis tried again. "You did report the same thing she has."

Luella's eyes snapped up to his, hot and dark. They could've murdered him on the spot. "I was mistaken. I tried to retract it. That new deputy—Altaha—she must've kept it on file anyway."

"How could you be mistaken about something like that?" Eveline asked.

"Maybe I was a little too friendly with the tequila that evening," Luella excused. She reached up and wiped her brow with the back of her hand.

"You don't drink," Ellis reminded her.

"How would you know?" she asked. "You and that little woman of yours are a double whammy. Her telling everyone I'm a home-wrecker and you sniffing around here trying to prove her right."

Wolfe motioned for her. When he snagged her attention, he spoke to her as only he could.

She seemed to deflate. "I don't need this right now," she said, wearily. "I didn't see *anything*. And I don't want any of you here. No!" she shouted when Wolfe lifted his hands again. "Stop trying to appeal to my good nature, Wolfe Coldero. I no longer have one. Leave! Please!"

Eveline saw the dejected look on her brother's face. As Luella went back to butchering, he watched with sad eyes that told Eveline everything she needed to know about how he felt about Luella. Wolfe opened the door at their back, and Ellis placed his hat on his head and murmured, "I'm sorry, Lu."

"For what?" she asked, sour. "For Liberty running her mouth about me or for not doing anything to stop it?"

His throat worked around a swallow. "I'm sorry," he said again, quieter.

"Just go," she said.

"Let's go, Ellis," Eveline said gently, grabbing Ellis's hand. "Come on."

He followed her urging, ducking out the door into the sun. He let her hand slip from his as he retreated.

She wanted to cry for him. Heartbreak was written all over him. She hadn't seen it until now. One run-in with Luella Decker had broken his demeanor.

Wolfe held the door open for her. She paused. She pressed her hand low on his belly, stroked. "I need a minute," she whispered.

His brows rose. He began to shake his head.

"I'll be all right," she told him. She smiled. "Take Ellis back to the truck. I'll meet you there in a minute."

When she didn't waver, he nodded slowly. With one last look at Luella, he put on his hat and closed the door at his back.

Eveline faced the woman on the other side of the table. "I don't buy it."

"You'd do well not to insult me while I'm doing this," Luella said mildly, slicing the meat.

"You saw the same thing I did." Eveline was certain of it. "Jones told you you were crazy. Like he did me. So you tried telling yourself you didn't see what you saw because it's better not to be seen as the village crazy person on top of everything else."

"You don't know a damn thing about me," Luella told her.

"I know you're as scared of this thing as I am," Eveline said. "That's why you won't talk about it."

Luella tossed the knife down. She came around the side of the table, wiping her hands on her dirty apron. "I'll tell you something," she said, advancing.

Eveline checked the urge to put her back against the door behind her.

"If you break Wolfe like your brother broke me,"

Luella warned, glittery intent in her eyes, "I will make you wish I gave you the mercy that I gave this one here."

Eveline stared at what remained of the deer. "I would think as Whip Decker's daughter, you'd know better than to make threats against me or my kin."

Luella's head whipped back at that, as if slapped. "My father was a raving lunatic," she said. "Before he hurt your mother and your sister, he hurt *me*. For *years*, he hurt me. I'm *nothing* like him."

"Then why're you saying things like that?" Eveline said. "I'm Jo Coldero's daughter. How am I supposed to take that?"

Luella was silent for several seconds. Then she said, "I *don't* want to see Wolfe heartbroken."

"I don't want that either," Eveline replied.

Luella weighed the sincerity behind that statement. She raised her hands, studied the lines and the mess left behind. "You know you'd do better to leave town again. Fuego isn't the place for someone like you anymore. And this thing will leave you alone if you go."

Eveline's lips parted slowly. She pressed them together, then opened them again. "I thought you said it wasn't real."

"Maybe it wants to be left alone," Luella suggested. "Wolfe will be better off, too, if you leave. You can't make me believe you're willing to face the scrutiny just so you can be with him."

Eveline frowned. "I might surprise you."

"People rarely do," Luella replied. "It's how I've survived." She pointed to the door. "You know your way out."

"She knows something," Eveline claimed when she met both the men back at the trucks.

Ellis's arms rested on his tailgate. "We shouldn't have come here."

"Maybe you shouldn't have," she acknowledged. At that, he looked away, out over the empty riverbed. "But she knows something she's not telling us, and I think you know that."

Wolfe shifted his feet and looked to Ellis. Worry was plain on his face.

After a while, Ellis moved toward the cab of the truck. "We should be getting back."

"Wait," Eveline said. She pressed her lips together. "I'm... I'm not ready."

Ellis looked between the two of them. He sighed and opened the door. "Hurry it up, at least."

When he shut the door, she turned to Wolfe. "I don't know what to do. She was our only lead. My only chance of proving to everybody that I'm not frickin' crazy."

He shook his head. With one finger, he reached out to trace the shape of her face all the way around.

She closed her eyes and didn't open them when his touch lifted. "I—I miss you," she breathed. "I miss you so much I might be crazy with it. You realize... I'm not going anywhere, right? I'm not going to leave. You may have convinced me to stay at the Edge. But I'm not going to back down from this. I'm going to stand up to it—everything—until either I'm proved right and it's caught or I end this whole thing alone."

When she opened her eyes, he shook his head again, this time more firmly.

She tried to smile. "Ellis won't admit it. But I'm getting better at target shooting. I know. In the moment, it's different. But I'm not going to back down, because I'm determined to be with you. No matter what *anyone* has to say about it."

He searched her eyes. Then his gaze touched on her mouth. He framed her face in his hand.

She turned her lips into his hard palm. "It's okay... not to be too patient." She smiled as she tilted her cheek into the cradle of his palm, framing the back of his fingers with her own to strengthen the bond. "It helps... knowing that waiting is as excruciating for you as it is for me."

He didn't have to answer that. Or, he did, rather, by bringing his mouth down on hers and kissing her until she came up to her toes in response.

She hung in the moment because it was perfect—so perfect tears pinched the backs of her eyes as they had when he'd held her moments ago. She felt everything. It was life-affirming, this treacherous waterfall of emotional upheaval...when she'd felt chronically empty before.

He broke away. She stumbled, tangled up. He steadied her.

She looked at him and felt soft. Softer and stronger than she had in her whole life. "Wait for me," she whispered.

He bobbed his head in a nod and ran his hand down her arm before breaking away.

Chapter 20

Eveline found both of her brothers behind the desk that had been their father's. They looked up from the set of blueprints spread across the tabletop. A new bunkhouse, she'd gleaned over the last few weeks.

"Don't you knock?" Everett asked.

"I don't need to knock," she snapped. "Here," she said and tossed the target paper she'd carried from the gun range on top of the desk.

"What the hell's that?" Everett wanted to know.

Ellis turned it right way up and raised a brow. "Well, someone's improved."

"I told you I would," she said. She pushed her hands through her hair. She had no doubt she looked disheveled. She'd been dividing her time between Griff, the horses, the shooting range and the sorting pen. This morning alone, she'd been chased up the fence by no fewer than three crazy-ass heifers. She'd taken it as a personal victory when she hadn't missed one calf while operating the squeeze chute. Everett hadn't had a single insult for her for the better part of the day. "I told you I'd pull my weight and you wouldn't regret me working the Edge," she said to him. To Ellis she added, "Just as I told you I'd learn to protect myself. I didn't miss the center circle once in a whole clip."

"Damn," Everett said. He caught her stare and ran his tongue over his teeth. "Not sure them fancy people in New York would recognize Eden Meadows if they saw her now."

It was as close to a compliment as she was ever going to get from him. She smiled at him—actually smiled.

By some miracle, Everett hadn't heard the rumors about her and Wolfe. The news was rife in town. On a trip to the tack store a week ago, she'd practically been mobbed by the speculative questions about their relationship. Thankfully, Javier had escorted her on the outing, wanting her to pick the right cinch for Sienna Shade. He'd nearly had to beat them all off with his belt to get her back to the truck.

Her big brother had been well insulated at the Edge. If the hands knew—and it was a good bet that they all did—they didn't dare bring it up around him.

But that was all likely to change, because tonight was Naleen Altaha's wedding at The RC Resort and the whole county was expected to attend. Paloma had declined Ellis's offer to go along as his plus-one. She had come down with the same stomach bug as Javier's family days before and, although back to her old tricks in the kitchen, hadn't felt well enough to attend.

Everett checked his watch. He beamed. "You know what?" He grabbed one edge of the blueprint and began to roll it up tight. "Why don't we cut out early, get cleaned up? Then we can head on over to The RC together. As a family."

Eveline balked at him. "Are you drunk?"

He laughed, reaching out to slap her shoulder companionably. "Meet you downstairs in an hour?" he asked.

Eveline watched him exit, then rounded on Ellis. "What did you give him?"

"Nothing," Ellis claimed.

She shook her head. "Does he like weddings?"

"Hates them," Ellis clarified. "He normally cuts out or spends the night moping at the open bar."

"Then how do you explain Mr. Rogers?" she asked, jerking a thumb over her shoulder.

Ellis thought about it. Then his eyes shuttered and closed and his expression shifted into dread. "Ah, hell. We may have a problem."

"What?" she asked.

He walked around her, closed the office door and planted his hand on it for good measure. "Four days ago, we got a notice from Lionel Bozeman. True Claymore and his wife, Annette, are talking about reclaiming that parcel of land between our rangelands."

She remembered her conversation with Everett about the Claymores on the way to the state park. "The same one they tried to take from Dad after his first heart attack?"

Ellis nodded. "Now that Dad's gone, they want to try for it again—try to get us with our guard down while we're all still in grief."

"That's...dirty," Eveline said, curling her lip in disgust.

"You can't put anything past the Claymores," Ellis revealed.

"The wedding is at their guest ranch," Eveline recalled.

"Yes," Ellis acknowledged. "And all of Fuego and the surrounding counties are invited. People are already calling it the wedding of the year."

Eveline splayed her fingers across her face because it struck her, too. "Everett's going to cause a scene, isn't he?"

"I believe so," Ellis said with a grievous shake of his head. "It would explain why he's been so chipper lately. The thought of kicking True's ass from here to Mexico must have been playing in his head for the better part of the week."

"Do you think Everett can take him?"

"Without a doubt," Ellis said. He had gone to the sidebar and began to pour himself a tall shot of whiskey. He downed it swiftly. Then he poured a second and handed it to her. "It's been a minute since his last bar fight, but he could always hold his own. The problem is True Claymore's security. They're the ones we need to worry about."

"He's a small-town mayor," Eveline said, holding the shot glass in both hands. "What's he need security for?"

"We've always wondered," Ellis considered. He cursed. "I thought I was going to have a hard enough time tailing him and curtailing any gossip about you and Wolfe. This makes my job a whole lot harder."

"Call Javy," she suggested. "He could tell you how many hands are coming along tonight. We could get a tighter detail for Everett…"

The thought seemed to amuse Ellis. He tilted his head. "Wrangle the boss instead of his cattle." He nodded and might have begun to smile if he'd been inclined to. "I like it." He pointed to her shot. "Drink up. You're going to need it if you're going to survive the night."

"Look at us," Everett said. He was dressed in black tie. His belt buckle shined in the lights of the parking lot outside The RC Resort and he was wearing a hat that wasn't browbeaten or dirt streaked. At six foot five, he looked down for a good time. Those around him knew better. He hooked an arm around both Ellis and Eveline, pulling them into the crook of his arm. "The burnout, the cheater and the hard-ass about to blow this party wide open."

"It's a wedding, Everett," Ellis said, running his hand over his tie. He looked spiffy with his hair slicked back from his brow. He covered it with his Stetson and exchanged a look with Javier on his right. "Tonight's about the soon-to-be Mr. and Mrs. Gains."

"Ah," Everett said with a dismissive sweep of his hand. "It's a party." He fingered the cuff links on one wrist. "And I aim to have a damn good time." He leaned down to Eveline's level, pressing a hard, smacking kiss to her cheekbone. "Let's do this."

Eveline hung back as Everett moved toward the entrance, flanked by half a dozen hands. "It's like Taylor Swift's *Reputation* album on legs. We aren't going to be able to keep a lid on him."

Ellis sighed, sinking his hands into his pockets. "Look on the bright side. The more attention he brings to himself, the less people will be talking about you."

"That's the thinnest silver lining I've ever heard." Nonetheless, she linked her hand in the curve of his elbow when he offered it. "You clean up good, for the record."

"You, too, kid," Ellis said with a wink. "Though

that's less of a surprise, seeing as you're the one used to wearing haute couture."

She fingered the wide neckline of the dress she had chosen. "That life seems a world away now."

"Not from this angle," he said, eyeing her sparkly silver rhinestone ankle boots.

She smiled. "I did splurge on the shoes."

They came to the entry queue. "You ready?"

She frowned at The RC Resort logo above the door. "I'll let you know."

Wolfe stuck to the outskirts of the reception. The dance hall of The RC Resort was crowded enough that his presence went largely undetected.

He'd been stunned when he'd received the invitation to Naleen Altaha's wedding. Normally, he was saved the effort it took to politely decline. But she and her fiancé had indeed spared no one the chance to attend—not even the town felon.

It was Eveline's text that had changed his mind about not attending. It had come with a photo of a target paper with the center obliterated. Underneath, she had typed the words, Meet you there?

It's a date, he'd replied without much hesitation.

He didn't like mingling with town folk—especially since the news of his and Eveline's relationship broke. He'd waited, however. Now he was done waiting and ready to reclaim what was his.

Mine, he thought as he watched her swept into a two-step with the groom himself. Wolfe's hand tightened on the snifter of liquor he'd snagged from the bar.

Her dress was the same color as her eyes. It had a wide neck that did nothing for once to hide the scars along her shoulder and collarbone. While he'd caught others whispering and staring at the display, he'd been transfixed at her bravery—at how she shined in her glittery boots. She was a Hope Diamond in a sea of cubic zirconia.

He watched her gaze linger over Terrence's shoulder at the bar where her brothers had been holding up the wall for the better part of the night. Everett was making an ass of himself, drinking liberally and growing louder by the minute. Ellis was having a hard time curtailing any shenanigans on his part.

Not for long, Wolfe wagered. Ellis had informed him in a snatched conversation shortly before the reception that Everett had it out for True Claymore and was bound to have his say before the end of the night.

Wolfe didn't much care if he did. The mayor had done his best to run Wolfe out of town when he'd returned. Neither he nor his wife had quite managed it, though they were the reason he'd bought the parcel of land so far outside town limits and not something closer to town and more convenient.

Somebody ought to put them both in their place. If that someone was Everett Eaton, then so be it.

The song ended and Eveline pulled away from Terrence with a smile—the kind she didn't quite mean.

He'd seen the smile she meant. It was enough to bring a man to his knees.

She glanced around as she made an escape from the dance floor, wary of more suitors. They'd kept her busy from the moment she graced the dance hall. It was as she was searching for a path to freedom that her eyes found his.

He lifted his glass, dipping his chin just enough that he could still see her underneath the rim of his hat.

She smiled. Not the fake smile—the real one. And

nearly brought him to his knees, as she always did. Veering out of the way of partygoers, her footsteps quickened. He held up a hand to stop her. When she did, he checked that no one was looking and tilted his head in the direction of the exit.

She nodded, ever so slightly.

Wolfe took a moment to finish his drink, then took the escape route. It was a night much like the one they'd had together—inky black sky lit only by stars. There were some clouds with lightning in the distance. He watched the storm heat, growing sterner over the mountains. The light show was spectacular, more so than the fireworks display promised for later.

Naleen and Terrence had gone all-out. Wolfe would bet they'd paid a fortune for the use of the Claymores' facilities.

Wolfe thought weddings should be simpler. There was nothing intimate about a wedding where everyone came to gawk, stare, point and eat and drink on your dollar.

"Nice night."

He turned to watch her come out of the dark. The sparkling shoes appeared first. Then the pale skin, punctuated by the green sheath. Her hair was twisted up on the back of her head and trapped there with diamond clips. He'd noticed that during the ceremony. He'd stood at the back of the chapel, as there was standing room only. She and her brothers had sat five rows from the back.

Everyone had watched the exchange of vows. He'd watched her and contemplated how much longer he would have to wait to hold her again.

His heart pumped in anticipation. He wanted to tell her she looked like a million dollars, that he hadn't been able to sleep a wink the night before knowing they'd be together tonight.

He wanted to tell her how he felt.

Not yet, he thought. *Not quite.*

She spread her hands to either side. "You clean up good, cowboy."

He glanced down at the suit. He'd had it cleaned. It'd been a minute since he'd worn it. His shoulders strained against the constraints of the jacket. He was bigger there than he used to be.

She closed the distance. Her scent swept over him and his body tightened. His molars ground together as her fingertips teased a line across his middle. "I can't remember ever seeing you in a tux before," she contemplated, drawing a line up his tie.

Her hand reached his collar and gripped. He followed the summons of her mouth as she brought it up to his.

He kissed her in the dark while lightning crackled in the distance and his blood fired under his skin. His hands rested low in the dip of her waist. As her arms twined around his neck, bringing his head down farther, he let them sink over the curve of her ass.

Voices reached their ears, not from the dance hall but the happy, distant chatter of children. They looked around and saw their faces lit by sparklers. Snap Dragons popped and shrieks and giggles answered. So close was it to what he remembered of being a child of the Edge, he smiled.

She smiled back and took his hand. "This way."

They stole across the dark lawn. The door of the stables was open, even though the long aisle was empty of workers or visitors.

"Everything's so Spartan," she observed. "How do they manage it?"

He peered into the tack room. He whistled lightly and tugged her through the door.

Trophies and plaques lined the walls, along with photographs of the Claymore family through the ages of expansion—from the black and whites of RC Ranch in its infancy to the glossy professional photographs of The RC Resort today. Tack wasn't so much the focal point of the room as it was an afterthought.

"Oh, I can't take anyone seriously if they don't have cobwebs and dust everywhere," she observed as he closed the door, leaving the low glow of the sconces burning around the room. She tugged open the drawer of a cabinet and hummed thoughtfully, pulling out a bottle of bourbon. "Fancy," she remarked. She held it up for him to see the expensive label. "Shall we partake?"

He didn't respond. He was too busy admiring how she looked in this light.

The top of the bottle squeaked slightly when she tugged it off. "No glasses," she said, checking the cupboard again. "Oh, well." She tipped the bottle up to her mouth and drank it straight.

His blood wasn't just crackling. It was burning.

She lowered the bourbon and offered him a nip by extending it to him. She raised her hand to wipe her mouth.

He latched on to it instead of the bottle. When she froze, her gaze riveted to his, he brought his open mouth down to hers.

Her taste was devastating—bourbon and champagne and the underlying thrill of Eveline Eaton. His arm twined around her waist and he brought her up hard against him. His tongue scraped over hers when she offered it and his hands roamed, free, all over her.

A happy noise sounded in her throat. She melted

into the kiss, letting him maneuver her between him and the sideboard. Letting him dig his fingers into the neat, taut knot on the back of her head and litter diamond pins on the rug where she'd dropped and spilled the bourbon bottle, paying it no heed. Her hair rained free into his palm.

His heart raged against hers, churning like a piston. He ran his hands over her regal shoulders, pushing the straps of her dress over the slopes so that they fell limp at her elbows.

Her hands raced across his front jacket, fighting against the lapels to open it and unknot his tie like she'd loosened his restraint. Her fingers tore at the buttons underneath. One popped off and rolled across the floor and her touch came up against his skin and the brunt of his heat.

He skimmed hard palms over the tops of her thighs, up her waist and ribs. She bowed back, exposing her throat, and he panted. He nipped the underside of her chin, then the creamy expanse of her neck as his thumbs traced the curve of her breasts across the line of her bodice. His fingers flexed, spreading.

When his name came out of her mouth, he thought he'd implode. The heat between them had turned suffocating but he still wanted more. His groan vibrated across her lips. His eyes crossed behind closed eyes when she raked her nails against his scalp, dislodging his hat.

The dress didn't move when he gave the bodice a tug. Her laugh echoed through the room. "Hang on," she said, breathless, reaching around. "There's a zipper."

He followed the urging of her hands, locating the zipper and pulling it all the way down the line of her back. Her breasts spilled free and his hands were there to knead. "*Ooh*," she murmured, her head reclining against the wall behind her. Her teeth came together. "That's good."

He managed to slide the dress the rest of the way down, unveiling her inch by exquisite inch. Breath backed up in his lungs and his heart was throwing itself against the wall of his ribs. When she bent one leg and then the other to let the dress go completely, he held the garment in one hand and looked his fill.

His mouth went dry. A thin swatch of silk was the only thing obstructing his view. Hooking his hand through it, he lowered it, too, more gentle this time. It was so delicate, his rough hands could rend it in two. Now she was just wearing her glittery boots.

She sensed him gentling. The playful light in her eyes gave way to need and plea. There was a fine sheen of perspiration cloaking her skin. She pushed the lapels of his jacket wide so that it fell from his shoulders. He let it go, kicking it aside. She undid the buttons on his shirt that she had missed before and parted it across his chest. He planted his hands on the sideboard on either side of her so she could go to work on his belt and the snap and zipper underneath.

Slower now, the giddy rush lost to something more, something that flamed deep and blue. Their lips meshed, molded, opened and dipped. He boosted her onto the edge of the sideboard so she was just the right height.

She arced like a current when he touched the place between her legs and stroked. He indulged her as her hips worked against his hand. Watching her move worked him up so fast and bright he was forced to stop right before she came apart.

He was beyond the brink of waiting anymore. He was mad for her.

She'd already sunk her hand into his pocket to find the gold wrapper he'd stuffed there for safekeeping when he'd left the RV. He tried to take it from her, but she held it over her head. "Uh-uh," she taunted, ripping a corner off.

He nearly lost his mind as she rolled the condom down over his hard length. She did it slowly, watching the muscles straining against his jawbone.

They moved together now, him driving, her accepting on a keening cry. She was a wet, velvet glove clenching him in a hot fist and he was the one who was crazy.

He could have died at that moment, knowing she was his—knowing he'd driven her to heaven and beyond. Hair clung to his damp brow. She swiped it aside in a loving motion.

When he only held her, she stilled. Her chest rose to meet his as she breathed raggedly. "Are you okay?" she asked, caressing his face.

He prayed his pulse would come down before his heart combusted altogether. He shook his head.

"Wolfe," she murmured, concern playing across her face. "What's wrong?"

He licked his lips. Then he parted them and ground some semblance of speech from the back of his throat. "E… Ev…"

She stopped breathing altogether, her gaze racing from his mouth back to his eyes. They pinged back and forth, left and right as he cursed himself. His voice was rough, like rust on a truck. He hated it. But he drew her name out as best he could.

"E-Evie…"

"I hear you," she whispered. Tears filled her eyes. "I hear you," she repeated, gentle.

He rushed to catch the tears on her face. He licked

his lips again. The muscles of his throat worked, harder than they should have, maybe. He couldn't be sure. "I..." He stopped, pressed his lips together. "I... I...love you. Evie." It washed out on a harsh whisper and he closed his eyes, wishing it had sounded stronger. Surer. As sure as he was that it was right.

"Oh, God," she breathed. "Oh, God, Wolfe." She kissed him once, then again, longer, deeper. A sob broke across her lips, shaking them both. "I love you, too."

Distant booming reached his ears. Fireworks, he realized. The oohs and aahs of the wedding party reached through the stable walls as they held each other.

They began to move together again to the cadence of the concussive reports. He lost what little of himself to her he had left. He gave it all away as she broke apart in his arms, shining like the diamond she was. His erection thrummed and kicked. The skin at the small of his back drew up tight. The resulting combustion was damn near nuclear, so much so he almost collapsed.

She held him. She held him in the aftermath until he could believe again that he'd have some strength and sanity at some point. Until then, she held on and he didn't think of letting go.

It was the door opening and banging back against the wall behind it and bright light piercing the room that caused them both to jump. And it was Everett, bleeding from the nose, and Ellis, jacket ripped, and a circle of stunned Edge hands around Wolfe and Eveline that made them freeze in place, caught.

Chapter 21

Eveline jerked the blanket Deputy Altaha had offered her at the police station over her shoulder. There were other uniforms in the room and they were staring.

She hadn't forgotten her dress in the tack room at The RC Resort. Nor had she forgotten her dignity. She wore it like a cloak now, fighting hard not to snap at the bland looks from the men in the bullpen. "Any way to get them to look elsewhere?" she asked Deputy Altaha, who sat on the other side of the desk in the maid of honor dress she'd been wearing when she and Sheriff Jones had broken up the stable brawl then arrested both her brothers, several ranch hands and Wolfe.

Altaha jerked her chin up. "Hey!" she snapped. "This ain't no rodeo! Butt out!"

The men respectfully turned away, going back to their computers or their coffee.

Eveline sipped her coffee from a Styrofoam cup.

"What are the chances of springing Ellis and Wolfe?" she asked.

Altaha blew out a weighty breath. "Not good. Jones is determined to keep them all overnight. The mayor's insisting. He's already threatening charges against Everett." She hid a smile in her own cup of coffee as she lifted it from the desk. "Ol' True's missing a few teeth after that skirmish on the dance floor."

"I'm sorry I missed it," Eveline said. Although, she wasn't. If she'd stuck around for Everett's *Justice League* moment, she'd have missed what had transpired between her and Wolfe in the tack room.

I...love you. Evie.

She closed her eyes as the words sang through her all over again. They'd be singing—for a long time to come. "Wolfe's part in the stable brawl was self-defense. Everett attacked him. Ellis was just trying to break it up. Javy, too. They were just trying to stop the two of them from—"

"Killing each other," Altaha finished. "I'm shocked it took this long for Everett and Coldero to come to blows. How long's that feud been going on? Fifteen years?"

More, Eveline thought to herself. *From the beginning.* "You can keep Everett as long as you want. But I insist... The others should be allowed bail."

"It's Jones," Altaha said again. "And not just because he's got the mayor in his ear. He hates when things get Western around here. Your brother is the definition of Western."

"I hate this," Eveline hissed. "This never would have happened if—"

"If you'd just told the truth, Miss Evie," Paloma said as she pushed through the doors into the station.

Eveline stood up. "What are you doing here? It's past midnight and you said you're still not feeling well."

"Wheest!" Paloma said, waving her hands in dismissal. She hauled her purse over her shoulder, looking ready for war. "If you'd just told your brother about you and Wolfe in your own time, we might not be in this mess."

"He went to the wedding looking for trouble," Eveline told her. "You have to know that."

"I don't condone what he did to True Claymore," Paloma said. "That was low. But you have to admit, what transpired between him and Wolfe might have been prevented if the two of you had just come clean."

Eveline was very aware that everyone in the bullpen was now looking at her once more. She fought the urge to cover her face. She was tired. So tired. "I didn't know how to tell him without him running off to throttle Wolfe."

"Oh, he did that anyway, didn't he?" Paloma asked. "And right where everyone in town could see it for themselves, along with you in an indecent state."

"I will not be condemned!" Eveline said. "What happened between Wolfe and I wasn't cheap and I will not hear it talked about that way!"

"Don't get your dander up, too, Miss Evie," Paloma warned. "We don't need another scene."

"You know," Eveline considered, "I don't care. I don't care who sees or who hears. I don't care what anyone thinks—the sheriff, Everett...*anyone*! I'm Wolfe Coldero's woman. And there's nothing anyone can say or do to change that!"

Paloma quietened. A splash of pride struck her. "Well," she said, tucking her purse satisfactorily against her middle. "I'd say that's a win for lost souls every-where."

Eveline found a smile climbing her face to match Paloma's. The woman held out her arms and Eveline went willingly into the embrace.

"That's my girl," Paloma murmured, stroking her hair. "Speaking her truth like she's known it all along. Your daddy would be so proud."

She laughed because she doubted he'd be happy with the roundabout way she came around to it. "I was naked as a jaybird in the Claymores' tack room."

"And you don't regret a mite of it. Do you?"

She shook her head, remembering Wolfe and *I love you* and him quickening inside her, letting her hold him in the upheaval. "No. None of it. But what are we going to do about Everett? He's never going to let us be happy."

"Never's for nonbelievers," Paloma told her as she pulled back "I happen to have more faith."

"In Everett?" Eveline asked, doubtfully.

"In fate, child," Paloma answered.

"Jones is too far in True Claymore's pocket for a county man," Paloma said in the passenger seat. She had her eyes closed. Her head was resting on the passenger window and she'd drawn her shawl across her chest.

Eveline had seen how tired Paloma was at the police station so she had offered to drive them both back to Eaton Edge until nine o'clock the next morning, when Sheriff Jones had agreed that Ellis, Everett, Wolfe and the others would be released. "Are you okay?" she asked, wanting to reach out to take Paloma's hand.

"I'll keep," Paloma assured her. "Just need a little rest, is all."

It was still dark, well after midnight. Main Street was dead. All the surrounding homes were dark at the windows. Once they were out of town, the streetlights faded. Paloma was silent. She had likely fallen asleep and Eveline was alone in the dark with her headlights.

She gripped the wheel of the truck harder and took several careful breaths because panic was starting to take hold in her belly. She kept her eyes on the dashed line in the center of the old road until her pulse evened out and she could block the images of something furred, fanged and matted from her mind.

They were a mile from the turnoff to Eaton Edge when she saw the object in the road. It wasn't an animal, she thought, squinting. Or at least that's what she told herself. It wasn't walking on four legs or two either. Whatever it was was lying prone across the center stripe.

When Eveline realized it was a person, she jerked the wheel.

Paloma started awake, just in time for the pickup to go into the ditch.

Too fast, Eveline thought, gritting her teeth and biting down on the urge to scream.

The vehicle went over the side and tipped. Before she knew it, they were rolling down, down, down to the bottom of the hill to the familiar and chilling accompaniment of breaking glass and crunching metal.

"Paloma!" Eveline shouted.

The truck was upside down at the bottom of the ditch. She could smell smoke and motor oil.

She was choking on her fear, but she shoved it out of the way as best she could because—*Paloma*. Paloma wasn't answering.

"Oh, please," Eveline begged. She unbuckled her seat belt. Gravity took over and her head hit the ceiling. Beating back the airbag, she tried untangling herself from the awkward position she was in. She was bleeding—she could smell it, and there was something wet on her face.

She couldn't think about that now. She groped for Paloma's hand. "Talk to me," she said. It was too dark to see. The dash lights were out. Even the headlights weren't working anymore. "Please, talk to me." Sobs worked up from the pit of her throat. She could no longer control her breathing. The shock was setting in, all too real.

She thought of the person in the road. She'd seen a face, pale and oval. Eyes, wide and desperate. The arms and legs at a strange angle…like they were hog-tied.

There was a noise from the space beside her. A moan.

"Paloma?" Eveline cried.

Another moan. "Evie… Are you all right, *niña*?" Paloma asked, her voice small.

"I'm okay," Eveline rushed to assure her. "Are you okay?"

There was a pause. "I've had better days."

Eveline, crazily enough, found a breathy laugh escaping in a short burst. It careened to a halt because the smell of smoke and gas was growing stronger. "We need to get out of here. Can you move?"

"My door's jammed. Can you get yours open?"

Eveline felt for the handle. The door opened but only by an inch. "Not really," she said. Fighting the trapped feeling she had felt in a wrecked car before, she felt for the driver's window. "The window's broken. Hang on. I'm going to shift around…"

She turned. The tinkling of small bits of glass fell

around her. As she propped her hand on the ceiling and worked around the crushed constraints of the cab, she positioned her back to Paloma and her feet to the window. Kicking, she felt the other parts of the glass give way. "We can squeeze out, I think," she wagered. She crouched down on her arms and army-crawled through the tight space. She grimaced when bits of glass nicked the undersides of her wrists and elbows.

The grass was tall, the ground slightly wet. She smelled the earth over the smoke. When she heard herself starting to sob again, she tightened down on the urge to let panic have its way. *No.* She had to keep thinking. If she wasn't thinking, she couldn't act and Paloma was still trapped in the vehicle.

Getting down on all fours next to the window, she called, "Can you come over to my side?"

There was some grunting, more moaning. Paloma was hurt, Eveline knew. She bit the inside of her cheek hard to stop tears. If she could get Paloma out of the truck, she could see what was wrong and find a way to get help.

Paloma's arms reached out of the truck. Eveline grabbed hold of her wrists. "I'm going to pull you out, okay? One...two...three..."

She tugged and pulled, digging her new boots into the muck until they were buried up past the toe. When Paloma's shoulders were free, she repositioned, grabbing her under the arms before pulling again.

Finally, Paloma's hips emerged and she lay in the grass, panting. She reached out, taking Eveline's hand. "It's all right now," she murmured.

Eveline wanted badly to break down, to lie on the ground with Paloma and cry. Her hands were shaking from effort, from panic, from shock. Every part of her was shaking. "Where are you hurt?" she asked. "Do you know if you can make it back up the hill?"

"Give me a moment," Paloma said, sounding calm— so calm. She breathed carefully for several moments. Then she sat up with some effort. "What made you go over the edge?"

"There was someone in the road," Eveline explained. She looked up at the top of the hill. "I should go check on them."

"Go," Paloma told her.

"Are you sure?"

"Go. They may need you more than I do." Paloma watched Eveline stand, tottering on her half boots. "Be careful, *niña.*"

Eveline climbed the hill, using her hands at one point for purchase. When she came to the roadside, she looked wildly around.

No one was there.

"What…" The question got lost. She pushed her hands back through her hair. There *had* been someone. She stalked out into the center of the road. *Right here.*

A bright light blinded her. She reached up for her eyes to shield them. "Who…who's there?" she asked. "Please. I can't see."

The light didn't budge.

She stepped toward it. "There's someone down in the ditch. She needs help. Will you help her?"

The light wavered slightly. It bobbed, drunkenly.

She smelled something foul over the smoke. She heard a growl.

Fear crashed into her. She had no choice but to feel it this time. She stumbled backward, arms milling. She tripped on her heel and fell.

The blacktop came to meet the heels of her hands and

the back of her hips. It hurt, but she scrambled backward as a figure took shape in the moonlight. It was advancing on her.

A cold, hard grip closed over her ankle. It locked, preventing her from escaping.

Something arced over the figure's head. For a second, the surface of it glinted.

Metal. Silver.

A pistol, she recognized, just before it swept down and connected with her temple.

Chapter 22

Wolfe slept sitting up in the cell he shared with Javier and a couple of other longtime wranglers from Eaton Edge, Spencer and Mateo. Once, he'd bunked with these men, branded cattle with them, chased horses and dug ditches with them.

They were good men with families of their own now. They'd found a way to accept him as lead wrangler when he'd worked the Edge. They'd learned to communicate with him—and vice versa.

They'd sat on his side of the courtroom during the trial following Whip Decker's demise.

Still, the fact that they'd all fallen behind him in the brawl with Everett Eaton, the man who signed their checks, knocked Wolfe flat—much as Eveline kissing him on the ladder in his barn had knocked him flat.

Wolfe shifted on the hard bench against the wall of the cell and peered through the bars to the next one over.

Ellis was there with Everett and three other hands—
these newer and younger. One of them, Lucas Barnes,
was still in high school. The other two had started working at the Edge after Wolfe's sentencing.

Wolfe saw that Ellis was awake, despite the fact that
it had to be three o'clock in the morning or more. He
made sure the men around him were still dozing and
lifted his hands. *If your brother fires these men, he deserves to rot in hell.*

Ellis didn't say anything or lift his hands, not for several minutes. Then he rocked forward on his seat and
signed back. *I'll make sure they stay on.*

Wolfe nodded. After a while, he motioned, *Thank you.*

Ellis frowned at him for a long time. *Do you love her?*

Wolfe stared. How did he put all he felt for Eveline
into words or motions? He didn't have enough signs
for that…

Ellis went on, *You better love her after what I saw.*

Wolfe pressed his hands into his knees, wondering
how much to reveal. This was his friend. However complicated things were between Wolfe and Ellis's family,
they would always have that bond. *I'd like to marry her.*

Ellis's eyes looked large in the dark. He blinked several times and shook his head. *One day you'll have to
explain how this happened so fast.*

Wolfe lifted his shoulders. *I don't know if she's ready.
But I want marry her.*

Ellis rolled his eyes. *You're not going to ask my per-
mission?*

You think she needs it? Wolfe asked him.

Ellis's mouth twitched at the corners. A smile hovered there, even if his eyes were tired and troubled. *No.*

Wolfe hesitated for a long time. Then he signed,

Would you mind your sister being married to some-one like me?

Any trace of a smile vanished. Ellis was dead serious when he signed back, *Name someone better.*

Wolfe didn't know how to react to that. It was acceptance, if cautious. But acceptance all the same. He tipped his head in gratitude.

Ellis tipped his back, crossing his arms over his chest and laying his head back against the bars behind him. He closed his eyes.

Noise echoed down the passage from the bullpen. Wolfe heard shouting, then other voices. The men stirred around him and Ellis. Everett, stretched out across the floor of his and Ellis's cell, groaned. "What now?" he mumbled.

Deputy Altaha appeared, rattling keys from her belt. She'd changed from her maid of honor gown to her buff-colored deputy's uniform. Sheriff Jones was on her heels, looking displeased, with Paloma behind him.

Everett sprang to his feet when he saw her condition. "What happened?" he asked, incredulous. He gripped the bars as she came to stand in front of him. His voice went low and dark. "Who the hell did this to you?"

"There was an accident," she explained. There was a gash on her cheek, another on her arm. Her voice was hoarse, shaky. She laid her hand over his. "Don't you worry about me. It's Eveline."

Wolfe stood up, edging toward the corner of the cell where he could best hear.

Ellis spoke up. "What about Eveline?"

"She was taken," Paloma said. Her breathing hitched. "I don't know what it was. I don't know where it took her. But it dragged her off into the dark…"

Everett bared his teeth. "What are you doing here,

Sheriff?" he demanded. "Why aren't you out there looking for my sister?"

For once, Everett's mind and Wolfe's were on the
same page. He pulled at the door of the cell. It didn't
budge, but it made enough noise to get Altaha's attention. He pointed at the lock.

She rounded on Jones. "We have to let them out, sir."

"Like hell," Jones argued. "They're not due for release until nine. No exceptions."

"We don't have enough men for a search party," Altaha informed him. "Everyone's gone home. These men
are ready and willing."

"She's right," Ellis spoke up. "You have our arms in
the safe. Give them back to us."

Jones scoffed. "You think I'm arming you after what
happened this evening at The RC Resort?"

"Did you see us use any of them against True Claymore or anyone else?" Javier challenged. "We use those
weapons for protection, Sheriff. Like any other person
'round these parts."

"We'll spread out and search the area," Ellis added.
"You can't afford to leave us locked up." He pointed to
the next cell. "That there's the best tracker in high desert country."

Jones gave Wolfe a long, cool assessment. "He can't
be armed. He's a felon."

Wolfe signed quickly and Ellis delivered the message.

"He says he doesn't need a gun."

Altaha nodded. "That's fair by me." She took the
keys off her belt, sorted through them and stuck one in
the door of the other cell.

Jones didn't say anything as Everett, Ellis and the
hands surrounding them were released. Everett took

Paloma's face in his hands, studying every inch of it. Ellis enveloped her in a gentle hug.

When Altaha reached for Wolfe's cell door, Jones brought her up with a hand on her shoulder. "You think you can vouch for this criminal?" he asked her in a low, warning voice.

She jerked her chin at him. "I'll stake my job on it. Sir."

Jones took a breath. He eyed her, then Wolfe in turn. Then he said, "It's on your head if this goes south, Deputy." He turned on his heel and left.

Altaha unlocked the door and pulled it open. She let the others pass but stopped Wolfe. "He wants me gone. That's the only reason he's agreeing to this—to see us both sent on down the river if things go bad."

Wolfe wished for Ellis. Then he could tell her in no uncertain terms, *It won't*. Instead, he held out his hand.

She took it for a firm shake, then stepped back to let him pass.

Eveline was aware of being dragged. She'd been dragged across rough terrain for some time.

Her head was on fire and the backs of her legs weren't much better from being raked across rocks and brush. She was aware of the harsh sound of breathing, the smell of something that should've rotted a long time ago. Her arms were tied at the small of her back.

Her booties had been lost at some point. There was something over her mouth—something that smelled and tasted as foul as whatever had taken her off into the brush.

Thoughts swam in her mind. She saw the moon and clouds passing across its face, obscuring the light so that she was lost in the night with…

When she made a noise, it stopped, dropping her unceremoniously to her back. It hovered over her. She could see the outline of a muzzle. Ears.

Why didn't it just kill her? Shouldn't it have done that by now—killed her and eaten her?

She thought of the bones at Coldero Ridge. The animal skull Wolfe had shown her. The pronghorn she'd seen it dragging off into obscurity.

Mountain lion, Ellis had told her.

Mountain lions didn't collect trophies, she thought. Or play with their food. They went in for the kill. The meal. They weren't evil. They just followed their biological urges.

What are you? she wanted to know.

It reached up. She feared something coming at her face again. Like before…

The gun. There had been a gun. Why would an animal wield a gun?

It dawned on her slowly with her mind scattered by pain and confusion.

An animal *wouldn't* carry a gun.

Hands came up. They weren't furred at all. They grabbed the muzzle and pulled, dislodging its head entirely. The furred face she'd come to know dropped to the ground next to her. She heard the drone of flies swarming it.

The moon broke free of the clouds.

Standing before her wasn't an animal at all. It was a man with thin arms, bony shoulders and a haggard face. He had a long, grizzled beard and his head was hairless. He looked old and wizened but his eyes… They were *evil.* Black with evil.

She knew this man, she realized after a minute's staring.

She knew him but could make no sense of it.

If she wasn't mistaken, she was looking into the eyes of a dead man.

He spoke to her in a voice that didn't sound right—a quiet voice that went straight to her bones.

"Not too much farther, mousey. Not much farther."

Chapter 23

Wolfe stood on the roadside. The truck was upside down in the ditch, just as Paloma had said. But whatever had happened to Eveline had happened on the road.

He crouched on the edge while the others shouted to each other around the truck below. Using the flashlight Altaha had given him, he went over every inch of ground.

The grass was tall, so it was easy to see the indentions left behind by feet and something else. Something bigger.

Like a body.

"Wolfe!" Ellis called. "You got anything?"

Wolfe whistled for him and waited for Ellis to approach before jerking his head at the trail.

"That's good," Ellis said, nodding. "Trust you to find the answers in the dark."

Wolfe looked off in the direction the trail went. They were going to need light. The indentation went off to the west. Over empty terrain. Over the desert with nothing between it and the Colorado Plateau except...

He narrowed his eyes on the silhouette of canyon walls in the distance. He jerked himself around to Ellis and thrust the flashlight at him.

"What is it?" Ellis asked, gripping the light and turning it on Wolfe.

He signed as fast as his hands would move. *I know where she is!*

"Over here!" another voice called from the other side of the road. It was Altaha. "We've got someone over here!"

Wolfe and Ellis broke into a run. They met the others on the far side. Jones pushed through them, making his way to the front. "Is it her?" he asked.

Wolfe laid his hand on Javier's shoulder. The man stepped aside so he could see.

In the beam of the lights, a woman lay on the ground. Her hands and feet were tied. Her hair was loose and auburn. There was a gag in her mouth, which Altaha quickly freed her from.

Ellis's voice cracked. "Lu?"

Luella coughed. Wolfe crouched next to her as Ellis did, too. They helped her sit up once Altaha freed her feet. For a moment, she heaved into the grass. Her hands, unbound, shook wildly as she raised them to her head, pushing back her disheveled hair.

"Lu," Ellis said again. He touched the back of her neck. "What did this to you?"

"I tried to tell her," Luella groaned. "She wouldn't stop looking..."

"Who?" Everett asked from above them. "What are you talking about?"

"Your sister," Luella said, raggedly. She seemed fragile in a way Wolfe had never seen her. "I tried to tell her. But she didn't stop . I knew he wouldn't like it…"

He? Wolfe shook his head. He drew her eyes up to his and signed, *An animal didn't take her?*

Luella swallowed and winced because it hurt her throat to do so. But she said plainly, "That's all he is now. Don't you understand? All he *is* anymore is animal."

"Lu, *who*?" Ellis wanted to know. "Who took Eveline?"

She licked her lips, which were dry and cracked and bleeding. She looked at no one when she said, "My father. My father, Whip Decker." Then she shuddered, made a faint noise like a strangled cry and dropped her face into her hands.

"Your…father?" Ellis repeated. His gaze streaked over her head and locked on Wolfe's.

Holy shit. Whip Decker was still alive? Wolfe automatically looked to Jones.

Jones was already staring at him. His jaw was taut. "You said you killed him."

"There was no body," Ellis said. "There was nothing left at the cabin…"

"…except his blood," Everett finished, grim. "Goddamn it, Coldero! You couldn't have finished the job before they sent you up for it?"

"Easy, boss," Javier cautioned.

But Everett was right, Wolfe realized slowly. Excruciatingly. Whip Decker had been alive when he left him at Coldero Ridge to go find help for Jo and Angel. He'd still been alive…

"We need to get the trauma unit out here," Altaha told Jones, holding Luella up with Ellis's help. "She needs to be checked out."

"She needs to answer more questions," Jones refused.

"Like how long has she known her father's been on the loose?"

"Not now," Ellis demanded. "Are you kidding me, Sheriff? Does she *look* like an accomplice?"

"Could be," Jones considered.

Ellis looked to Altaha for help. "Call it in. Have them send the EMTs. Whatever questions you have can wait."

Altaha nodded agreement. She grabbed the radio on her shoulder and turned her head to report, "11-41. Repeat. We need a bus ASAP on Highway 11, three miles north of Main Street, Fuego."

"You know where they've gone," Ellis said as Wolfe stood.

He nodded. He exchanged a look with Jones, then Everett. He nodded in the direction he'd seen the trail and motioned for the men to follow him.

His blood ran cold. If he was right, Decker had taken Eveline back to where it had all started seven years ago.

He'd taken her to Coldero Ridge.

The stench of sulfur flooded Eveline's nose. It assaulted her senses and she knew instantly where they were.

Whip Decker had brought her back to Coldero Ridge.

She began to struggle.

He cackled. His was a high-pitched laugh. "Smart mousey."

She tried talking through the bind around her mouth but the words were muffled and the cloth bit into the corners of her mouth. She kicked her feet even though they were tied at the ankles.

"She was in that little vegetable patch when I found her," Whip was saying. "Tending to those spicy peppers she used to sell at town gatherings."

Eveline stilled. Was he talking about her mother?

"She was wearing something red, if I recall, and the little one was sitting in the shade in her overalls with her dolls."

Eveline didn't want to listen. But she couldn't not. She closed her eyes, trying to shut herself off from the fount of his memories.

"She told the girl to go inside when she saw me," Whip continued. Another high-pitched laugh. "Like that was going to save either of them." He laughed some more.

You son of a bitch, Eveline thought. *You* sick *son of a bitch*.

"She was tall, your mother. Much like yourself. But she wasn't strong. Not strong enough, anyway. I dragged her in that house—like I'm dragging you now, mousey. I dragged her in, tied her up. Found the little one hiding under the bed. I told her if she came out, real nice like, I'd give her a treat." He laughed at that. "Now that one…she had some gumption. 'Bout bit my finger clean off."

Eveline whimpered, struggling against the rope around her arms. If she could inch it down to her wrists, she could maybe slip free.

"I took care of her," he said. "Tied 'em together. I didn't cover their mouths, though. I wanted to hear 'em. Hear 'em scream."

Something dark and bitter welled up from Eveline's chest. It clawed over her neck and face, hot. She shouted through the bind, telling him exactly what she thought of him.

He laughed some more. "You should have heard 'em. Once the smoke went up around the exterior…once it started sneaking in and they smelled it…they sang like birdies. I wonder…if you will, too, mousey."

As he dragged her farther between canyon walls,

Eveline eyed the sky. The sulfur smell burned her eyes and they teared. But she hoped that what she saw was the clouds growing lighter. If the sun came up, maybe she'd be able to get away. Maybe she'd be able to find a way to escape.

Whip Decker wasn't going to murder another member of her family. She couldn't let him succeed again.

The canyon walls were dark even as the soft, pale blue that proceeded daybreak was approaching. Wolfe checked the ground around the canyon, trying to pick up the trail.

"Are you sure they came through here?" Everett asked. He, too, was looking around as he loaded his pistol.

Wolfe nodded. He pointed to a line in the dirt. *That way*, he indicated by pointing.

"That's the direction we went the day we searched the place," Ellis noted, grim.

Wolfe frowned. If Decker took Eveline to the place in the rocks he and Ellis had found, they'd have little chance of getting to her.

"That's a lot of cover for him," Ellis said, mirroring his thoughts. "And not a whole lot for us."

Wolfe nodded agreement. The valley between the walls of the box canyon had nothing for cover.

"Do you think we can get a four-by-four out there?" Altaha asked. She pointed to the sheriff's vehicle. "It's not armored. But it'll hold up to some firepower."

Wolfe thought about it. The steep decline into the valley—it might not be too much for the SUV. He nodded.

"Do you have any rope?" Ellis asked. When Wolfe narrowed his eyes, he added, "There's only one way in and out of the arch. Unless someone approaches the site from above."

Wolfe lifted his chin as understanding dawned. Then he looked to Altaha and Jones for an answer.

"We might have some in the back," Jones admitted. He motioned for Altaha to go and check.

"We should load up," Everett said, taking the safety off the gun. "We're not far from daybreak. That's less cover for us." He frowned at Wolfe. "Aren't you going to ask for a weapon?" When Wolfe only stared at him, he said grimly, "If we're going to flush this jackass out, you're going to need more than those brick fists of yours."

As Everett stalked back to the sheriff's wagon, Wolfe looked down at his hands. They were balled, as they had been since he'd left the station.

He caught Jones watching him. Planting his hands on his hips, he ducked his head and moved back to the truck.

The stars were starting to wink out, shy at the coming of day.

Whip had his back turned. He was digging a hole at the base of a tree. Eveline took the chance to try sitting up. Her arms were starting to cry out, twisted too far past a comfortable angle for too long. How long had it been since he abducted her?

Paloma. Was Paloma okay? Had she been rescued or was she still down at the bottom of the ditch?

Eveline tried to sit up, using the wall behind her to help. Her arms itched from the cuts they'd received. Her legs weren't much better. She felt filthy and ragged. How she wanted to slap herself so she'd stay alert. Mostly, she needed to watch Whip. How else could she anticipate whatever he had planned for her?

He'd lit a small fire in a circle of stones at the center of the clearing. It was a natural indention in the rocks, accessible through a thin archway.

She couldn't see an escape other than the way they'd come in. She tried to gauge how high the walls were. Twenty feet? More? They were smooth, sanded by wind and time. No handholds or footholds. Things didn't look good for her. She swallowed to wet her throat. Her mouth was bone dry and she was sure the bind was causing her to bleed at the edges of her mouth. They hurt enough.

Whip grunted as he used his shovel as a fulcrum to bring something large up from the bottom of his hole. A heavy metal box tumbled end over end and came to rest next to the fire.

He panted and wheezed. In the firelight, she could see everything seven years living under the harsh desert sun had done to him. The top of his head was red, the skin there wrinkled and marred. There weren't wrinkles in his face but crags deep enough to cast shadows. His eyes were red lined and they seemed to protrude from their holes.

His smile was black when he bared it. He fell on the box and opened it. He laughed darkly as he piled things out of it.

She stopped moving. He had ammo. Lots of it. The clips piled on the sandy floor of the clearing.

A voice, far away, made them both freeze. It echoed, canned, through the canyon.

"JACE DECKER. THIS IS SHERIFF JONES. SEND OUT THE HOSTAGE AND COME OUT WITH YOUR HANDS WHERE WE CAN SEE THEM."

"Like hell," Whip muttered, picking up a gun and one clip. He ejected the used clip from what looked like an old Colt 1911, tossed it aside and slid a fresh magazine into place with lethal motions. For someone who had been living off the land under the radar for seven years, he looked like he'd been practicing. "Don't move, mousey," he told her before edging along the wall to the archway.

Eveline tried counting the magazines in the dirt. She shook her head. The sheriff and his party didn't know what they were up against. They were walking into a trap.

"JACE DECKER! SEND OUT THE HOSTAGE UNHARMED AND WE WILL NEGOTIATE."

In the shadows of the arch, Whip crouched. He looked long down the barrel of the pistol. Eveline counted twenty seconds before he fired.

"DECKER! STAND DOWN!" came the response.

Whip shouted, "You can have the woman over my dead body, Sheriff!" Then he fired another round.

No return fire came. As they waited, Eveline holding her breath, she heard the slight sound of whirring. She looked up at the opening above and whimpered at the sight of the reconnaissance drone hovering in midair.

Whip raised his Colt to the sky and squeezed the trigger. It hit, dead on center. He cackled and danced as the drone fell and crashed into the fire. "Gotcha, birdie!" he said and whooped.

Eveline groaned, laying her head back against the wall. She saw Whip positioning himself in the shadows again, ready to pick the sheriff's men off one by one.

They had no way in. She had no way out. Desperate, she struggled with the bind at her wrists anyway, wriggling furiously. She wasn't going to die like her mother, tied up like a steer.

If she was going to die today, she wasn't going down without a fight.

It had been a while since Wolfe had used ropes for anything but cattle roping and horse training. Ellis helped him set up the rappelling system some fifty feet from Decker's position.

From the radio on Ellis's hip, he heard Altaha. "Eaton, do you read?"

Ellis stopped what he was doing so he could take the radio off his belt. He raised it to his mouth. "Loud and clear, Deputy."

"He shot the drone but we got some footage. She's there. Looks like she's tied up against the east wall."

Wolfe met Ellis's stare. Ellis blinked several times. "Copy that."

"How long until you and Coldero scale that wall?" she asked.

Ellis looked at his work. "Couple minutes."

"Copy," she returned. "Once you get to your position, remember—do not move until we give the signal."

"10-4," Ellis replied. He placed the radio back on his belt. He eyed the wall in front of them. "All right. I'll go first. I'm going to need to get the top rope anchors in before you can follow."

Wolfe frowned. He'd been counting Decker's shots. *We don't have much time.*

"Unless you can jump the cliff face, we don't have any other options," Ellis told him. "We'll get to her, okay?"

Wolfe nodded.

Ellis positioned himself against the wall. He was rigged around the waist. Wolfe held the loose end of the rope as Ellis fitted his hands into the small grooves and tiny crags in the unforgiving rock. "Tight rope," he grunted at Wolfe when he reached the first position where the wall was too smooth for free-climbing.

Wolfe tautened the rope and held it tight as Ellis secured the bolt for the top anchor into place with the power drill he'd tied to his belt.

It was time-consuming work between drilling and building the top anchors all the way up to the cliff edge to the chorus of Decker's never-ending gunshots. The longer it took for Ellis to get to the top, the longer Eveline was alone with that monster.

What would happen when Decker ran out of firepower? What was going to happen when Decker realized he was cornered? A desperate man was more dangerous than any predator Wolfe had ever encountered.

Wolfe was so tense by the time Ellis reached the top, his jaw was locked up. "All right," Ellis called. "Come on."

Wolfe followed the same path up to the first anchor. The rock hit into his hands and fingers, but adrenaline pushed him. He had to tell himself to slow, to think about what he was doing as he clipped in. If he didn't do it right, he would go plummeting backwards off the rock face.

He grabbed Ellis's offered hand at the top and pulled himself over onto the flat summit. As he caught his breath, Ellis unbolted them both, then straightened out the ropes. At this point, he pulled the gun out of the sheath Altaha had given him. He checked to make sure the chamber was loaded. Holding it firmly, he nodded across the flat surface to the opening fifty feet west. "Ready?"

Wolfe palmed the handle of the knife he'd sheathed at his hip and gave a nod. They crept carefully across the top of the cliff. It was ten feet at the widest point from one side to the other and four feet at the narrowest. The south side tumbled away for a hundred feet or more. Rockfall and boulders littered the base. A fall over that way would kill a man.

As they approached the opening that was Decker's hideaway, Wolfe clapped a hand on Ellis's shoulder.

"We have to wait for the signal," Ellis hissed, even as Wolfe moved ahead of him.

Wolfe went down on his belly. He fitted his fingers over the edge, then slid closer so that he could peer down into the cell.

Decker was covered, damn it. The lone tree in the clearing was blocking him from view. Eveline, on the other hand, was clearly visible. She lay on her side just where Altaha had said, against the east side of the clearing. For a split second, Wolfe saw the blood on her temple, the tiny rivers of it on her arms and legs, and thought the worst.

His world centered on her. The gunshots ceased to his ears. They rang and tunnel vision set in with Eveline dead set in the middle.

Then he saw her move, lolling to her other side with a grimace. He saw her wrists working where she was tied. Her ankles, too. She was alive and fighting to free herself.

Wolfe took several careful breaths, pulling himself back from the edge. Sweat poured down his cheeks. Panting, he answered Ellis's questioning stare with a nod. *She's okay.*

Ellis signed back. *Where is he?*

Can't see him, Wolfe motioned.

Ellis's lips tightened. He got down on his belly, too, and army-crawled to the edge. He took a look, gun ready. He shook his head as he pulled himself back. *I don't have a shot*, he told Wolfe.

Wolfe jerked his chin to get Ellis's attention. When he had it, he signed, determined, *Plan B*.

Ellis eyed his rope belt. Then, reluctantly, he made sure Wolfe's harness was secure before feeding the ropes into place, tying them tight. "I hate this," Ellis muttered under his breath. "You've got no firepower and, from what I could see, he's got enough to secure his position until nightfall. If he sees you, you're dead."

I'm going, Wolfe told him in no uncertain terms.

Ellis did curse. He was sweating, too. It ran from his hairline in rivulets. "I don't have it in me right now to mourn anyone else." He thumped Wolfe hard on the chest with the heel of his hand to bring Wolfe's focus back to him. "Take the gun."

When Ellis offered the weapon, Wolfe stared at it. He shook his head. *I can't.*

"I don't give a crap about Jones," Ellis whispered through his teeth. "I'll take whatever blame there is for what goes down. Now you'll take this *goddamn* gun or I'm going down there to rescue her myself."

Wolfe looked at Ellis. He looked at the gun. He thought about Eveline.

He didn't have what it took to save her.

Resigned, Wolfe closed his hand over the butt of a gun for the first time in seven years.

Relieved, Ellis breathed raggedly. Then he patted Wolfe on the shoulder. "I'll give Altaha the all clear. Wait for the signal and don't forget the safety, brother."

Chapter 24

Every voice in Eveline's head told her to give up. She was Whip's prisoner. He'd tied her too well, too tight, and she was never going to be free again.

The trouble was all those voices pissed her off so much that no matter how badly she hurt, no matter how long it took to make any progress, she didn't stop trying.

She pushed her feet into the ground and rolled so her hands were underneath the small of her back. Biting down on the cloth in her mouth, she pushed with the heels of her feet so that the rope around her wrists met the curve of her hip.

She needed resistance—just enough to slip the bind over the heel of her palm. From there, she might be able to...

Something arced over the wall above her. It fell, bounced and rattled as it rolled across the clearing to Whip's position to one side of the arch. Before she could identify what it was, it exploded in a cloud of smoke.

She ducked, curling herself away from the onslaught. She closed her eyes to protect them and took shallow breaths against the dirt.

Smoke curled up her nostrils, regardless, and she coughed. She could hear Whip coughing, too, furiously. She wondered if he still had the Colt.

A hand, hot and damp, slipped over her mouth.

She shrieked and bucked against the hold.

Then her hands were suddenly free. Her shoulder joints screamed as she lifted her palms to her face, trying to clear the smoke away.

A cheek pressed against hers. "Evie," a voice whispered against her ear.

She nearly sank back to the ground. *Wolfe.* Where had he come from? She reached for the wrap around her mouth. He placed his hand against the side of her head. *Hold still*, it seemed to say. She held very still.

The cold slide of a large knife fit between her cheek and the cloth. She sobbed when he torqued it hard, as far away from her skin as he could manage. The bind bit further into the corner of her mouth.

Then it loosened, too. She opened her mouth wide. Her jaw protested, but she wiggled it. "Wolfe," she cried.

His hand clamped over her mouth again.

The smoke was clearing, she realized. She lifted her ankles so he could cut them free, too.

She could still hear Whip coughing, but he was cursing now, too, crawling toward them—toward his pile of ammo next to the fire.

Wolfe positioned her behind him.

As she opened her eyes, she saw the glint of steel in both his hands: the knife in the left. A Ruger that looked a lot like Ellis's in the right.

The wind picked up, catching up the smoke and funneling it away. The air was clear. Whip had stopped coughing. Stopped cursing.

Wolfe was tense—so tense, Eveline held her breath. Her heart racked her ribs like a sledgehammer. "Did you take off the safety?" she whispered between his shoulder blades.

Wolfe hesitated.

Eveline closed her eyes in dread.

"Son of a bitch!" Whip cried out. Then, louder, "*Son of a bitch!*" And he laughed in the way only he could. The laugh arced up the canyon walls and echoed back to them, a living thing itself.

Wolfe fumbled, trying to take off the safety. He dropped the knife.

Eveline dove between his feet to pick it up. She needed a weapon. *Give me a weapon!* Her hand closed over the handle as Whip took aim at the center of Wolfe's chest.

Wolfe took a step back, backing Eveline up toward the wall behind her.

"That's right," Whip said with a broad grin. "That's it. You back up. It's me who has the high ground this time..."

Wolfe backed up, obedient. He was holding the gun up in surrender. Eveline gripped the knife, wanting to use it. Too shaky to use it. "*Wolfe?*" she said, grabbing hold of his belt at the small of his back. Whip was going to shoot him. He was going to shoot him right in front of her...

A shot rang out, loud in her ears. She screamed, dropped the knife and gripped Wolfe's shoulders. "Oh, God," she sobbed.

But it wasn't him who fell. Whip toppled headlong into the pile of ammo.

Wolfe stepped away from her to kick the gun from his hand, out of reach.

In a state of shock, she watched him roll Whip and press two fingers to his throat.

Nothing happened. Eveline breathed through her teeth. "He's not…still alive, is he?" she asked, her voice not her own.

Wolfe closed his eyes after a moment. He shook his head. Then he stood up and angled his chin up, giving a whistle. Eveline looked up, too.

She couldn't help it. At the sight of Ellis, she gave way to all the terror of the last few hours. And she didn't stop—not when Wolfe took her into her arms and held her, rocked her, kissed her. Depleted of her strength, she could do nothing but let him sway her over the spot of the clearing with his body between her and Decker.

Others flooded the hideaway. She recognized voices but couldn't give them names. It was several moments before words began to make sense again.

"Everett…ambulance…"

"What…" She fought to speak. "W-what's wrong with Everett?"

"He took a hit," Deputy Altaha said again, slower.

"Is it bad?" she asked. Why was nobody answering her?

Finally, Altaha said, "Some officers took him to meet the chopper. He's been airlifted to the county hospital. We'll need to take you there, too, to get checked out."

Eveline, Paloma and Ellis waited in the waiting room of the Fuego County Hospital. Eveline had been questioned and stitched and bandaged and questioned. She couldn't count the questions. But all she could think about was Everett on the operating table in the next room.

They'd gotten to see him, just before the orderlies had rushed him off to the OR. He'd been white as the sheet he'd lain on. *Shot in the chest*, they'd reported. *Emergency surgery.* She'd barely been able to process it. Except how he'd taken her hand.

"You're okay?" he asked, his lips barely moving.

"I'm okay," she assured him. "And you will be, too."

"You're...staying," Everett said, his hand tightening on hers and his brow steepling with the effort to stay present. "You're...not going anywhere..."

She shook her head, fighting against the need to sob again. Everett didn't want her to leave like all the times before. He wanted her here. At his side. "I'm not going anywhere," she promised. "I'll be here when you wake up. And I'll be here every day after, okay?" When he didn't answer and his eyes didn't open, she raised her voice. "Everett?"

In the waiting room, she lowered her face into her hands. They were heavily taped to cover all the cuts she'd received. Her wrists were already bruised, as were her face and ankles from being restrained for so long. There was a heavy bandage on her temple. She'd had to be sewn up once more where Whip had hit her with the Colt.

She hurt everywhere. But none of it meant anything. Everett had been in surgery for hours. And she was so, so afraid. "I can't lose him," she said. "He drives me crazy. But I can't lose him, too."

Paloma took her hand in a firm grip, but not even she could muster words of comfort. There were bandages on her arm and face, too.

Ellis pushed out a shaking breath. He raised himself to his feet, then ran his hands through his hair. He looked worn thin. His eyes were hangdog eyes. They'd seen one too many things today—enough to rattle his soul. He dropped his hands and paced. "I need a cigarette."

"You smoke?" she asked, confused.

"Devil's candy," Paloma opined, her voice quiet and thin.

"I'm not perfect," he said. "I've never been perfect."

Eveline watched him, the way his shoulders hung. The way he looked at everything and nothing.

Even if Everett came out of the OR alive, Ellis would have to be chief of operations at Eaton Edge for a while.

He carried so much on his shoulders already, Eveline thought woefully. She licked her lips. "You saved my life," she murmured. She thought of Wolfe between her and the madman. And Ellis, like an angel, above. "You saved both our lives."

When he said nothing to that, she got up to stop him from roving restlessly over the floor and hugged him.

Someone passed through the doors. It was Luella Decker. Eveline had heard how they'd found her on the side of the road near the place where she and Paloma had flipped into the ditch. She must have been the one who'd been lying in the road—the reason Eveline had jerked the wheel and wrecked.

Ellis opened his mouth to say something, then stopped when he saw Jones at her back.

Eveline realized that Jones had cuffed her and was marching her out of the hospital.

"What are you doing?" Ellis asked him. "You can't do that. She didn't do anything."

"Out of the way, Eaton," Jones barked. "Get ahold of yourself. She's been aiding and abetting her old man for the past seven years."

"It's not true," Ellis said. His gaze fell on Luella, his

voice gentling. Everything about him gentled like he was talking to a spooked horse. "Lu. I know that's not true. You wouldn't help him. Not after everything he did to you."

Luella couldn't meet Ellis's eyes. Eveline saw how hard she tried to make her expression blank, but emotions worked over it, anyway. Her chin wobbled. "Get out of the way, Ellis," she told him, sounding small.

"The hell I will."

"Ellis!" Luella shouted. She'd fixed her face so that it was hard, as hard as it had been the day he, Wolfe and Eveline had gone to see her at Ollero Creek. "I'm not worth saving. I don't *want* your saving. So stop. Stop trying."

"Out of the way, Eaton," Jones told him. "Or I'll have my deputy bring you in, too. I don't think you want that. Not with your brother on the operating table."

Paloma placed her hand on Ellis's back. "Back away now, *niño*. There's nothing you can do."

Ellis stood his ground for another moment, then two. Eveline felt her bottom lip quaver when his posture caved and he moved aside.

The way he looked at Luella, it broke her heart. *Oh, Ellis*, she thought but couldn't bring herself to say.

Jones took Luella away. Paloma rubbed circles over Ellis's spine. "You have to let her go," she murmured.

Ellis kept his head down, his hands braced on his hips. "I, uh…" His throat clicked as he swallowed. "I need a minute. If the doctor comes…"

Paloma nodded away the rest. "We'll come and find you."

He nodded once before he moved to the door and disappeared. To get a smoke. To pace or curse or shout. Whatever Ellis did to pull himself together.

He was always together. That was why seeing him broken was too much.

Eveline did know one thing for certain. Her brothers and Paloma needed her. Whatever life looked like at the Edge from this point forward, she'd be there. She wasn't going to walk away again. How could she—when everything she wanted was right here in Fuego?

The doors opened again. Eveline sat up straighter, thinking it was the doctor. Her lips parted when she saw Wolfe, instead.

He looked at her—simply looked—as the door swung shut behind him. He studied her bandaged hands. Her face.

He looked beyond the details. He looked into her eyes. Her heart. And he looked relieved beyond belief.

She stood as he crossed the room. She lifted her arms and pulled him in as his went around her, too. She held him as she'd been unable to after the shootout with Whip Decker. Seaming her eyes closed, she pressed her face against his shirt. He smelled like gun powder and smoke. But most of all, he smelled like Wolfe and freedom.

He smelled like hers.

Relief, crystalline, broke apart inside her. For a moment, she'd thought he was hit. She'd thought her life—the new life she'd been building for herself, the one she was meant to live—had been struck down in the high desert canyons of her and his youth. It had devastated her. And she'd cried. She'd cried like she never had before.

She kissed his throat. Then his jaw. Holding his face in her hands, she breathed against him as he breathed into her. Seeking, she raised her mouth to his and took his whispering kiss.

When she broke away, she felt off-balance and deeply moved as he pressed his cheek to her cheek and swayed with her, side to side, as he'd done with Whip's body at their feet.

She shuddered. Was she ever going to stop shaking? She could still feel it—how close they'd come to losing everything.

What must he have felt facing a man he'd thought he'd killed long ago, whose death he'd served time for? What must he have felt when he realized he'd forgotten to take the safety off the gun?

"It's over," she whispered, moving her hands over his back in a caress. He was holding her so tight. "He's really gone now. Isn't he?"

He gave a small nod but didn't let go.

"I'm okay," she assured him. She rocked him now. "We're both going to be okay."

He didn't move for a while. Then he eased back. Looking down at both her damaged hands, he didn't take them. He lifted his hands under them then raised them, as if afraid holding them would hurt her any further. He bent down enough to touch his lips to the back of the left, then the right. Then he turned them up and kissed the bruises on one wrist, then the other.

She stitched together a watery smile. "I don't think you can kiss every part of me that's hurt. You'd never get to the finish line."

His fingers traced the undersides of her arms, up and down, in a lulling caress that brought her to the brink of relaxation. Her head bobbed and she dropped her head to his shoulder again.

"Evie."

She did smile now, broad and true. Now that was the

sweetest sound. Her name on his lips. "Yes, Wolfe?" she whispered back.

He didn't say anything else. She lifted her head and stilled. He looked sure and certain. Determined, even. But she saw the nerves in his eyes.

He opened his mouth, closed it. Then opened it again, taking her hands once more. He took a breath, then dropped to his knees.

Paloma made a noise.

Eveline stared. *Is this...? Is he...?*

He didn't say the words. He simply held her hands. He waited, watching.

She felt the way his thumb traced the base of the third finger on her left hand. Where she'd wear a ring. His ring.

She thought of everything they'd lost. Everything they'd beaten together. She thought of everything they would build—together. She wet her throat. Then she slipped her hands from his. Raising them to his face, she held it for a moment, taking her gaze over every one of his stunning features. Then she lowered her mouth to his. "I will," she answered.

He lifted his hands to her face, too, and held it. Held her. Then his hand swept back into her hair as he stood, and he kissed her. He kissed her hard and hot and fast, as if she'd change her mind.

She wasn't going to change her mind. Her life was here. With her family. With her brothers. With Wolfe Coldero.

No. Nothing was going to change her mind.

"Ms...er... Meadows, is it?"

She looked up and found a man in scrubs standing in front of the swinging doors to the OR. "It's Eaton," she told him. "My name is Eaton." But not for long, she thought, keeping her hand firmly in Wolfe's as he stood tall beside her.

"Ms. Eaton," the doctor said. "Your brother is out of surgery."

"Oh, thank Jesus," Paloma sighed tumultuously.

"How is he?" Eveline asked, and dread crept back in because the moment had been too perfect. Too perfect to last. "My brother, Everett? How...is he?"

"We removed the bullet and stopped any internal bleeding. He's lost a lot of blood. He'll need to be kept under observation for a while. But he's strong and seems to be a very stubborn individual, which will help him in his recovery."

Paloma sobbed, burying her face in her hands. Wolfe drew her in under the solid line of his shoulder and held her close.

Eveline caught a laugh escaping her throat. "He's going to be okay?"

"I think so," the surgeon said with a nod. "He's got a long road to get there. But he should be just fine."

Paloma beamed. "Thank you, doctor. Thank you so much." She turned to Wolfe. "Ellis," she said. "I need to find Ellis. He'll want to know..."

Wolfe nodded away the rest. First, though, he kissed her temple. Then he took Eveline by the shoulders. He gave them a squeeze.

Everything's going to be all right. For the first time, she realized that everything and everyone was going to be okay. She hadn't lost another member of her family. Whip Decker and the monster that had stalked her asleep and awake had been vanquished. And she was free to live the life she wanted—here—with her family and this man.

She'd live. They'd live. And not to spite the person who'd tried and failed time and again to take it all away. Because they were free to do so. Because they deserved to live the life they wanted in the time and place they chose.

Eveline knew that she and Wolfe would do all that and more. They would raise horses, love each other and build a fine life together in the rough country of the high desert plain.

* * * * *

Don't miss another exciting romantic suspense novel by Amber Leigh Williams:

Hunted on the Bay

Available from Harlequin Romantic Suspense!

Get 4 FREE REWARDS!

We'll send you 2 FREE Books plus 2 FREE Mystery Gifts.

FREE Value Over "$20"

Both the **Harlequin Intrigue®** and **Harlequin® Romantic Suspense** series feature compelling novels filled with heart-racing action-packed romance that will keep you on the edge of your seat.

HARLEQUIN
PLUS

Try the best multimedia subscription service for romance readers like you!

Read, Watch and Play.

Experience the easiest way to get the romance content you crave.

Start your **FREE TRIAL** at
<u>www.harlequinplus.com/freetrial</u>.